Dying Words

A Ghostwriter Mystery
(Book 4)

C. A. LARMER

Larmer Media
ISBN: 978-0-9924743-2-4
Cover design: Stuart Eadie

For the early surveyors of the world
who smoothed the path for all of us,
and their families who smoothed
the path for them.

ALSO BY C.A. LARMER

The Ghostwriter Mystery series:
Killer Twist (Book 1)
A Plot to Die For (Book 2)
Last Writes (Book 3)
Words Can Kill (Book 5)
A Note Before Dying (Book 6)
Without a Word (Book 7)

The Murder Mystery Book Club series:
The Murder Mystery Book Club (Book 1)
Danger On the SS Orient (Book 2)
Death Under the Stars (Book 3)
When There Were 9 (Book 4)
The Widow on the Honeymoon Cruise (Book 5)
Gone Guest (Book 6)

The Posthumous Mystery series:
Do Not Go Gentle
Do Not Go Alone

The Sleuths of Last Resort:
Blind Men Don't Dial Zero
Smart Girls Don't Trust Strangers
Good Girls Don't Drink Vodka

PLUS
*After the Ferry: A Gripping
Psychological Novel*

An Island Lost

CONTENTS

ACKNOWLEDGEMENTS

Thanks to my family and friends, as always.
And a special mention to Graham Matheson, past
Surveyor General of Papua New Guinea whose real-life
quest for a missing photograph in his final days
inspired this fictional tale.

.

PROLOGUE

Everyone in the room thought the old guy was dead and at least one of them was happy about it. But then he went and opened his eyes again, and the tiny, ponytailed woman who was quietly sobbing over his chest, drew back and gasped.

"Mah darleeng, you alive!"

He looked at her, this slip of a thing with oily black hair and deep brown eyes, as though he had no idea who she was and why the hell she was there. He glanced slowly around the room, to the other faces gathered at his bedside. Ah, there was his daughter, looking anxious as always, her husband standing behind her like a stunned mullet, and his stepson, bored and desperate to flee. *Typical.* Behind them all, loitering by the door was a young man in a royal blue uniform.

Now why was there a policeman here, he wondered? Oh, that's right.

He tried to talk and his son-in-law stepped forward.

"Just relax, Berny, everything's going to be okay."

"Oh for goodness sake, let him speak," snapped the daughter, grabbing her father's hand with trembling fingers. "What do you need to say, Dad? Just spit it out."

"Please, leave him be," the other woman sobbed and the police officer cleared his throat.

"Did you have something to say, Mr Tiles?"

The old man tried to nod. "Get ... get ..."

"Yes?" said the officer, his eyes wide with anticipation.

"Water!" announced the son-in-law, reaching for the brown plastic water jug that had been placed on a table to the side.

The old man tried to shake his head, wasn't sure he'd pulled it off. He was having trouble functioning and he couldn't get the right words out. It was like he was stuck in wet cement, his mouth full of sand and gravel. A straw was now being shoved through his cracked lips and he managed to swallow a little which seemed to help. He tried again.

"Get Rah ... Rahhhh ..."

"Renata?" The daughter glanced back at the other woman with a frown. "Renata's here, Dad."

Still sobbing, Renata stepped towards her husband again, more tentative this time.

"I here, Berny, no you worry, I here for you."

He groaned. This was going to be harder than he thought. *Oh why had he been such a fool?* If only he'd listened, if only he'd understood how important it was. What it meant to them all. He swallowed hard again and tried to sit up, but it was useless, nothing was working properly anymore.

The daughter choked back a tear. "Dad, we're all here, we love you. Honestly we do. You need to know that."

And you need to listen to me, he thought. *All of you, you need to listen!* But they were turning away now, talking amongst themselves. He heard the words, "Terrible tragedy" and "Not long now" and he felt his heart plunge.

He took a final, crackly breath, pulled his head up as far as he could from the pillow and said, "Roxy!"

"What?" The daughter swung around to face him, her eyes wide, her cheeks flushed.

"Roxy Parker," he managed this time, swallowing hard before adding, "She ... has ... it ..."

Then he slumped back with a final gasp of breath before descending into the darkness.

CHAPTER 1

Roxy Parker was busy gasping for breath when she reached her fourth-floor apartment, and that, coupled with one too many merlots, was probably the reason she didn't flinch when she opened her front door and spotted the dark figure hovering by the window, a ghoulish silhouette against the distant moonlight.

In fact, Roxy's first reaction was to laugh out loud. He looked like a poorly drawn character from a *Scooby Doo* movie, his hands held out like claws in front of him, his back hunched over, and what looked like grotesquely oversized ears drooping down on either side of his head. All that was missing was a pair of glinting yellow eyes and some fangs.

"What the ...?"

She didn't manage to finish that sentence (let alone that thought) before the ghoul was rushing towards her like a Mack truck. She tried to step back but he was faster and clearly more sober, and she was barrelled over as he made a dash for the door. By the time Roxy pulled herself back up—no mean feat under the circumstances—he was gone, vanished into the night, and for a moment there she wondered if she'd just conjured up the whole thing.

Roxy's entire body told her otherwise. Her heart was thudding like a jackhammer, blood thumping in her ears, prickles of fear racing through her spine and down her legs, which now felt like tree trunks as she stepped tentatively towards the open door.

Still gasping for breath, she peered out. Nothing. The corridor was dimly lit and deathly quiet, not so much as a swinging door or a puff of smoke to show that anyone had passed by.

"What the ...?" she said again before instinct took over and forced her to slam the door shut, secure the lock and find the nearest chair.

She fell into it gratefully and steadied herself. Had she just interrupted a burglar? And if so, *why!?* Of all the joints in all the land, surely he could do better than hers? She had nothing of value in her tiny unit, apart from some moth-eaten vintage clothes, a cheap, digital TV and her laptop.

Her laptop! Roxy got up and staggered into the sunroom, switching the light on as relief flooded through her. It was still on her desk. Thank God. It wasn't a particularly fancy computer, but it was home to several large projects she had been working on and she didn't need the agony of trying to retrieve it all.

"Yes, yes," she thought irritably. "I'm supposed to back up regularly but I'm also supposed to visit the dentist annually, and like *that's* ever gonna happen."

Roxy glanced at the clock, the reporter in her now taking over despite her intoxication. It was 1:22 a.m. That meant Big Ears had broken in some time before 1:20 when she'd arrived home. She hadn't meant to come home. She was supposed to be staying over at Max's place, but had decided at the last minute to head back to her own bed. She couldn't decide now whether this had been good fortune or bad.

She breathed deeply and assessed the situation. It didn't look like he'd taken anything or done any damage. There were a few cupboards open, and three drawers, but she couldn't remember if she'd left them like that in her haste to meet her boyfriend for dinner that night. She wandered around unsteadily, checking all the drawers, her jewellery box, her little crystal bowl of keepsakes, and sighed with relief. Everything was in its place.

Had she only just interrupted him? And how the hell did he get in? She staggered back towards her front door. It didn't look tampered with, but she was too nervous now to open it and check. What if he was still lurking around?

She thought of the cops. Should she call them? And say what?

"Hi, guys, there was this really creepy burglar in my apartment."

"And what did he take, Madame?"

"Er, nothing ..."

"Well, do you at least have a description of this man?"

"Yes, have you seen the latest episode of *Scooby Doo*?"

She shrugged the thought away, scooped up her walkabout phone and dialled. After several rings, it picked up.

"I could've been fast asleep then, you know," Oliver Horowitz said, his voice raspy down the line.

"Yes, and I could be on the latest cover of *Sports Illustrated*, but let's stick to reality, shall we? I know you're up, you'll be up for hours yet. I have a problem."

"And you wonder what keeps me up. Okay then, but first tell me, have you been hitting the turps again?"

She sighed. "What has that got to do with anything?"

"Okay, chill, I just like to know who I'm dealing with."

"Huh?"

"Normal Roxy or Sloshy Roxy. It helps."

She ignored this. "I think I just got burgled."

"You *think*?"

"Let's put it this way. I just got home, there was a man lurking in my lounge room and he took off as soon as he saw me."

"You sure it wasn't Max getting a good look at you at this hour?"

"You're hilarious. Can you take this seriously, please, it was very unsettling."

There was a pause. "So you *are* serious?"

"Yes, Olie, I'm serious. I'm not into prank calling my agent at one a.m. There was some weirdo in my home. What should I do?"

"Christ! Are you okay?! Is he gone?"

"Bloody hope so."

"Did you lock the door?"

"No, I left it wide open with a 'Don't be shy' sign out the front."

"Cut the sarcasm, Rox, I'm tryin' to help. Did you get a good look at him?"

She thought about this. "Not really. He was largish, wearing a bulky coat of some sort, I think, weird long ears drooping down."

"Long ears? What, like a rabbit?"

"Okay, it was dark, maybe I got that bit wrong. But it's odd. He stared right at me, pushed me over in fact, but I can't picture any of his features."

"Perhaps Bugs Bunny was wearing a ski mask?"

She groaned. "Olie, this is serious."

"I know, I'm sorry. Did he hurt you? Is anything missing?"

"No, no, nothing like that."

"Want me to come over? I can be there in ten."

He wasn't exaggerating. Oliver's apartment was a quick stride away in a seedy suburb called Kings Cross, but she wasn't in the mood for more visitors tonight.

"No, no, no. I can't see how it would help, but thank you. I guess I just need to tell someone so I don't wake up tomorrow thinking I'd imagined the whole thing. Look, sorry to disturb you, I'm fine. He didn't hurt me, he didn't appear to take anything, but I'll double check. You attempt to get some sleep and I'll do the same."

"I'll come over in the morning."

"By morning you mean lunchtime."

"Yeah, that's what I said. Oh, and Roxy?"

"Yes?"

"Check your fridge. Maybe he raided your carrot supply."

He chuckled as he hung up and she shook her head at the telephone. *Honestly, her literary agent had the sensitivity of a gnat.* She looked around her now well-lit apartment and wondered what to do. Eventually, she gave up wondering and managed to find her way to bed, but not before double-checking her front lock several times, and sneaking a bread knife under her pillow. If Scary Bunny came back, he'd have more than Shaggy and the crew to worry about!

CHAPTER 2

Roxy's first thought when she awoke in the morning was not of ghoulish bunnies or her thumping hangover, but of Max. Why, she wondered, with a pang of guilt, hadn't she phoned her strong, strapping boyfriend of eleven months (and four days) last night instead of calling up pudgy, older Oliver who was about as useful with his fists as a feather boa? Was it because Olie lived so close, or was it something else, something deeper?

She decided not to let that thought develop—she was really good at leaving thoughts in the proverbial camera—and she struggled out of bed and into a shower, popping a couple of paracetamol on the way. She needed to work out what exactly had happened last night and she needed to do it minus a headache and plus at least one cup of coffee.

Ten minutes later, dressed in blue denim jeans and a floppy white T-shirt with the tablets denting the drumming in her brain, she padded into her kitchen and reached for her ancient Atomic coffeemaker. As she made a good strong brew, she leant across the cabinet and chewed her lower lip, deep in thought.

A man had broken into her apartment. That much was clear. He clearly wasn't interested in her, or her belongings, as far as she could tell. So what did he want?

She shook her glossy black hair, which now hung down past her shoulders in thick, chunky layers. He was obviously *about* to rob her, and she had interrupted him. It was that simple, so why did she need to make it more complicated? She stalked across to the front door, peered through the peephole to the empty hallway and then unlatched the lock. She slowly opened the door and looked out. Emptiness again. She studied the lock. *Ah yes.* It had been slightly jemmied, there was paint scraped off and there was a tiny bit of damage. She hadn't noticed it when she let herself in the night before. She returned to her bedroom, retrieved her smartphone and then took a few quick snaps. Evidence, she didn't know of what.

"Running out of sunsets?" a deep voice said and she jumped.

Max Farrell was standing behind her, his hands shoved into the pockets of his baggy trousers, a well-fitting, grey hoodie covering his long, lean chest, blue and white gym boots on his feet.

"Jesus, Max, you scared the crap out of me!"

"Sorry, just wondering why you're taking photos of the most boring aspect of your apartment."

"Does this lock look tampered with?"

He inspected it. "Maybe. Dunno, why? What's happened?"

Roxy's green eyes darted around then she pulled him in before shutting the door.

"I got burgled last night. Well, kind of."

"What?" Instinctively, Max grabbed her into his arms and held her in an embrace. "This is why you should have stayed at my place."

She ignored that comment, counted to three then pulled back just as the Atomic started spluttering like an old drunk.

"Want a coffee?"

She switched the Atomic off and poured the murky brew into two cups, then added milk as she told Max exactly what had happened, deliberately omitting her late-night call to Oliver.

"So you phoned Gilda?" he asked.

"Gilda? No, of course not." She reached for the sugar bowl and scooped two large teaspoons into her coffee then reconsidered and added a third. "Why would I bother a top homicide detective with something as menial as B&E? I mean, it's not like he took anything or hurt me or even damaged the door. Although I will get that lock changed. I need something more heavy duty. He probably just jemmied it with a bloody credit card."

"This is serious, Parker," Max said and she eye rolled him. "You should have stayed at my place last night."

"Yes, you already said that but if I had, he would have had free rein of the place, and I could be returning home today to a cleaned out apartment. Or a trashed one. Who knows?"

"Better than returning home to get trashed yourself."

"I was already trashed, if you recall. That's the last time I let you talk me into that second bottle of merlot."

"Parker, this is serious."

"I know, I know, but I honestly don't think he wanted to hurt me. I mean, he could have if he'd wanted. I walked straight in, half tanked, but all he did was freak out and scuttle off into the night. Like the rat that he is. Or should I say bunny rabbit."

"Sorry?"

"Don't worry."

"Still, it's pretty scary. Maybe he's a stalker."

She sighed. "Max, this isn't Hollywood. I don't have a stalker. Listen, I can't have you making a big fuss about this. I'm not even going to tell Mum because she's even worse than you, so please, just chill out, okay?"

He stared hard at her. He was good at those hard stares—the clenched jaw, the piercing eyes. If he wasn't so bloody attractive when he did it, she'd punch him. His jaw loosened.

"Fine. Want to grab some breakfast?"

She considered this. It would be a good distraction. She swallowed her coffee in one gulp. "Let's do it."

On the way out, Roxy popped on a slim leather jacket, hoop earrings and some lip-gloss, then sent a quick text message to Oliver. It was almost 10:00 a.m. and she assumed he'd still be snoozing, but she wanted to tell him where to find her, just in case. By the time she got to her local café, Peepers, however, he was already there, slouched at a table outside under a giant, white umbrella that had the word *Vittoria* across it.

It was chilly out. Despite it being the early days of spring, the weather had not noticed and it still felt like mid-winter. Oliver, too, had missed the memo and was wearing little more than a thin, cotton Hawaiian shirt, baggy black jeans and a beat-up old Fedora.

"Goodness, you're up early," Roxy said as Max stayed on the sidewalk to take a call on his mobile phone.

Oliver looked up at her with tubby jowls and three-day growth and grimaced. "No choice, Rox. Got an early morning call—"

"I know, I'm sorry. But can you keep that to yourself? Max ... well ... he probably would have preferred I called him—"

"I'm not talking about your call, it's not *all* about you, you know? About nine this morning, some chick rings and demands your details."

"*My* details? But I thought you said it's not all about me." She bat her eyelids at him and he smirked.

"Yeah, well, she wakes me from the deepest bloody sleep. I nearly told her where she could stick your details, except she sounded needy. You know what I'm like with needy chicks."

He offered her a lopsided grin and she laughed, taking the seat beside him. "So who is this damsel in distress? What did she want? You didn't just hand over my—"

"'Course I didn't, I'm not an idiot." He looked offended for about a second. "Said her name was Sandra Lang or Lane or something. I got her number and said you'd call her back when you had some free time."

He reached into his pocket to retrieve a scrap of paper on which he'd scribbled a mobile number. Max appeared then, looking harassed.

"Sorry, that's me done. I've got to go and collect Caroline—she's woken up in some strange guy's bed and has no idea how to get home."

Oliver laughed and Roxy shook her head. "Who's the guy?"

"I don't know. She's started some new hobby and I suspect he has something to do with that. And stop laughing, Oliver! This is just typical of Caro, she gets to have all the fun and I get to pick up the pieces."

"Like *we're* not having any fun?" Roxy said, eyes squinting.

He shrugged. "We didn't have any fun last night."

She let this one pass. "You men and your damsels. Okay, well good luck and I'll call you later."

He hesitated, looking down at Roxy through tangles of dark, unruly fringe. "You're sure you're okay? Maybe you should stay at my—"

She held a hand up. "I'll be fine, honestly." She jumped up and gave him a long, lingering kiss, which seemed to cheer him up, not to mention catch the eye of a few passing pedestrians. He rewarded her with one of his thousand-watt smiles, then waved them goodbye and strode away.

"That Caroline's a piece of work," said Oliver.

"I know, I love Max's sister, she's a hoot, but I wouldn't want to be related to her."

"You might be if all goes well with you-know-who."

He raised his bushy eyebrows a few times provocatively and she scowled back at him. She wasn't lying. She did love Max but marriage was not a topic she had any fondness for.

"Anyway, enough of that, I need a greasy ham and cheese croissant and I need it now. You want anything?"

He shook his head and Roxy jumped up to place her order at the counter. By the time she returned, she'd forgotten all about marriage to Max and strange visitors in the night, and for just an hour or so, life returned to normal. It would prove to be short-lived.

CHAPTER 3

The policemen stood out like sore thumbs. Dressed in cheap, ill-fitting suits with wrap-around sunglasses and short back and sides, they looked equally uncomfortable in Roxy's bohemian, inner-city suburb of Elizabeth Bay, and her heart skipped a beat as she walked up towards them. One was standing beside her car, which she'd parked outside her building at a particularly dodgy angle the night before, the other pressing on a buzzer that looked suspiciously like hers from a distance.

Oh God, she thought. *I'm gonna get done for sloppy parking.*

As she approached, they both turned to watch her for a few seconds before one said, "Roxanne Parker?"

She braced herself. "Yes?"

The man who had spoken produced a police identification card from his jacket and flashed it in front of her. He had a protruding beer belly, grey bags under his eyes and looked about 105. When he spoke, his voice was breathless and croaky. "Detective Sean Leary, Cremorne Area Command."

"Yes?" she repeated.

"Is that your vehicle?" He indicated the dark blue VW Golf and she felt her stomach lurch.

"Yes, yes, I know it's a crappy park. It was a really tight spot and I got in late last night so—"

"Can we speak to you inside?"

Oh for God's sake, it's just a dodgy park! "Look, Detective, I've got the keys on me and I can straighten it up now."

His expression did not change. "We're not here to talk about your parking skills, Miss Parker."

"Oh, right. So why ...?" That's when it clicked. "Oh, you heard about the break-in?"

Detective Leary glanced at his partner, a much younger man with carrot-orange hair and a face splattered with dirty brown freckles, then back at Roxy.

"Break-in?" he now repeated.

"It's not that big a deal, really. It's not like he took anything, at least not that I can tell."

"Did you report this?"

"Well, no, as I say, he didn't take anything. I must have disturbed him."

He looked bored suddenly by this conversation. "We're here about a separate matter, Miss Parker."

"What separate matter?"

"Inside, if you don't mind," the younger man spoke now, waving a hand towards the entrance.

"Fine." She unlocked the door. "It's four floors up."

She wondered if the old guy would make it; it was hard enough for *her* these days. Roxy's usual fitness regime—a daily speed walk/jog on good days—had taken a real beating of late. Not only had she been preoccupied with her latest ghostwriting assignment, but Max had been monopolising the rest of her time and her walking shoes were probably covered in cobwebs by now.

She led the way up, Leary panting heavily behind her, and stopped outside her door. The last time she'd opened it, a strange man had been lurking inside. Today, she was inviting two more strangers in. She hoped their credentials were legit.

She swung the door open and peered inside tentatively, before stepping in and heading straight for the lounge room. Before she could offer the men a seat, Leary had already dropped into a dining chair, red-faced and sweaty.

"Are you okay?" she asked. "Would you like a glass of water? Cup of tea?"

He waved her off and produced a small notepad, taking a few croaky breaths before opening it and whipping through several pages. Eventually, after a few more breaths, he said, "What is your relationship with a Mr Bernard John Tiles, please?"

"Bernard John Tiles?" The name rang a bell but for the moment Roxy could not work out why. "I'm not sure ...?" They stared at her blankly. "Can I ask what this is in relation to? His name sounds familiar but—"

"It's a straight forward question, Miss Parker. You either do or do not know a," he glanced at the pad, "Mr Bernard John Tiles."

She shook her head. "Well, I can't—" She stopped. "Oh, do you mean *Berny* Tiles? The surveyor?"

They looked at each other again but did not answer, so she said, "I know a Berny Tiles. Not well. I interviewed him recently for a book I was writing on Sir Wolfgang Bergman. You know, the mining magnate? It was a pretty brief interview with Berny, though, just one hour over lunch. Why?"

"Do you own any other motor vehicles, Miss Parker?"

His sudden change of tack caught her by surprise and for another moment Roxy's mind went blank. Eventually she managed to shake her head, no.

Detective Leary kept reading from his notepad. He clearly had a set of questions written down and he intended to get through them.

"Have you driven any other motor vehicles in the past six days?"

"No. Unless you count a couple of cabs."

He stared hard at her. "You *drove* those cabs, did you, Miss Parker?"

"Obviously not," she replied, restraining a smirk.

He referred back to his pad. "Where were you on the evening of Sunday, September the second?"

"Sorry?"

"Six days ago, Miss Parker. Where were you between the hours of 9:00 p.m. and midnight?"

She considered this and then felt a small lump in her throat. "That was Father's Day, right?" He nodded. "I was with my mother."

"On *Father's* Day?" said the younger man, his freckles scrunching up into one big, brown blob around his nose.

"Yes, well, I would have preferred to be with my dad, but he's six feet under." She tried not to look too smarmy. "So I let my mother talk me into celebrating that evening over dinner with my stepdad, but, well, that was a barrel of laughs as always. You want their number?"

Leary nodded and she recited it by heart. "Try not to freak her out when you call. She does tend to overreact."

"I'll keep that in mind," said Leary.

Roxy felt suddenly tense. "Look, she's going to think the absolute worst, is there any way you can tell me what's going on? What all these questions are about?"

The elderly detective snapped his notepad shut. "We're not at liberty to say, Miss Parker, but we thank you for your time. We'll be back in touch should we need anything further."

She stared at him stunned, not sure what she'd actually given him. "This is all very cryptic. You're not even going to give me a clue?"

"Just clearing up a few issues for an investigation. We may be in touch."

And with that they opened the front door and departed, leaving a very perplexed Roxy Parker in their wake.

CHAPTER 4

Unable to shake off a strange sense of foreboding, Roxy decided it was time to get her fitness back on track. Exercise always helped calm her thoughts and right now they were on overload.

Why, she wondered as she changed into a tracksuit and joggers, did two policemen show up at her door asking some very strange questions about her car and her whereabouts? And why on earth did they mention boring old Berny Tiles?

Exchanging her beanie for a cap and her black Rayban spectacles for prescription Gucci sunglasses, Roxy recalled the seventy-something retiree and his kindly face—ready smile, steel spectacles, scruffy grey hair—and couldn't think of any reason why the police would be making enquiries about him. Or, at least, nothing that was very positive and she wasn't in the mood for negative, so she thrust him from her mind, grabbed some small change and her keys, and headed out again.

It had been months since Roxy had walked, but the route was a familiar one—past the steamy Laundromat, newsagency and a Chinese takeaway, crossing the road at Peepers, down a back alley and a set of stone stairs, and into the lush green park of Rushcutters Bay. There she usually picked up the pace and began to jog, but she was already puffing from the power walk so she decided to stick to that today, knowing her body would thank her and torture her in equal measures later.

After fifty-five minutes and several buckets of sweat, she peeled off her cap, wiped down her brow then returned up the steps, through the alleyway and onto Elizabeth Bay Road again. She zigzagged across to the newsagency where the oversized Greek owner was now perched precariously on a stool out the front, a glass of espresso in his hand.

"Ullo, Miss Roxy!" Costa called out as she approached. "You come for your papers at last!"

"Yep, I forgot to collect them earlier. They still there?"

"We always save 'em for you, you know that!" He then bellowed into the shop, "Rocco, get papers for Roxy!"

"Huh?" came a voice from inside.

"Roxy Parker, you moron! Look for name on top!"

He shook his head at Roxy as if to say, "You can't find any decent help these days."

A minute later, Costa's muscle-bound son Rocco burst out of the agency with Roxy's two Saturday newspapers in his hands.

"Ullo, Roxy," he said, giving her a flirtatious grin.

"Hi, Rocco," she replied, handing him the change. "Been working out, I see."

He beamed proudly, suddenly feeling the need to scratch the back of his neck, thus allowing Roxy another good look at his bulging right bicep. She almost laughed but decided Rocco might not take it so well, and simply smiled, wedged the papers under one arm and continued on to her apartment.

She was just reaching for her keys when a very thin, very pale woman with startling red lipstick stepped out from a nearby doorway. Her greying brown hair was pulled into a tight ponytail, large ears protruding out, and she was clutching a shabby brown leather handbag in front of her chest.

"Roxy Parker?" she asked, her voice barely a whisper and for a moment Roxy thought her ears were playing tricks on her. She glanced around.

The woman was staring keenly at her, so she said, "Beg your pardon?"

The woman stepped a little closer. "I'm looking for Roxy Parker. Are you ...?" She let it dangle there and Roxy stepped back.

She was getting a lot of odd visitors of late. "Yes, I am, can I help you with something?"

"I'm Sondra Lane. I ... I rang your agent this morning?"

"Oh yes, he mentioned something." But he shouldn't have given her address out. "What's this about?"

The woman glanced around. "Can we talk, please? Inside, if you don't mind?"

The woman indicated the front door that Roxy had not yet opened and she sighed. *Could no one have a conversation outdoors anymore?*

Sensing her hesitation, the woman added, "I promise not to take up too much of your time. It's very important."

It's very bloody odd is what it is, thought Roxy, but then again, it had been a very odd twenty-four hours.

She let her in and led the way up to her apartment feeling a case of déjà vu as she did so. She also felt the same sense of wariness as she opened her front door, and she wondered whether a shiny new deadlock would make a jot of difference. Had the creepy burglar stolen her apartment's innocence forever?

"Excuse the mess," Roxy said as she headed for the kitchen. "I wasn't expecting guests. I don't know why. They're a regular occurrence these days."

"It's perfectly fine," the woman replied, glancing around herself.

She looked as though she, too, expected a crazy man to appear out of the shadows and Roxy decided a good settling cup of tea was probably in order for both of them.

She dumped the papers and her cap on the kitchen bench, switched back to her Rayban glasses and popped the kettle on.

"How do you like your tea?" she called out, reaching for an antique blue and white china teapot.

"Oh ... er, white and no sugar, thank you. If it's not too much trouble?"

"No trouble at all. Please, pull up a pew, make yourself comfortable."

Roxy feared the strange, pale woman would drop. She had that broken bird look about her—bony limbs accentuated by a flowing woollen dress, pale features amplified by stark coloured lipstick, the only makeup she appeared to be wearing. Yet Sondra stayed standing until Roxy joined her with the tea and then sat down across from her on one of the sofas, her handbag in her lap. For a few minutes neither woman spoke and Roxy was beginning to regret ever letting her in.

Eventually Sondra said, "This is most unusual, I don't know, really, where to begin."

You can say that again, Roxy thought, but she simply nodded and encouraged her to continue as she poured them both a cup of tea.

"The thing is, I wouldn't bother you with this, only ... it was so strange, you see. I just had to ... I had to ..."

"Yes?"

The woman stood up and began walking around the room in a kind of circular motion. Despite this, she was clearly trying to get her thoughts straight.

"I need to know ... I'm sorry if I'm prying but ... do you know my father?"

Roxy picked up her teacup. "Your father? Well, it would really help if you gave me his name." *Like, really.*

"Oh, goodness, I'm sorry, I'm all over the shop, as you can see. His name is Bernard." She stopped and turned to look straight at Roxy as though waiting for some sign. When Roxy kept blinking back at her blankly, she said, "Bernard Tiles."

The flash of comprehension in Roxy's eyes was all she needed; a look of horror swept across her face and she placed a hand to her mouth.

"Oh! How ... how long?" she stammered.

"Sorry?"

"How long have you ... and he ...?" She let it dangle there again, barely able to meet Roxy's eyes.

Now Roxy was really confused. The police had just been there, asking about Berny Tiles, now his daughter was standing in her lounge room doing the same. *What was going on?*

"I'm not following."

Sondra folded her arms in front of her chest. "You're not going to make this easy for me, are you? How long did you and he ... *know* each other?"

She shrugged. "Not long. It was really brief."

"Well it obviously meant something to him."

"Really? That surprises me but that's nice to hear. Considering it was only an hour."

The woman's eyes widened. "An hour?! Are you ... was he ...?" Her eyes began darting around the room again. "You're a *prostitute*?"

Roxy nearly spat her mouthful of tea across the room. "Prostitute?! What the hell—"

The woman held up a hand. "I apologise, escort or whatever you call yourselves these days."

Roxy leapt to her feet. "Hang on a minute, I'm not an escort or a prostitute. I'm a writer."

"Writer?"

"You know?" She pretended to scribble in the air. "I write books and articles for a living. I don't know what your dad told you but I interviewed him for a book I just wrote.

One hour max, over lunch at Giardineto's. About three, four months ago. That was it. Him, me, two plates of linguine and a digital recorder. Sure, they took a happy snap of us, they do that there for some reason, but that's as close as we got. And I can assure you, not one item of clothing was shed!"

Sondra turned as red as her lipstick and a bony hand returned to her mouth, aghast. "I am so sorry ... I thought ..."

"I know what you thought! It's not true." Roxy stopped. "Oh, God, do the police think that too?" And then. "What's all this about? I am really confused! What has your father been *saying* about me? I have a good mind to ring him up and tell him off!"

"He's dead."

Roxy blinked. "Sorry?"

The woman's face had paled again. "My father died. Last Sunday night. We buried him yesterday."

This stopped Roxy in her tracks. "Oh, right ... Oh God ... sorry."

Sondra looked equally deflated and they both slumped back down on the sofa.

"It doesn't make any sense, then," Sondra said, staring into her tea as though that might somehow clarify things. For Roxy's part she just wanted to know what the hell was going on.

She cleared her throat. "Look, I'm really sorry to hear about your dad, he seemed like a sweet guy when we met, but I didn't really know him at all. I'm sorry if someone gave you that impression."

"He did," she said softly.

"Huh?"

"My father. He mentioned you, just before he died. He said your name. Roxy Parker. Then he ... then he ..." She searched for a tissue in her handbag but Roxy beat her to it, finding a box on the mantelpiece and handing it over. Sondra took it with a grateful smile and helped herself, giving her nose a delicate blow. As she did so, a strand of slivery hair loosened from her ponytail and got caught up in the tissue. She swiped at it irritably.

Roxy sat back and thought about what Sondra had said. "Your dad, Berny Tiles, said *my* name? Before he died?" Sondra nodded, fluttering a look at Roxy. "That's it?"

"Not quite. He was dying ... we had all gathered by his bedside, and by the time we did, he was ... well, he wasn't good. It was clear, though, that he wanted to tell us something, something really important to him, but when he did all he said was, 'Roxy Parker has it.'"

"Roxy Parker has it?" She nodded. "Has *what*? Exactly?" Sondra shrugged a bony shoulder in the air. "Perhaps you misheard him? Or maybe he was talking about a different Roxy Parker?"

"I considered that. But you're the only Roxy Parker I can find in the entire phone book. And ... well ... you just told me you did know him."

"Yes, but as I said, just fleetingly." Roxy was beyond baffled; she was in cuckoo land. "Okay, so let me get this straight. Just before your father died, he told you that I have something that belongs to him?" Sondra nodded. "I'm sorry to disappoint you, but I don't have anything of your father's. Nothing."

"Nothing at all?"

She shook her head. "Look, I don't mean to sound rude, but does it actually matter now?"

"I think it does matter."

"But why? Maybe he was hallucinating, or it meant nothing ... I can't see why it should matter now that he's ... gone."

"It matters," the woman said, more firmly this time.

"Why?"

"Because my father was murdered, Roxy, and I think it has something to do with you."

CHAPTER 5

Roxy felt her blood run cold. Oh God, she thought, here we go again. *What is it with all her clients dropping dead?* Okay, this guy wasn't, strictly speaking, a client—he was a friend of a client—but it was close enough.

Her next thought was to declare her innocence and send the woman packing, but there was grief in Sondra's eyes and genuine confusion. It mirrored hers. Roxy wasn't sure if she was being accused of murder, or if that's what the cops believed, but she didn't like the woman's implications.

"So that's why the police were here," she said, more to herself than Sondra. "Listen, you have to believe me, I met your father once. We had a lovely lunch at a restaurant in North Sydney, he gave me some quotes for a book I'm writing, but that was all it was. An interview."

"I don't think you killed him, if that's what you're worried about," the other woman said and Roxy felt her heartbeat relax.

"Then why ...?"

"That's what I want to know. *Why?* Why did my father mention you of all people before he passed away?" She held a skinny hand up. "Don't tell me he was rambling, please, that's what my husband says and I refuse to believe it. My father was *determined* to say your name, he was adamant. It took him a while but he did it. He said your name. And he said you had it, whatever 'it' is. Did he give you something? Anything that day you met for lunch? Any documents? Old letters? *Anything?*"

"No, just some colourful anecdotes, that's all." *And they weren't even that colourful.*

She looked bitterly disappointed. "Can you at least tell me what you were working on with him?"

Roxy nodded. "I'll go you one better and get you a transcript of everything he said to me. I taped the entire conversation, although, to be honest, I don't remember it having anything to do with you or your family. You see, I've been ghostwriting a book—"

"Ghostwriting?"

"That's what I do for a living. I write other people's autobiographies." The woman still looked at her like she was speaking French, so Roxy explained. "Basically, a client who can't or doesn't want to write their own story hires me to do it for them and I usually keep my name off the book. That's why they call it ghostwriting, or ghosting."

"So it looks like they've written it themselves."

"Yeah, well, it's not exactly an honest living, but it pays the bills. Or most of them. Strictly speaking, it was Book It Publishing who hired me to do the bio on Sir Wolfgang—"

"Wolfgang?" her eyes fluttered again and she appeared to pale even further.

"Yes, do you know him? Your dad was an old acquaintance from Indonesia."

Roxy had spent the past six months researching and writing the mining magnate's life story. Wolfgang Bergman had made and lost and made his fortune again in the wilds of Southeast Asia. Mostly oil and gas, but there was a little copper and gold thrown in for good measure. Sir Wolfgang was as rough as the terrain he had pillaged, and despite being close to eighty-five, was as frisky as a young mare, and Roxy spent most of their interview time ignoring his leering looks, sleazy innuendo and wolfish grin, which is why she came to nickname him 'Wolfman'. Of course, she didn't tell Sondra any of this, but it was fairly clear that Sondra wasn't his biggest fan either and from the second she mentioned Wolfgang's name, a frown had settled on her porcelain forehead.

"Yes, I know Sir Wolfgang," she said. "My father was his biggest fan. Although he didn't even bother turning up to Dad's funeral." There was an edge in her voice now, a cold, distant look in her eyes. "I didn't realise Dad was involved in that book."

"Only in a very small way. He had a few stories to tell about their days in Jakarta and Irian Jaya, nothing very exciting. As I say, I'll get you the full transcript and you can read it for yourself. Maybe I've forgotten something. Maybe he told me something he wants repeated to you guys."

Roxy didn't believe it for a moment but it seemed to placate the woman and she stood up, clutching her handbag.

"Thank you. That would be very kind. I have taken enough of your time."

She reached into her bag and retrieved her purse. From it, she plucked out a small business card and handed it to Roxy. It was illustrated with a bright red rose and had the name *Blooming Bros* in a fancy script across the front.

"That's my husband's business, really, I just help out when I can. Use the e-mail address at the bottom; it will get to me. If you could send the full transcript there."

Roxy nodded and took it from her, then began to show her out when she suddenly remembered the photo. *But surely it couldn't be about that?*

"There is one thing," she said and the woman turned back, a look of hope squeezing out the anxiety in her eyes. "Sorry, I completely forgot about it because he didn't actually *give* it to me, *per se*, he sent it—"

"What?!" she interrupted, her eyes as wide as saucers now.

"The photo."

"What photo?!"

"Your dad sent me a photo to go in the book. It was the only picture he had with Sir Wolfgang and he said I might like to use it. I never actually received it myself, you see, I asked him to post it to my agent, and then he forwarded it on to the publisher."

"That must be it! What was in the photo, did you see it?"

"Yes, just briefly at my agent's office." Roxy thought about it. "It was a pretty boring picture, Sondra. If I recall correctly, it was a really old black and white portrait taken of your dad, Sir Wolfgang and a couple of other people at some conference or something. Nothing very exciting. In fact, I don't think it even made the book because I can't recall seeing it in the final mock-ups."

Sondra's red cheeks and animated eyes showed she didn't think it was unexciting at all. "Can I see it?"

"Of course. In fact, I'm sorry it hasn't been returned to you."

"Do you have it?" She looked around anxiously again.

"Oh, no, not here, I don't."

The woman's shoulders drooped and Roxy thought then of a kite. Sondra seemed to dip and soar on Roxy's every word. She was clearly in a very brittle emotional state and Roxy felt for her. Losing your father was always a struggle, losing him to murder was unthinkable. "I can easily find it for you. It must still be with the publisher. Even if they didn't did use it, they'll have it in their files. I'll track it down."

The shoulders straightened again. "Oh please do, as soon as you can. It's very important."

"Of course, but the publisher won't be there today; I'll call them on Monday, first thing."

Again, the woman thanked her and headed towards the door.

"Just don't get your hopes up," Roxy called after her. "It's a really ordinary shot."

Sondra stopped and turned back. "Perhaps it wasn't so ordinary to my father," she said.

CHAPTER 6

"I'm going to give her five minutes and then it's onto *my* work," Roxy decided after Sondra left and she had put a call through to her local locksmith. He would be there within the hour and she couldn't wait. She still felt uneasy and couldn't help darting wary glances at her front door, fearful it might burst open at any point.

She shrugged her fears away, pulled off her sweaty tracksuit and threw herself under a shower. Ten minutes later and another furtive glance at the front door, she strode into her small sunroom-cum-office and switched on her laptop. As she watched the screen dance to life, she thought of Sondra's visit and what it could possibly mean.

Sondra Lane seemed to be on some wild goose chase but she was clearly desperate and Roxy felt for her. Having lost her own father so young, Roxy understood the need for answers, but she had never got any herself, and she wondered whether Sondra would. Shivering a little, she recalled the woman's earlier words:

'My father was murdered, Roxy, and I think it has something to do with you.'

She sat back and thought about this. How bizarre that a dying man would utter *her* name in the last moments of his life. Of all the things he could have said, of all the names he could have called, he called out hers. She didn't feel flattered, not at all. If anything she felt uneasy, as though she had just been thrust, unwillingly, into someone else's torment, and a small chill trickled down her spine.

"Stop it!" she told herself, trying to shake it off. Sondra's husband was right. It was probably just the final, delirious ramblings of a dying man. Or maybe he was just trying to get all his ducks in order, so to speak.

Roxy scrolled through her files and located a folder dubbed "Wolfman" and double clicked. Inside she opened a file named "Boring Berny" and felt a flush of guilt. She hadn't meant to sound so mean, but he really had been rather dull, the last man she would have expected to get caught up in a baffling murder mystery. Roxy opened it, curious now as she glanced through the content.

It was just a few pages, a fairly brief interview about Berny's dealings with the well-known mining billionaire. Long story short, Berny had done some surveying work for one of Wolfgang's Indonesian copper mines in 1973, and they had started a friendship that, as far as she could tell, seemed more lopsided than anything else. Berny had nothing but gushing praise for the older magnate, while the magnate had very little to say about Berny other than that he was a "good bloke" who might have a good quote or two to contribute to the book. In fact, Wolfgang hadn't mentioned Berny at all and it was only after Roxy had pressed him for more colour—mining books were dreary by nature—that he had suggested Berny for an interview.

She recalled later wondering why. Apart from the gushing praise, Berny had little to contribute and, if anything, seemed almost protective of his old mate. He did confess that they both drank and gambled way too much for their own good, but that was as colourful as it got. It wasn't exactly X-rated stuff.

As she reread the transcript now, Roxy got the same impression she had when she first interviewed Berny, the strange feeling that he was holding something back. She had forgotten about that. Several times Berny had gone to say something and had checked himself, retraced his words and changed the subject. She hadn't thought much of it at the time—most friends and family were guarded when a tape recorder was rolling—but she wondered now if there was more to it.

Or was she just reading into it for Sondra's sake?

Roxy finished the transcript and sighed. Berny Tiles was just as she remembered, sweet but dull, and she couldn't see anything particularly exciting or alarming in the copy, certainly nothing that should interest his progeny. There were no loving words of wisdom, no mention of changed wills or where he might have hidden the family jewels. It was all about Wolfgang, and all pretty benign. She closed the file, attached it to an open e-mail and then popped Sondra's husband's business address at the top.

As she watched it whiz off to the *Blooming Bros* e-mail in-box, she went back through the PDF layouts of the entire Bergman book that had been sent to her by the publisher. She always kept "mock-ups" of her books on file. While Roxy's job was officially over once she sent the text in, she liked to be involved in the editing and layout process, just to make sure her words had been transplanted correctly. She wasn't just being a perfectionist. Roxy's reputation was also on the line. Her name might not be on the cover, but it was always the writer who copped the blame when the editing work was sloppy.

In Bergman's case, however, she had been particularly fastidious. Despite his old age and sleazy overtures, he was a cunning businessman, not someone you wanted to get offside. At least, that's the impression Roxy got. She did not want to feel Wolfman's bite.

Wading through it all again now, it was clear that Berny's photo had not made the final layout, just as she'd thought.

Roxy stood up and stretched her long, lean body out like a cat, then stopped and stared at the sun that was just starting to set on the glistening bay below her window. Her apartment might be small and shabby but it had a lovely harbour view and she regularly had to remind herself to soak it up, lest she forget. It was one of the reasons she had bought the place, was breaking her back to pay the hefty mortgage, and it was also why she was reluctant to move in with Max, despite his many offers.

Max's warehouse might be four times bigger and a great deal slicker, but it didn't have this intoxicating view, and she reminded him of that whenever he pressed the point. He said it was just an excuse and he was probably right, but she wasn't about to admit that to anyone, least of all herself.

She shook all thought of Max from her mind, picked up her phone and dialled. After five rings, a cheerful voice answered.

"And there I was thinking Max had locked you up in a dungeon somewhere, never to be seen again."

Roxy laughed. "Sorry, Gilda, I've been pretty preoccupied. How have you been? How's homicide working out?"

Detective Superintendent Gilda Maltin had been promoted from the Mosman Area Command, in Sydney's swanky North Shore, to the Homicide Serious Crime Squad in the heart of the city, a little over six months ago and had barely had a spare moment since then.

"Busy, too, but not with fun and games like you," she said.

"They haven't got you working on a Saturday have they?"

"You of all people should know that crime never sleeps."

Gilda was one of Roxy's best friends, had been since they cracked a murder case together, over two years ago, and Roxy adored her. She was smart, funny, and as unlike a police officer as anyone could get—a tiny, blonde thing with a cunning brain and bawdy sense of humour. They had shared many a good laugh together and it warmed Roxy's heart to know she had one of the city's top cops on speed dial. She didn't normally like to abuse it, but her curiosity was now piqued.

"Listen, I hate to disturb you at work but I do have a work related question."

Roxy heard a clicking keyboard in the background. "Just a sec," Gilda said. There was more clicking and then everything went quiet. "Shoot."

Roxy filled her friend in on the bizarre visit from the two officers earlier that day, then on her chat with Sondra Lane. "Says her dad was murdered, do you know anything about the case?"

"Hmm ... sounds a little familiar but I'm not working on it if that's what you mean. Did she say her dad was murdered or she just *thinks* he was?"

Roxy considered this. "The latter, I think. I mean, she seemed pretty confused, grasping for straws."

"I will never understand people, Roxy. Why would they prefer to know their loved one was murdered rather than just dying innocently? I mean, surely that's a little more soothing."

"Maybe they need to know it was avoidable or want someone to blame?"

"Yeah, or maybe humans are just plain nutty. Okay, leave it with me and I'll get back to you. So it was Detective Sean Leary, you say?"

"Yep, although I can't remember the other guy's name, sorry. Not even sure he told me."

"I know Leary, he's an old-timer from the Cremorne branch, near my old stomping ground. Was his partner a young redhead, wet around the ears?"

"Yep, looked about twelve."

"That'd be Eddie Calhoun. Okay, I'll hunt them down and find out what's going on. I wouldn't worry too much. Sounds like they were just crossing t's, dotting i's, that kind of thing. Hey, why don't we get together tonight, chat about it then and catch up at the same time? That is if Max will let you out of the dungeon."

"He won't have any choice," Roxy said. "Where do you want to meet?"

"How about that cool little wine bar you used to go to a lot. Pico's?"

"God, I haven't been there all year. You're right. Max has been monopolising my time. I barely ever go out anymore."

"Right, well, come out tonight and we'll catch up. Eight p.m. would work for me. Oh, and Roxy?"

"Yes?"

"Leave your violin at home with Max."

Roxy laughed as she hung up the phone.

CHAPTER 7

Pico's hadn't changed one bit since Roxy was last there. It was still a shabby, bohemian-style wine bar perched on the grungier side of the city, and a favourite amongst artists, musicians and other creative types. Max had first introduced Roxy to the bar over three years ago, and they had made it their own, and as she strolled in and looked around today, she wondered why they hadn't been here of late. It was home to many of their happiest memories. It was also the place where they first fell in love.

She groaned. They had barely been anywhere over the past eleven months (and four days), their life narrowing down to a five-kilometre radius between his place, her place and the Indian restaurant in between. *Sort of like the Bermuda Triangle,* she thought gloomily as she pulled out a leather barstool and sat down.

"Hey, Roxy Parker," the barman said, smiling widely. "Long time no see. What're you after? Merlot?"

She laughed. "Hey, Pedro, you remembered?"

"You're the only one who ever drinks it," he said, winking. "I'm sure we've got a crusty old bottle here somewhere."

As he turned to prepare the wine, she rummaged through her handbag for her iPhone. Gilda was running late and had sent a text message to that effect, so by the time she got to the bar, Roxy had polished off half her glass of wine and was already nibbling on potato wedges.

Gilda looked stunning as always, her golden blonde hair wispy around her face, dark eye shadow smudged around her wide, brown eyes. For a forty-something policewoman, she was surprisingly stylish, too, in tailored woollen trousers, black and white striped top, and killer heels that looked incapable of chasing down bad guys.

"Love your hair!" Gilda was saying, swooping in to plant a quick kiss on her friend's cheek before ordering a gin and tonic. "What happened to your trademark bob?"

"Time, or lack thereof," Roxy replied. "Easier just to let it grow out."

"Goodness, Max really is monopolising your time. Well, it looks fab. Shall we grab a table?"

They collected their stuff and slipped into a side booth where they could have a little more privacy and space to spread out. Gilda produced her phone and placed it on the table.

"Did I mention crime never sleeps?" she said by way of apology and Roxy waved her off.

"So did you find out anything on Berny Tiles?"

Gilda's smoky brown eyes lit up. "Oh yes I did, and no wonder everyone's knocking on your door." She paused as Pedro brought her drink across, thanked him then continued. "You're right, the Cremorne branch is still handling this one at this stage. I'm not sure what the daughter told you ... Sandra was it?"

"Sondra. And not much."

"Okay." She took a gulp of her drink, the ice rattling in her glass. "According to Leary and Calhoun, Bernard Tiles definitely died from injuries sustained by a hit and run."

"So *that's* why they were checking out my car, looking for suspicious dent marks. Cheeky buggers."

"Yes, well, they obviously didn't find any and the only witness—a very vague, very elderly neighbour of the deceased's—said something about a white van. So your navy blue Golf is off the hook, for now."

"But what about me?" She remembered the detectives enquiring about other cars she might have driven in the past week.

"They have to keep an open mind, Rox. The deceased did say your name before he slipped off this mortal coil, so they'd be remiss not to look into it."

"I get that, but they'll see I have an alibi and I couldn't possibly have done it."

"Already checked out. Your mother and Charlie have verified that you were with them that night. Good thing you slept over."

"Yes, well, I have to get completely trashed to survive an evening with Mum, you know that. Then I was over the limit and I would *never* drink and drive."

"Always the model citizen." Gilda smiled.

Roxy thought about her mother then and wondered why Lorraine hadn't called. The visit from the police would surely have unsettled her and she would no doubt give her daughter the grilling of her life over lunch tomorrow. Roxy cringed at the thought, but she felt grateful, too, that she had an alibi. She knew how these things went. Oliver had recently been through a similar ordeal, and Roxy didn't like the idea of being on the receiving end of suspicion and false allegations, all because you didn't have anyone at home to vouch for you.

"Have they got any suspects at all? Any idea of motive?"

"Not yet, no. According to the witness—who has cataracts, by the way, so I doubt her evidence will ever see the light of day, excuse the pun—she heard an almighty 'thunk' just outside the victim's house, and looked out her window and spotted some bloke jumping into a white van just before it sped away. She hobbled out and found Mr Tiles severely injured on the road outside his front gate."

"And when was this?"

"About 10:15 p.m. on Father's Day. Last Sunday. According to the daughter, he'd been home alone all night. Apparently she was supposed to meet up with him, as you do on Father's Day, but he cancelled at the last minute, said he wasn't feeling well or something like that."

"So what was a sick man doing hanging outside his house at that time of night?"

"Exactamondo!" She took a swig of her gin. "Very suspicious. Leary and his lot are continuing with their enquiries."

"So it's not considered a 'serious crime' yet?"

"Still being investigated. Obviously Leary's team has to look at all the options before they hand it over to us, if they ever do. I mean, hit and runs are tricky crimes, Roxy. They happen more often than you'd care to know, most by innocently bad drivers who have no idea they've just wiped out an old guy crossing the road. Maybe he'd gone for a late night stroll or something. But these cases do tend to remain open until the driver is located and motive is eliminated. I mean, the guy was old but he wasn't *that* old, and the fact that the driver never stopped and rendered assistance, and that someone else was present at the scene and fled with the driver, makes it all look very, very dodgy."

"I wonder why I didn't read about this."

Gilda smiled over her gin and tonic. "Didn't make your Book of Death, eh?"

Roxy squinted her emerald eyes. "I call it a Crime Catalogue, and you know that."

"Whatever helps you sleep at night." Gilda winked. "Shall we order some decent food?"

Roxy glanced down at her plate of wedges. "God no! I'm thoroughly enjoying my high carb overload, but you go right ahead."

Gilda plucked a menu from a nearby table. "I need something heartier than that."

"So, what you're saying is, I'm officially in the clear?"

"Thanks to your mum, yes, but my hunch is, somebody was out to get this poor man. They weren't mucking around. Any idea why? Or, more importantly, why he said *your* name—of all the names in all the world—just before he died?"

"I've been madly racking my brain trying to work that out. I can only guess that Sondra's hubby was right and he was delirious at that stage." She only hoped the detectives believed that too. "I had recently interviewed him for the Wolfgang Bergman book I was writing. I told you about that book, right?"

"Yes, you had some charming name for him if I recall."

"Wolfman. I also like to call him Sir Sleazebag on occasion."

Gilda laughed. "Sounds like half the blokes I work with. The other half are married." She sighed. "Anyway, yes, that explains how you know him, although it doesn't explain why he said your name at such a critical moment. You'll probably hear from Leary about the transcript. He'll want a copy, I'd say."

"And he can have one. But what else should I do?"

"Nothing! I know that's hard for you, Miss Super Sleuth, but the Cremorne branch is on it and you need to leave them to it. Why the victim said your name right before he died, nobody knows, but Leary's more interested in the hit and run angle, so let him work that angle and see what he finds. If they do manage to uncover the driver, it will probably all make sense. And if it doesn't, it's probably not relevant. Just step away."

"Gladly!" Roxy said.

She'd made a promise to both her mother and to Max almost a year ago that she'd had enough crime and misadventure for one life, and would steer clear of it in the future, and she intended to keep that promise.

Gilda's big brown eyes watched her closely for a few minutes as though she didn't believe her, then she signalled the waiter over and ordered a Greek salad.

"Let's move on to more exciting topics. How's it all going with Max? You moved in yet?"

Roxy finished off her merlot with a large gulp and said, "Think I need another one of these first. You?" Gilda agreed and Roxy signalled the barman with two fingers. He nodded and set about making their drinks.

"Oh dear, this doesn't sound good."

"He wants me to move in."

"And that's *not* good?" Roxy shrugged. "You're not ready?"

"We've been going out less than a year, it's not long."

"You've known each other over three years. Doesn't that count for anything? What's the problem?"

"There's no problem."

Gilda cocked a blonde eyebrow at her just as the drinks arrived, followed soon after by Gilda's salad. She popped a chunk of feta cheese in her mouth before saying, "So what's going on?"

"What do you mean?"

"Roxy, it's me. 'Fess up."

"Nothing's going on ... I don't know. I just love my apartment. I love my space, my freedom."

"More than you love Max?"

She groaned. "Why does it have to be one or the other?"

"Look, I agree with you. There's a reason I'm still single, and it has little to do with the fact that most of the guys left on the market are cast-offs, not worthy of a garage sale. I, too, love my own space and I can't imagine finding anyone who deserves to clutter it. But you have found someone very worthy. He could clutter my place any time he likes." She sighed dreamily. "He's one of the good guys, Rox. He's trustworthy, he's sweet, he's a giant bloody spunk. That's like the full trifecta. I honestly don't know why you aren't running towards him with open arms. Actually, scrap that, I do know why."

Roxy looked up from her glass warily. She had a feeling she wasn't going to enjoy hearing this next bit.

"You obviously don't love him. Not really."

This surprised Roxy. She was expecting the usual lecture about her inability to commit, her immaturity or selfishness, but a lack of love had not occurred to her. She didn't like the sound of that.

"I do love him. Very much," she replied sulkily.

"Not enough, though, to move in with him." Gilda took a swig of her drink. "Listen, I always say when you know, you know. Well you obviously don't. It took you forever to get together with the poor bugger, now you're hesitating *again*? Riiiing, riiing, that's a warning bell, Missy, that you are with the wrong guy." She held her hands up, revealing recently polished nails. "Sorry, but it has to be said."

Roxy chewed over this as she chewed on her wedges. She didn't agree with her friend; it was ridiculous. But she was not in the mood to argue either, so she eventually said, "Can we let it drop? Move on?"

"Please yes, or I'll slip into a coma." Gilda forked some salad into her mouth and began chewing while she said, "Wanna hear about my riveting love-life instead?"

Roxy eyed her suspiciously. "I thought you said there was no love-life."

"Well, I use the word under advisement, but I have been dabbling a little online."

"Go girl!" Roxy said, cheering up enormously. "Okay then, give me every scintillating detail."

Gilda proceeded to fill Roxy in on her adventures on a popular dating website and the "disaster dates" she had recently "endured" and they spent the rest of the night laughing hysterically and drinking far too much alcohol. Max was now the furthest thing from Roxy's mind as she slipped into buddy heaven and let it roll over her like a warm blanket, or a glass of 2004 Barossa merlot.

CHAPTER 8

"It's ridiculously cold in here," Lorraine Jones announced, taking the spare seat beside Roxy at the Flower Pot Café where they met every second Sunday for a bite to eat and a few nibbles at each other.

Roxy glanced around at the motley collection of pot plants and garden furniture, each with a price tag attached. "It's an outdoor café, Mum."

"Doesn't mean they can't get some of those fabulous gas thingies, you know the ones I mean? The tall stand-upy ones that light up."

"You should work in a hardware shop," she deadpanned. "I think you mean patio heaters, the 'thingies' that contribute more to global warming than the entire island nation of Vanuatu."

Lorraine glared at her daughter. "We are *not* going to start on that topic, are we?"

Roxy shuddered, remembering too many heated conversations with her conservative mother and stepdad. "No, no, I've learned my lesson there. No sex, religion, politics or climate change."

"How about crime then, that seems to be the recurring theme in your life." Lorraine's eyes squinted and Roxy knew what she was getting at.

"Why don't we order first? I can't manage this on an empty stomach."

After Roxy had placed their orders—two vegetarian focaccias, a latte and a sparkling mineral water—she returned to her seat and found her mother still eyeing her dubiously.

There was no more avoiding the topic, so she launched in. "Okay, so I gather the policemen have been in touch. Well, if you're wondering what they were on about, I'm as clueless as you are."

Lorraine pursed her bright pink lips and began to play with her gold chain, the look on her face saying very clearly, "I know you, my dear, don't even try."

"Honestly, Mum, it has nothing to do with me."

"So why, then, do I have two very frightening police officers show up at my door yesterday?"

"Mum, one of them looks like he should still be at primary school, the other's a geriatric. There's nothing frightening about either of them."

Lorraine ran a hand through her neatly straightened, ivory blonde bob. "Their questions were rather scary."

"They just wanted to know if I was with you last Sunday night, right?"

"Yes, but why, my dear? They simply refused to elaborate, quite outrageous, and I did explain to them that we are good friends with the deputy police commissioner himself."

"*Good* friends?"

She blinked several times and dabbed a serviette at the corners of her mouth. "Well, we met him once at a party with Harold and Tina Donaldson, but anyway, that's not the point. The point is, why were these policemen asking about you? What have you been up to?"

"Nothing. Honestly! Look, they didn't tell me anything either. All I know is, some poor guy I interviewed once, really briefly for a book I was writing, showed up dead outside his house on Father's Day. Cops are looking into it, just speaking to anyone who had any dealings with the man over the past few months. It's really nothing to worry about."

She didn't mention the small matter of the man uttering her name in his dying breath, and her mother clearly didn't know about that, because she said, "I guess they have to interview everyone and with your record of dead bodies, I'm not surprised they've come knocking. Luckily I could verify your ..." she hesitated, her nose crinkled a little, "*alibi*. I was only just saying to Charlie how lucky you are to have been with us that night."

"Yes, really lucky to have spent Father's Day with a man who is not actually my father."

"Now don't you start on Charlie—"

"I'm not knocking Charlie. I'm just saying, I miss Dad, that's all."

Lorraine reached over and patted one of Roxy's hands. "Of course you do, sweetie, we understand that. That's why we had you over that night. Now," she sat back as the food arrived, "how's that Max man going?"

"Max Man is good, thanks," Roxy said, not sure this conversation was any safer than the last.

"Is there a ring on that finger yet?" She glanced down at Roxy's bare hand. "Or is he just getting all the gain, no pain."

Roxy sighed. *Here we go again.* Her mother liked her boyfriend, she knew that, but she was also stuck somewhere in the 1950s and believed there was really only one good use for a man, and that was a good marriage proposal, and the sooner the better. Anything less was just "taking advantage". The fact that Roxy was enjoying being taken advantage of was beside the point.

"I'm just saying, he should make an honest woman out of you."

Roxy glanced at her watch. Just thirty more minutes to go.

CHAPTER 9

The rest of the weekend was fairly uneventful, if you didn't count two loads of washing, some online banking and a much needed grocery shop, and by Monday morning, Roxy was back at her desk, trawling through her diary, reviewing her work schedule.

She had a bunch of magazine articles lined up, but the deadlines were some weeks off as she had expected to still be working on Wolfgang Bergman's biography at this stage. There was nothing more motivating than an unlikeable client, and she had finished the book in record time.

The fact that she was now free to get started on her freelance work was cause for happiness. Roxy loved the early process of article writing, the research, the setting up of interviews and the construction of thought-provoking questions. Everything was shiny and new and full of promise. The fact that many interviews turned out less than inspiring, or the writing didn't always flow freely, was a problem for a future day.

Speaking of problems, Roxy sighed. First, there was the small matter of Sondra Lane and the missing photograph. She began scrolling through her address book for the publisher's number when she had a better idea. She picked up her phone and dialled Oliver.

"I have a bone to pick with you."

"Bloody hell. What have I done now?"

"I thought you said you didn't give out my details to Sondra Lane."

"Who?"

"Needy woman. Woke you early Saturday morning, trying to track me down."

"Oh, right, her. No, I didn't. I promise! Why?"

"She tracked me down. Cornered me outside my apartment block."

"Shit, sorry. Must have *Googled* you. Can't be too hard to find your address."

Roxy considered this then she thought of the police and wondered if they'd handed her address over. "Yeah, I s'pose."

She filled him in on her strange conversation with Sondra, the police visit earlier that morning, and the juicy details she'd got off Gilda on Saturday night. She finished up by asking, "Do you know where Berny Tiles's photo has ended up? I think maybe that's what all this is about."

"Must be an award-winning photograph. Remind me what it looked like."

"Nothing worthy of an award, I can assure you. It's just a boring black and white shot of a bunch of people sitting around a table, I think, at some survey conference in Indonesia, circa 1970-something. It came to your office, I had a quick squiz at it, it was about A4 size—"

"Oh, yeah, that's right. I sent that on to the publisher, or at least Shazza did, which is the usual procedure. So it has to be with them. Want me to track it down for you?"

"That would be great, thank you, I really have to get on with some work."

"Yeah, like I'm sitting here twiddling my thumbs."

She ignored this and said, "When you track it down, do me a favour and ask them to Express Post it straight to Sondra. Easier that way."

She retrieved Sondra's card and repeated the address over the phone to him. It was obviously for her husband's floral business, but she figured that was better than nothing, then she hung up, hoping to give it no more thought.

Five minutes later Oliver was back on the line. "You want the good news or the bad news?"

Roxy snarled. She hated that question. The good news was usually just a Band-Aid patching up the gaping, bloody wound that had been left by the bad news. It never did the trick. "Let's start with the bad news then," she said, bracing herself.

"You will not believe this, but the publisher tells me they got broken into last night and a whole bunch of photos got stolen."

Roxy sat forward with a start. She wasn't expecting that. "My God, you're kidding? What's going on with this city! Thieves are out of control."

"Yep, they are still going through the damage but they tell me it looks like the box of stuff relating to the Bergman book was amongst the stuff that got stolen. Including a bunch of photos."

She considered this. "But why would they take those photos? Or any photos, for that matter?"

"Oh I think they nicked a few laptops as well but, yeah, you gotta wonder what value some old pix might have. Maybe someone was trying to get hold of some shots that are worth a bit of dosh. Maybe sell them to the tabloids or blackmail him? Bergman is a minor celebrity, after all." He chuckled. "Get it? Miner? Minor?"

She groaned again. "This is serious, Oliver. How weird is it that the publisher got broken into on the same weekend that I did."

He stopped chuckling. "You think that's what your burglar was after? Bergman's photos?"

"Makes me wonder. Okay, then, so what the hell is the good news?"

"They didn't actually take the picture you're after."

Again, Roxy was surprised. "Huh?"

"I described the photo to them just as you'd described it to me and they reckon that particular one is with Scott's Scanners in Strathfield, getting some dig' work done."

"In English please, Oliver."

He cleared his throat. "Okay, so the publisher sends all the pictures to a separate agency who does the high definition scanning for the book, right? Then the agency returns the scanned pix to the publisher. They reckon—and they're double checking this—that your photo was one of about seven or eight shots that needed rescanning so it is still at the agency. They never got it back. Hence, it never got stolen."

Roxy could have leapt for joy. "That was lucky!"

"Blood oath. I've got Scott's Scanners' deets so I'll give them a buzz and ask them to hunt it down and get it off to Sondra ASAP."

"Great," Roxy said, and then, "No!" She was beginning to hear that clanging bell sound in her head and she wasn't quite sure why; something was off, she could sense it. "Listen, I might head straight over to the scanners now and collect it myself. The way things are getting pinched around this city, it might be safer. Then I can get Sondra off my back and get on with my life."

"Suit yourself," he said, telling her the address and clicking off.

Roxy sat for a few minutes thinking about what Oliver had just told her. What a coincidence, she thought, that both her place and the publisher's were broken into on the same weekend. She didn't like coincidences, never had, but she didn't want to read too much into it either. Surely, a whole bunch of people fell foul of thieves over the weekend; she mustn't let her lively imagination run into overdrive.

Returning to her bedroom, Roxy changed into an oversized, burnt-orange jumper, black leggings and short boots, grabbed her handbag and the address Oliver had given her, and headed outside.

CHAPTER 10

Scott's Scanners was a dinky little business down an alleyway just off the main drag of the inner western suburb of Strathfield. There were several men in long-sleeved shirts hanging outside on the street, sucking on cigarettes like their life depended on it, and one of them held the door open as she walked up. She thanked him, stepped in and towards a small desk where a woman wearing an earpiece and very little else held a long finger up to silence her.

"Yes, Mr Karpathakis, we got that one, yep ... yep, okay, will get him onto it." She must have ended the call because she then flicked her thickly pencilled eyes to Roxy and said, "Can I help you?"

Roxy proceeded to tell her about the Wolfgang Bergman photos and her desire to get one back. "That is, if you're finished with it."

The woman pushed her chair back from the desk and stood up, dragging her super tight, super short dress down with one hand. It was a sexy little frock, more suited to a nightclub than an office block, Roxy thought then winced at herself.

My God, I'm turning into my mother!

"Follow me," the woman said and began to click clack down a badly lit hallway towards a back office.

Roxy dutifully followed and stopped with her at a door marked "Processing". The woman held her hand up again, indicating Roxy was to stay put, opened the door and disappeared inside, shutting it behind her. A minute later she opened it again and ushered Roxy through before departing.

Inside, a very young, very obese man was sitting on a swivel chair, working away on what was clearly a large flatbed scanner, adjusting a light over a series of transparencies, which had been placed side by side on the glass top. He closed the lid and held up a pudgy hand, too, obviously wanting to finish his job before Roxy spoke, and she wondered at all the sign language going on around here. As far as she knew, noise didn't affect picture quality. After a few minutes, a loud zapping sound and a flashing light, he reopened the lid then turned to Roxy.

"I'm Phil. Kylie tells me you're here to collect the Bergman shots?" As he spoke, he pushed his chair away from the scanner and towards an old, rusty filing cabinet.

"Not all of them, no, I just want to get one in particular." He looked around. "The owner of the picture has been hassling me for it, so I didn't want to wait until you got it back to the publisher. Hope that's okay."

He shrugged, opened the cabinet and began sorting through the files. "Which one?"

"It's a black and white photo of a group of mostly blokes in suits, circa 1970."

He turned back to her with a "Duh" look on his face. "That sums up half the shots. Got anything more specific for me?"

"Well, I was told you only have about seven or eight from the book, that you'd sent the rest back, so if you locate those shots ..." *"Duh" right back at you*, she thought.

He turned around and kept searching. Soon he was pulling out a thin manila folder and swivelling it across to his desk. He flipped open the folder and went through the pictures, producing one with a loud, "Voila!" as he held it out to her.

She frowned. "No, that's not it. Do you mind?"

She indicated the folder and he handed it over. Roxy flipped through them herself and realised he was right, there were five black and white shots of men in suits, one of a large muddy tractor and a final one of a very hazy mountain view with a man in a suit in front of it. It was obviously Sir Wolfgang in the '70s. His lascivious smile and pork-chop sideburns were a dead giveaway. The group shot she was after, however, was not in the file and she told him as much.

"Maybe we never got it."

"I hope you did. The shots that were still at the publishers were all stolen over the weekend."

Phil looked up at her then, his large ruddy face brightening. "OMG! What happened?" This news had clearly livened up his day.

"Well, I don't know the details, but a bunch of pictures and a few computers got pinched. The publisher says, though, that the one I'm after needed rescanning so it should still be in your files."

"That's my file," he said, glancing down at the folder in her hand. "If it's not there, I ain't got it."

"Could it be in transit?"

"Just the one shot? No way, José. These have already been rescanned and as far as I know the job is *finito*. They were all due to go back tomorrow if I hadn't heard differently from Johnno at Book It. I don't send them in dribs and drabs, they go as a unit."

Dammit, she thought. So where was the picture she needed?

"Can you show me which pic it is from the mock-ups?"

She shook her head. "It never made the final cut. But you did scan it, apparently."

He nudged his eyebrows towards a large desktop computer. "Then I'll have the original scan in here somewhere. We don't trash them. Want to look? I could even get you a print out and then you'd have a replacement at least."

"That'd be great, yes."

It wasn't quite the same thing as having the original and she was sure Sondra would not be satisfied, but it was a start. Besides, she was now very curious to see what all the fuss was about. Phil got to work on the computer, tapping his way through several folders until he found the one he was after.

"Here are all the pix from the Bergman book." Tap, tap, tap. "Here are the seven we rescanned." Tap, tap, tap. "Hang on a minute." He took the file from Roxy's hands and flipped through it. "Yep, seven images here, seven scans, so yours never made it to us, unless it got lost somewhere between Kylie's desk and mine, which happens, like, *never*. We'll go back to the first scans we did ... Let me see ..."

He continued tapping away slowly until he located another, larger file, then pushed his chair away from the desk. "Here are all the Bergman pix that came through on the first run. You'll have to go through them, yourself, see if you can spot the one you're after."

She stepped in front of him and leaned over the desk where a folder of dozens and dozens of thumb-size images had been opened on the desktop. A chair would have been nice, but he didn't look like he was about to surrender his in a hurry, so she stood and trawled through the shots for five full minutes until she found the one she was after.

"Here it is," she said, double clicking to bring the image to full size.

He moved his chair closer and they both stared at it for a few moments, not speaking. It was just as Roxy remembered—deadly dull and seemingly benign.

The picture was in a horizontal format and featured six people standing behind an oversized wooden desk. Along the bottom, in capital letters were the words: Indonesia Survey Congress, 1975, and below that, the names of the people featured in the shot. From left to right, W.K.

Bergman, Betty Reilly, G.J. Reilly, R.T. Brownlow, C.M. Holderson and B.J. Tiles.

Bergman was standing very close to Betty Reilly, a pretty young thing and the only woman in the shot, and this did not surprise Roxy one bit. She also noted that B.J. Tiles (aka Berny) was looking away from the camera towards Bergman and Betty, while G.J. Reilly, a tall, scrappy looking fellow with a bushy moustache and matching sideburns, was caught mid-blink with a worried frown on his face. The others were smiling widely, happily staring straight into the lens, as if they didn't have a care in the world, nor a secret to hide.

Apart from Bergman and Tiles, at least one other name sounded familiar to Roxy and she was just trying to work out why when Phil said, "I'll print you a copy, hey?"

She stepped back from the desk and he began tapping away at the computer again.

Roxy retrieved one of her business cards from her bag. "Can you also e-mail that image to me, so I have it on my files? Plus, if you could have a look around for the original print, maybe ask Kylie if she has any idea where it might be."

He took her card and nodded. "You never know your luck in the big city, maybe it got dropped down the side of the filing cabinet or something."

"One can only hope," she replied before taking the fresh print he had placed in an envelope, and thanking him.

Roxy then retraced her steps, back out to the reception desk, past Kylie who, surprise, surprise, simply waved a hand goodbye, and out the front where, she could swear, the same group of guys were still worshipping their tobacco god.

On the way to her car, Roxy snuck another look at the picture and was left even more perplexed.

How could such a mundane image be such a pain in the butt?

CHAPTER 11

When Roxy got to her car, she heard her smartphone beep and grappled through her handbag to retrieve it. There was an incoming text from an unknown number and she opened it to find a message from Sondra. It simply said, "Pls call."

Roxy unlocked her car, got inside and took a deep breath. *Might as well get this over with*, she thought as she tapped "redial". It was answered almost immediately.

"It's Roxy Parker, Sondra," she said.

"Oh, great, thanks for calling back. And for sending the transcript through. Although you were right, there doesn't seem to be anything of interest in it. Unless you're a fan of Sir Wolfgang Bergman's, of course."

And Roxy had already deduced that Sondra Lane was not. "You're welcome. Listen, I have some bad news on the picture front." Roxy proceeded to tell her about the missing photo, and the burglary at the publishers. "But don't worry too much because I'm almost 100 percent sure it wasn't at the publisher's when it got broken into. In any case, I have a very good copy of it and I'll get that in the post to you today."

"I really need the original."

"Yes, I appreciate that." She chewed her lower lip. "I'm just outside the picture agency now, and they are searching for it as we speak. I'm sure they'll find it—"

"How can you be sure?"

"Well, it has to turn up eventually. It can't just disappear off the face of the earth." *Can it?* She switched the phone to her other ear, and began to turn the key in the ignition. "I'm really sorry, these things happen occasionally when images are being sent backwards and forwards but—"

"Can I see the copy?"

"Of course, I'll post—"

"Can you bring it to me? Now? If you don't mind?"

She tried not to groan aloud. "Sure, what's your address?"

There was a pause. "Oh, um, how about we meet somewhere else. Wherever's convenient for you. I can even shout you lunch if you like. I just need to see that picture."

And so Needy Woman was back. While it might work wonders on Oliver, it only made Roxy feel irritable, but so did a hungry stomach and she was suddenly famished. She glanced at the digital clock on her car dashboard.

"Fine. Have you heard of Lockies Café in Surry Hills?"

Lockies was bursting to the brim when Roxy arrived but that didn't stop the owner, Loghlen, from finding her a quiet table up the back near the roaring fireplace. He'd been a good mate for years and he didn't let her down today. She was never quite sure how he managed to find a spare table. Did he send newer patrons scuttling, or did he keep one on reserve for his favourite patrons? She liked to think the latter but she wasn't betting on it.

"Thanks, Lockie," she said. "If a pale, jittery woman wanders in, send her over. I'm expecting her."

"Ai, will do," said the gangly Scotsman. "Cane get you a latte while ye wait?"

"Does the Pope wear a silly frock? Course you can. Thanks."

He laughed and dashed off to work his magic behind the espresso machine while she studied the overhead blackboard glancing through the delicious menu, knowing only too well exactly what she'd order.

He returned with the coffee and said, "Vegie focaccia then?"

She laughed. "One day I'll shock your socks off. But can you hold the order until my—"

"Hello," came a small voice behind them and they both looked up to see Sondra standing there, hands held in front of her stomach, clutching her brown leather handbag.

She was wearing a shapely blue skirt today, with a cream silk top, and had left her hair loose around her face, so she looked less startled and severe. Even her crimson red lipstick didn't look quite so alarming on her pale face, and the way she smiled now, her head held high, suggested to Roxy that the kite was on the way up.

Roxy did the introductions and Sondra ordered a soy latte from Lockie before taking a seat at the table.

"Thank you for meeting me," she said. "Did you bring the copy?"

"Yes, and I really am sorry about the original," Roxy told her. "But apart from sentimental value for your dad, I can't see how it would matter much to you or anyone in your family. I'll show you."

She reached into her own bag and produced an orange envelope, handing it across to Sondra. The woman pounced on it, pulling the copied image out and taking a long look at it. She turned it over and then back again.

"You know, this picture *is* familiar. I've seen it at Dad's place, I think. I certainly recognise some of these faces. But you're right. It's not really of any value that I can see."

"Exactly." Roxy took a sip of her coffee, winced, then reached for the sugar bowl and emptied two sachets into her cup. "What about the names? Recognise any of them?"

Sondra peered keenly at the typed names and squeezed her eyes shut momentarily as though trying to remember.

"Obviously I know Sir Wolfgang, although I note he's not a Sir here."

"He was knighted seven years ago. That picture's over thirty-five years old. Plus he's not a surveyor, so I'm not quite sure why he's even in it."

"Oh, Sir Wolfgang does exactly what Sir Wolfgang wants to do," she replied drily and before Roxy could ask her to elaborate, she quickly said, "C. Holderson has to be Clive Holderson, an old mate of my father's, but he died, oh, a good ten, fifteen years ago. Cancer, I believe. Um ... this man," she pointed to the short, stocky man on the right side. "It says his name is R. Brownlow. You know, I've definitely heard that name before."

Roxy sat forward. "Yes, I have, too, but I can't work out why."

"You didn't interview him for the book?"

"No, Sir Wolfgang only asked me to talk to your dad, said the others weren't important—his words, not mine."

Sondra flashed Roxy an inscrutable look then returned to the picture. "As for the two Reillys? They're obviously husband and wife."

"Oh, you think so? They could be siblings. She's really pretty, he's a bit shaggy for her I'd've thought." They both stared at the scowling bespectacled man with the oversized moustache and sideburns. "They could even be unrelated."

Sondra shook her head firmly. "I doubt it. Single white women didn't really go to Indonesia in those days. It's most likely they were married. I know my mother had to marry Dad before she went. It was the done thing back then. Betty could have been at the Congress with her husband or she could have been a secretary or a clerk or something."

"That might explain why she's in the picture," Roxy said.

"Oh yes, she wouldn't have been a surveyor. Certainly not in those days."

"And does her name, Betty Reilly, ring a bell?"

"Not at all, no. I don't know either of the Reillys, I'm afraid, or even if they're still around, although she looks younger than the men so the chances are she will be. Do you have a digital copy of this picture you can forward to me?"

"Of course, I'll e-mail you the image this afternoon. That hard copy is all yours."

Lockie appeared again with Roxy's focaccia in one hand and Sondra's latte in the other. "Sorry about the delay. It's like a noothouse in here today. Anything else before I take off agin?"

They both shook their heads and he returned to the coalface while the two women continued to stare at the photo.

Eventually Sondra took a deep breath and said, "I'd like to ask you something. A favour."

Roxy peered at her across the top of her cup. *Oh no*, she thought, *and here I was thinking I was about to make a clean getaway.*

"I'd like to hire you. To investigate."

Roxy dropped the cup back down with a thud. "Investigate? Investigate what, exactly?"

Sondra looked sheepish and began chewing on an already well-chewed fingernail. "I ... I don't know ... but my father mentioned you for a reason, I just know it. And I'm hoping you can find out why. There has to be something that we're missing."

Roxy considered this. "What are you hoping I will find? Do you think this is related to your dad's murder?" She indicated the photo that was still in front of Sondra. "Do you think I'm related to that?"

"I don't know what to think, but I know it's important. *You're* important. I know that sounds dramatic. My husband and Renata think I've completely flipped."

"Renata?"

"My father's new ... *wife*." She spat the word out as though it were bitter and distasteful. "They only got together a few months ago and got married almost immediately. Thank God he didn't—" She stopped and placed a hand to her lips as though trying to hold back whatever dark thought was about to be verbalised. "Anyway, Tony and Renata seem to think you don't matter a jot. No offence." Roxy nodded, showing that no offence was taken. "That's what the police have told them and so they think I should just let it go, but I know my dad. He mentioned you for a reason, Roxy. He was giving me a message and if I ignore it, then I'm a fool."

Roxy didn't look convinced, so she added, "What you have to understand is, my father was a man of very few words. I don't know if you recall that from your interview."

She thought back to that lovely, seemingly insignificant hour she had spent with Berny just a few months before he died, and she had to concur. He had been pleasant enough, but he wasn't chatty at all. In fact, she had been secretly annoyed that the restaurant provided crayons to decorate the paper tablecloths because he had seemed more interested in doodling than dishing the dirt.

"I could never get anything out of my father," Sondra was saying, her eyes clouded over. "Most surveyors are pretty quiet types, especially those old-timers who were used to endless hours in the bush. It was pretty dry, methodical work they did, often with only a local chainman for company and, even if he could speak English, he was usually a mile away holding one end of the chain. That's the way my dad liked it. It's the reason he chose that profession. Solid, no fuss. Yet, the night he died, he made a fuss. He said your name for a reason, Roxy, he said you had it—whatever *it* is. I want you to find out what he meant by that."

"Then you should really hire a licensed investigator."

"But you do investigations, right?"

Roxy almost laughed. "Well, not really, I mean, I'm a journalist but not a proper investigator."

"I read that you've helped solve several crimes."

Now Roxy did laugh. "Yes, because I'm a nosy bloody Parker and I butted in where I wasn't welcome. I'm not a registered PI. If that's what you're after, you really ought to—"

"I want *you*," she said simply, thrusting her hands under the table. "And I will pay whatever you usually earn per hour as a journalist. I'll match it. I just can't spare any more time and I know you're busy too, which is why I'll pay you. I have some money saved, plus my dad's inheritance. It's not much, but it's enough."

"But what do you expect me to find? I mean, where do I start?"

"You can start by trying to track down the original of this picture."

"I'll do that anyway, Sondra, for nothing. It's terribly unprofessional of us to lose it and we owe it to your father to return it. When I'm entrusted with a client's personal photos, I always make that commitment." She took another bite of her sandwich, although she was fast losing her appetite. "But I still can't see how the original will make any difference. What you've got there"—she waved her focaccia towards the print—"that's exactly what it looked like. Nothing's been cut off or altered as far as I can remember."

"Still, until we have the original, we won't really know, will we? Perhaps there was something on the back of the original? Or there's something in this image that we just haven't spotted yet?"

"What, an invisible code scrawled across it?"

Sondra placed her hands back on the table and pushed the photo across to Roxy. She looked at her with imploring eyes. "You don't understand. I don't just want the original photo, I want to hire you to track down the people in that photo. Maybe they will know what this is all about."

Roxy stared at the picture again and then back up to Sondra. "Do you think someone in this photo is responsible for your father's death?" Sondra shrugged slightly, a flicker of anxiety sweeping through her eyes. "You think that's why your dad wanted this picture so badly? To point the finger. If that was the case, why didn't he just name that person on his deathbed? Why go to all this trouble?"

Again Sondra shrugged. "Maybe there's more to this than meets the eye. Maybe he'd forgotten their name? Or maybe saying their name would not explain their motive. Maybe someone in this photo has the answers."

"We don't even know where these people are or if they're still alive."

"Which is why I want to hire you. I wouldn't ask for your help if I could do this myself, but I don't know where to begin looking and you're obviously good at this kind of stuff. You already have access to Sir Wolfgang; speak to him first. If he knows nothing, then track down the others. Just talk to them, ask them if they have any idea why my dad wanted the photo so badly. If they don't know, then so be it."

Roxy shook her head a little. She found the whole thing very confounding and was about to reject the assignment with a firm but friendly no, when Sondra said something she couldn't ignore.

"Don't you wonder about the break-in at the publisher's? And at your house? Don't you wonder if they're related and if they had anything to do with this photo? Seems like an awfully big coincidence to me."

Roxy squinted her eyes. She had already connected those dots and yes, she did wonder about that. "How do you know about the break-in at my place?"

"Your agent mentioned it, the morning I rang. He said you were busy with that and couldn't see me." She paused. "Did you get a good look at the burglar? Any idea who it was?"

Roxy shook her head. "He was tall and large, that's all I remember," she replied, omitting all mention of Scooby Doo and bunny rabbits. "Okay, but even if what you say is true— and I'm not saying it is—then has it occurred to you that this busy burglar may already *have* the picture? I mean, it's not at the publisher's, it's not at the scanner's. Maybe they beat us to it."

"And maybe they didn't," she replied firmly. "Please, Roxy, I've got too much going on at the moment and I promised Tony I would give him some time this week. We have three weddings coming up this weekend, and a flower expo early next week. It's more than we can cope with. I just can't spare a second."

"You guys run a florist, right?"

"We have a stall, down at the flower markets at Homebush, mostly roses. Tony's been covering for me since Dad ... and the funeral ..." She choked back tears again.

"So you work together? You and your husband."

"On and off. I'm actually an accountant, I'm supposed to just do the books, but Tony needs me on hand during the busy times. Things have gone a bit crazy lately, we really need to put on more staff but, well ..." She smiled apologetically and hesitated before she said, "My husband might be tiny, Roxy, the size of a gnome, but he has big plans. Too big sometimes."

The anxious look was back and she was nibbling hard on her fingernails again. "Please, can I hire you for the week? Just seven days focusing solely on this. Just try to find out what happened to the photo and who these people are." She glanced back down at the image of the six people beaming out at them from a bygone era. "If you can't find the original, perhaps you'll find some clues as to who stole it, and why. At the very least you might get a better grasp on why my father said your name the night he died."

I wish he bloody hadn't, she thought wearily.

Roxy normally liked a good mystery, but this one was way too obscure for her liking. Still, Roxy had to concede that she didn't have a large workload at present and could do with the extra money. It's not like she was going to get cracking on her freelance articles anyway. Her usual routine was to procrastinate (unpaid) until the deadline started looming.

"I'll double your daily rate," Sondra said, pleading. "Just one week. If you don't find anything, if no one in the picture has any light to shed, then at least I can let it go. I can get on with my life. Do you understand that?"

Again Roxy thought of her own father's death, and of the years she held tight to the idea that she could somehow change it, fix it or make it all better. She eventually realised she never could, but it was early days for Sondra. Plus there was a particularly frightening power bill sitting, unpaid, in her in-tray.

"One week?"

"That's all I ask."

"And that's all you'll get because any more would be a giant waste of my time and your inheritance."

CHAPTER 12

Where do wild goose chases start? Roxy wondered as she doodled idly on her desk diary. It was Tuesday morning and she was now seated in her office sunroom trying to get her head around Sondra Lane's request. She had spent the rest of Monday planting a few seeds for her future articles and generally clearing away chores so she could focus on the Berny Tiles case for seven full days, as promised.

Roxy scowled. *What on earth was she going to do in seven days?* She should have said no. *Of course* she should have said no. But the woman seemed so desperate and so suspicious. Normally, Roxy was the suspicious one and she did have to agree that all these mysterious break-ins and the picture's disappearance were rather *odd*. Then, of course, there was the mystery surrounding Berny Tiles's death.

"I'll start there," she said aloud, a side effect of living alone for so many years, and put a call through to Gilda.

"Oh, I've had a very interesting chat with old man Leary," Gilda told her, obviously chewing on something as she spoke. Probably chocolate.

"What did he have to say?"

"Well," she said, swallowing loudly, "they're looking for motive, right? Who would want to run down an old geezer? So they've been poking their nose into Tiles's finances, he had no life insurance, few savings, and the only asset of any value was his house, which isn't exactly a palace, apparently. And according to the will, it goes straight to his daughter who, sadly for Leary, has an alibi."

"What about the new wife?"

"Wife?"

"Yes, there's a new woman on the scene. Renata, I think her name was."

"Leary didn't mention any new wife." She sounded annoyed. "If she's new, as you say, then she probably didn't get written into the will in time, but she can certainly demand her share through the courts. That opens things up a bit, but that's not the interesting bit."

"Oh?"

"Tiles didn't have a lot of savings, as I said, he was on the pension after all, but there was a recent deposit that has rung some major alarm bells."

"Really?"

"Yep, a tidy sum of $200,000 cash was placed in Mr Tiles's bank account about eight weeks ago. No explanation, no idea at this point as to where it came from or why, but it's about the only lead they have, other than the half-blind neighbour, of course, so they're jumping all over it. We'll know more about that soon."

"Do they think it might be related to his death? Maybe he was blackmailing someone and they'd had enough, bumped him off."

"Yes, literally, with a white van," Gilda said. "I'm sure that's one angle they're working. Oh, hang on—" Roxy heard another voice in the background and then Gilda said, "Duty calls. I've got to go."

"Of course, thanks for that. I appreciate it."

"No wuzzers, you owe me a Cherry Ripe for that."

"I'll make it a family-size block, shall I?"

They hung up and Roxy returned to doodling. Then she clicked open a new computer file and began trying to make sense of the seemingly senseless.

What did she have? She had an old man who may or may not have been blackmailing someone, and may or may not have been murdered.

She had an old picture that may or may not be important, and may or may not have been stolen.

And she had a daughter who was clearly a Daddy's girl and was going to hunt down that missing shot of her father if it killed her. Roxy just hoped it wouldn't come to that.

She opened her e-mail account and noticed a new message from Scott's Scanners. Cheering up, she clicked on it but her good cheer didn't last long.

"Still no sign of your pic," Phil had typed. *"Here tis again. Attached. Let me know if you want to put compensation request through for missing image."*

"I don't want compensation!" Roxy hissed at the computer. "I want the original bloody picture!" Although why she wanted it, or more precisely, why Sondra wanted it, was still beyond her.

She clicked on the attachment anyway, and watched the old photo come to life again in front of her eyes. *What is it with this picture?* she thought, magnifying it considerably. Down at the bottom she reread the names that had been typed indicating who was who, and noticed for the first time that Betty's Christian name had been spelt out while the men were given initials. Was that sexism? Human error or inconsistency? Did it even matter?

She moved her eyes to the table in front of the group, wondering if a clue lay there. There was a large book opened, but she couldn't see what was on the pages, and below it, a white ink pad with what looked like brown leather corners. There didn't seem to be anything written on that, at least not that she could make out. To the right was an ashtray overflowing with cigarette butts, of course—smoking was practically compulsory back in those days—but nothing else. Behind the group was the bottom half of what was clearly a large map, probably of Indonesia, squiggly black lines indicating mountainous terrain and rivers. There was nothing else of note.

Roxy opened a fresh e-mail, attached the picture and sent it to Sondra. Then she thought about what Sondra had said and skimmed through her address book. She was right. There was one person who probably had a very good idea why this picture was so important and could clear it all up in a matter of minutes. She picked up the phone again and dialled the home number of Sir Wolfgang Bergman.

Wolfgang's wife, Virginia—"Please, call me Ginny!"—answered in her half-English, half-Indonesian accent, and seemed surprised to find Roxy at the other end of the phone.

"Oh, hello!" she said. "I thought you were all finished with my husband now."

"Very nearly," Roxy fibbed. "I just need to fact-check a few names I have on a photograph for the book."

"Oh yes?"

"Can I speak with Sir Wolfgang?"

There was a pause. "Now is not a good time, Roxanne. Perhaps you could e-mail him directly, and he'll get back to you when he can."

"I'd just rather speak with him, if you don't mind."

"I do mind, he's not well, he's bed bound at the moment."

That surprised Roxy; he'd seemed dangerously robust the last time they'd met. "I'm sorry to hear that. Is it something serious?"

"Naturally, or he would not be bed bound," she replied coolly. "I have to go. You have our e-mail, of course?"

"Yes, but—"

"Thank you, Roxanne." And she hung up.

Roxy stared at the phone gloomily. She hoped Mr and Mrs Bergman weren't going to be quite so taciturn with the media when the book came out. As a ghostwriter, Roxy was rarely allowed to get involved in the marketing process and had to rely on the client to sell the book for her. She had assumed that Wolfgang would be a great spruiker for sales, but not if ill health, and his buttoned-up wife, had anything to do with it.

She turned back to her computer and clicked on *Google*. She was going to have to do this the hard way. Roxy placed the first name, the most familiar, into *Google* and began scanning for information. She knew it wouldn't be easy and sure enough, within seconds she had millions of references to the word "Brownlow". She narrowed her search by typing in "R.T. Brownlow", "surveyor" and "Indonesia", crossed her fingers and waited. But she didn't hold her breath. Much of Roxy's biography work involved researching the older generation and they were exasperatingly private. Unlike Generation Y, this group didn't generally set up Facebook pages and pour their life stories out on blogs and websites for the world to see. They viewed the Internet with suspicion and it made her job so much harder.

Today, however, she was in luck. Not only was R.T. Brownlow (aka Bob) a vivid presence on the web—he had a Facebook page *and* a website to boot—but he had also recently made the news and a stream of newspaper websites flashed in front of her eyes.

She held her breath and clicked on the first archived article. It was a snippet from a free Eastern Suburbs newspaper, dated three weeks ago. It was not good news. Roxy read the headline quickly and nearly fell out of her chair.

"Local man dies after mugging gone wrong."

She clicked on the story and brought the copy up, quickly scanning through the text as an unsettling mixture of excitement and foreboding began tingling through her veins.

According to the brief report, an elderly Bondi Junction man named Robert "Bob" Brownlow was found brutally bashed on the street outside his terrace house, his wallet and a gold watch missing. A police spokesperson asserted that it was likely a mugging turned fatal.

So that's why his name had rung a bell!

Roxy reached down towards her filing cabinet and pulled out her latest Crime Catalogue, a scrapbook that Oliver (and now Gilda, it seems) mockingly called her Book of Death. True crime was a quiet, inexplicable passion of Roxy's and she spent many long Saturdays, cup in one hand, scissors in the other, snipping out the most interesting, obscure or baffling crime articles she'd read that week.

There were now twenty-five books in her catalogue, but this story would surely be in the latest, and she was right. She only had to turn back a few pages to find it. (Since hooking up with Max, it wasn't just her fitness level that was being neglected, she was finding less and less time for her morbid hobby, too. He would say that was a good thing; she wasn't quite so convinced.)

The article Roxy had clipped was as brief as the one on the screen, no picture, just a few quick paragraphs from the *Daily Telegraph* and she reread it several times trying to take it in. According to the article, Bob Brownlow was a seventy-seven-year-old pensioner who lived alone. "Bit of a character," one neighbour was quoted as saying. "This kind of thing never happens here," ranted another, adding, "What's the world coming to?"

Roxy tapped her nails on the desk. *What, indeed.*

She clicked on the photo Phil had sent her and sat back, staring at it again. This case was getting more interesting by the minute. Of the six people in the picture, three were dead, at least two under suspicious circumstances, and one was on his sick bed. Two others were still unaccounted for.

She peered into the faces of the Reillys and wondered how they were faring. Were they still alive and kicking?

Feeling more confident this time, Roxy returned to *Google* and placed the name Betty Reilly into the search engine. Once again, a million varieties appeared, so she tried narrowing her search, adding the words "Indonesia" and "survey congress", but nothing came up.

She repeated the process with G. Reilly and had even less success. Roxy groaned aloud; her confidence waning again.

"I don't have the patience for this," she decided, dialling Gilda's mobile number.

This time, the detective couldn't talk, but she promised to drop by Roxy's apartment that evening with the information she was after.

"I'll grab a bottle of plonk and some sustenance on the way. Will I get enough for Max, too?"

"Not sure." Roxy realised with a start that she hadn't heard from her boyfriend in two days. Technically it didn't bother her, but she knew Max, and she knew something was up. He was a regular phone call kind of guy.

"I'll get extra, just in case," Gilda said, "but I've really gotta go."

And Roxy really had to ring Max. She took a deep breath, dialled his home number and then smiled when a woman answered.

"Hi, Caroline," she said.

"Hey, Ms Parker! We were just talking about you."

Oh dear, she thought. "Discussing my insane beauty?"

Caroline laughed. "What else?!"

Roxy didn't want to know what else so quickly changed the subject. "Are you moving back in?"

"With grumpy bum? God no! Just house-minding. He's going away tonight, you knew that, right?"

"Of course!" she said, thinking, *shit, did he tell me that?* "So what else have you been up to? Max mentioned something about a new hobby."

"Hobby? He's such a patronising prat! I'm doing a course on the stock market, darling, trading and all that. It's no *hobby*, Roxy, it's going to make me rich!"

"I thought real estate was your pathway to the good life."

"Puh-lease! Way too much like hard work for me, I'm afraid. Plus they only pay you when you sell a house, which is *ridiculous*! No, no, the stock market is much more my style. Actually, while I've got you, I need a few guinea pigs for the course. Mining shares are on the up. Got a spare grand I can dabble with?"

Roxy laughed. "Sure, let me check the pockets of my mink coat and I'll get back to you."

"Oh well, worth a try. Hey, I'll get Cranky Pants for you, he's just packing his bag upstairs, hang on."

Roxy heard the phone drop and the clickety clack of heels on Max's polished wooden floorboards. A minute later, he answered, his deep voice still churning her insides as it had done from the start.

"Hey, stranger," he said.

"Sorry, Max, I meant to call. I've just been a little swept up with my work."

"What've you been up to this week? I thought you said it was going to be a quiet one, that you might drop over."

Really? She'd said that? She didn't remember that either. "Yeah, well, I got a last-minute assignment, quite an urgent one, so ..." Roxy decided not to tell Max too much more. He hated when Roxy steered away from freelance and into the murky world of crime. Best to keep that one to herself.

"So you remembered I was flying out tonight, right?"

"Yeah, of course!"

He paused. "To Melbourne? Got a Mercedes advertorial."

"Yeah, I know." *Nope, it wasn't registering.* How weird, she thought, that she had better recall for a stranger's death three weeks ago, than for her boyfriend's itinerary. "When do you go, again?"

"About an hour. Gonna see me off?" She glanced at her computer's clock. "I'm kidding, Parker. Don't stress. Caro's taking me to the airport, looking after the place while I'm gone."

"Okay, well, can I at least pick you up? When do you get back?"

He seemed surprised by this. "Okay, sure. I'm back Friday arvo. I'll text you the flight details. Thanks, Parker."

"Don't be silly! I'm your girlfriend, aren't I?"

"Are you?"

She shrunk in her seat, scrunching her eyes up.

"Sorry, ignore that," he said quickly, adding, "I love you, I'll miss you, and I'll call you when I get to Melbourne later this evening. Is that okay?" She could hear the wrench in his voice down the phone line.

"Of course that's okay," she scolded. "Safe travels."

After hanging up, Roxy felt that dreadful twinge of guilt again. Her mother was right. She really was appalling at relationships. No wonder she rarely had them. Then, keen to dissipate the guilt, she turned back to *Google* and began trawling through the search engine results for G. Reilly again.

After twenty minutes of hits and misses, she had a better idea. She switched her computer off, grabbed her coat and handbag and headed out again.

CHAPTER 13

What is it with the super rich, thought Roxy as she pulled her car up beside the fancy intercom at the front gate of the Bergman's mighty mansion. They couldn't just have a front door like everyone else. Oh no, they were all so obscenely paranoid they had to have high walls, steel gates and a security system befitting the White House. Sure, they had plenty to steal, but was it worth a life behind bars?

She stalled her car beside the front gate, pressed the buzzer and waited as she had done many times over the past six months. Eventually the intercom crackled to life and a woman's voice demanded, "Yes, who is that?"

Roxy's heart sank. She was hoping the kindly housekeeper would answer as she usually did and show her in with barely a word. She was out of luck today.

"Hi, Ginny," Roxy said, recognising the voice and knowing only too well that the tiny camera beside the speaker (not to mention the one on the gate) was showing Virginia exactly who was on the other end. "I was just passing and thought I might try my luck with Sir Wolfgang this arvo."

The crackling stopped then restarted. "I thought I made it clear, Roxanne. He's not well."

"Look, I'm sorry, I wouldn't normally drop in like this. But it is very urgent. I just want to show him a quick photograph, and then I'll be out of his hair. For good."

"What's this regarding? Exactly?"

"It's about an old friend of his. Berny Tiles."

That seemed to do the trick because the crackling stopped again and a loud beeping sound indicated that the gate was about to swing open. Roxy watched it widen, then revved her car up and drove through. Just up the driveway, she heard the gate clang shut behind her. At the top she found Ginny standing at the front door, hands on her ample hips, frown wedged below a stiff, beehive hairdo.

Roxy swung the car past the three-door garage and into a guest spot out the front, then leapt out before Ginny had a chance to change her mind and send her packing.

"This better be important," she snapped and Roxy tried for a warm, disarming smile.

She already knew not to underestimate Ginny Bergman, had seen her tear shreds off her Indonesian housekeeper several times, and it was not pretty. Part Indonesian herself with a little Dutch thrown in, Ginny was now in her fifties but had obviously been a trophy bride once—she had the unblemished skin and razor sharp cheekbones to prove it. These days, however, she was so much more than that. Not only had she produced Wolfgang's heir and "spare"—two strapping sons who were now running his operation in Indonesia—but she was also dubbed his "secret weapon" in the country. Roxy had already discovered how it worked and knew that, as a foreigner, Bergman would not have had a free pass to pilfer so many of Indonesia's precious resources without his locally born wife.

Ginny clearly knew it, too. She wielded a power, even over her formidable husband, that was often terrifying, and Roxy had to wonder as she glanced around for the missing housekeeper, if the poor thing had finally had enough.

"What's all this about Berny Tiles?" Ginny was demanding, bejewelled fingers still at her hips.

"Oh, I just need to track down the contact details for a few old associates, that's all."

Ginny eyed her suspiciously through long, fake eyelashes, then swept around, pushed the enormous Balinese-style front door open and strode through, her bum wiggling like two Miniature Poodles behind her. Roxy followed her towards the library, a large room crammed with bookshelves and stuffy sofas on the darker side of the house. This is where Roxy usually found Wolfgang waiting, glass of scotch and hungry smile at the ready.

She knew this routine by heart, having visited the Bergman's harbourside mansion at Point Piper at least a dozen times for the book, but today she was surprised to find the library empty and Wolfman nowhere to be found.

Ginny swept a few thick curtains aside to let in the light, muttering something about "blasted housekeepers" that Roxy couldn't quite catch, then swung back, the smile still stiff on her lips.

"I'll see if he's available but I don't like your chances!"

Roxy thanked her and watched her wiggle back out of the room and towards the circular staircase, which she knew led towards the master bedroom. So Ginny wasn't exaggerating after all. Wolfgang really was bed bound.

As she waited, Roxy wondered what had knocked him about so badly, and in such a short time. He'd seemed fighting fit the last time they'd met, just a few months earlier.

After five minutes, Ginny reappeared, her smile slightly softened, her tone a little more conciliatory. "He's coming," she said, then left her alone in the library.

When Sir Wolfgang eventually appeared, some ten minutes later, he looked considerably older and a lot less robust than before. Instead of his usual garb—crisply ironed office shirt, pleated trousers and boat shoes—he was in a velvet, maroon Polo sweatsuit, tufts of scraggly grey chest hair poking out at one end, protruding beer belly at the other, and had a pair of dark slippers on his feet. He shuffled towards Roxy but when he caught her eye, she noticed the cheeky glint was still in place and he was still clutching hold of his trademark glass of scotch. Wolfgang loved his whisky and Roxy wouldn't be surprised if they buried him with his thick crystal tumbler, the last dregs of single malt still warm in his belly.

"Roxanne Parker, you look ravishing as always," he said, his voice a little weaker and craggier than she recalled. "You've got my wife in a bit of a tizz, though."

"Sorry about that."

"Don't be. She gets het up over a broken fingernail. What can I help you with on this bright and sunny day? Let me guess, you just *had* to see me one more time."

He gave her one of his lecherous smiles, licking the bottom of his lip with a short, fat tongue and glancing down her body, across her long legs and up again. She felt instant revulsion and wished she could give his scaly bald head a good slap, but she knew how this worked and she smiled benignly as he shuffled slowly to his favourite lounge chair, a dimpled leather number with soft quilted cushions.

He dropped into it then turned back to her with his dissolute smile. "Bloody pneumonia," he said, coughing a little. "It's got me by the short and curlies, but it won't take me down, Roxanne, I can promise you that."

More's the pity, she thought, but said instead, "I'm sorry to drag you out of bed. I just need to ask you about the Reillys."

He scratched at a patch of skin on the top of his head. "Really? Ginny mentioned Berny Tiles."

"Yes, well, about him, too." She produced a copy of the photo and held it across to Bergman. He didn't look like he wanted to take it at first, but eventually he did and he stared at it now, his brow furrowed slightly.

"Where did you get this?" he asked.

"It's a copy of an original that Berny sent me for your book." She paused. "You did hear about Berny—"

He nodded firmly. "Of course. Poor bastard. Couldn't make the funeral, I was too sick, but I hear the police suspect foul play."

"Yes, a deliberate hit and run. But they can't find a motive as yet."

"Is that why you're here?" His watery eyes penetrated hers and she wondered how to play it.

"Not exactly, no. Sondra—Berny's daughter—has asked me to track down the people in that photo. She has her reasons, it's probably not important, but well, a job's a job, and I thought that if anyone knows, you would."

He continued staring at her for some minutes, sipping on his scotch and rubbing his head where the skin was flaking off. Roxy noticed there were white flakes on his shoulders and tried not to recoil.

She said, "I have already learned that two others are dead—"

"Yeah, Clive lost his battle with cancer some time ago, and Browny—Bob Brownlow—well, he also met a pretty grim ending. Only recently, I believe. You heard about that?"

"I read about that. Did you attend his funeral?"

"Why would I? Hadn't seen the man since ... well, probably since this photo was taken." He paused then added, "He wouldn't have amounted to anything."

The superiority in his tone shocked Roxy. "Really? Why?"

He shrugged, not interested in elaborating. "I can't see what any of this has got to do with Sondra."

"She's obviously very upset about her father. She's searching for a link, that's all."

She knew it was a vague answer and he knew it too. A slip of a smile crossed his lips and he said, "She'll find no answers here, and neither will you, my love. It's all just ancient history now."

"What about the fifth man, G. Reilly? Do you know where he might be?"

Wolfgang glanced back at the picture. "Gordo Reilly," he said slowly, his eyes squinting slightly but his expression impossible to read. "Nope. Lost touch with him soon after as well."

"Would he have amounted to something?"

Wolfgang shot a quick glance at her, his expression now clearly amused. "He was an alcoholic loser, so you decide for yourself." He took a long sip of his scotch, the irony clearly lost on him. "Oh, don't look so shocked, Roxanne. Have I ever minced my words with you?" He chuckled, coughing a little. "I've told you this before and I'll tell you again now: there were all types of blokes in Indonesia in those days, not just entrepreneurial types like me, or guys like Berny who were trying to make an honest buck; there were also plenty of cowboys and conmen, alco's and party boys. The wilds of Irian Jaya attracted them like flies to shit." He coughed and cleared his throat.

"So you're saying Gordon and Brownlow fell into the alco's, cowboys and conmen category?"

He shrugged but didn't say a word.

"Okay, then, what about Betty Reilly?" She indicated the photo. "Gordo's wife, I presume?"

He shook his head, the wolfish glint in his eyes again. "Not anymore. They split years ago, or so I heard."

"Do you know why?"

He sniggered. "I can guess why. Look at her. She was wasted on that man. Nice piece of work, a good sport, too." His licentious smile was back and he was doing that icky tongue licking thing that made her stomach churn.

"Do you have any idea where Betty might be now?"

"Far away from him, if she's smart."

He really had it in for the guy, she thought. "Do you know why she was in the picture? She couldn't have been a surveyor."

"'Course not."

"So why was she in this shot? Why were *you*, for that matter?"

He considered this. "She was obviously at the Congress with her husband, but why she was in this official photo I can't recall. I was there as an honorary guest of the Surveyor General. My company had been providing the bulk of Irian Jaya's survey work for many years. Bloody lucky to have me."

She smiled, well accustomed to his arrogance. "Do you know anyone who might know where Betty or Gordon ended up?"

"I'd say Berny Tiles. He kept up with everyone from those days. But ... well ... dead men can't speak, now can they?"

She felt a shiver race down her spine while he placed the glass to his lips and polished off his scotch. He dropped it on the table by his chair and cleared his throat again.

"I'm not sure what Sondra's playing at here, Roxanne, nor why you've agreed to be her puppet, but I'd let it drop if I were you. I really would."

He was half smiling now, but there was a steeliness in his eyes and she had a fleeting feeling he was threatening her. As if on some silent cue, the door swung open and Ginny reappeared.

"Okay, you two, that will do it!" she announced. "I'll show you out, Roxanne."

Roxy stood up. "Of course, I really appreciate you seeing me on such short notice, Sir Wolfgang."

She took the photo he was holding out to her and noticed as she did so that Ginny's eyes widened and she shot a quick glance towards her husband.

"It's quite all right," he said firmly.

As she was led away, Roxy had to wonder whether he was saying those words to her, or to his startled looking wife.

CHAPTER 14

There's nothing more delicious than a properly prepared Pad Thai, or at least that's what Roxy decided as she brought the overflowing fork to her lips. Gilda had come, as promised, laden with edible goodies, and Roxy had to ignore her friend for several minutes as she enjoyed the slippery flat noodles, crisp vegetables, slivers of marinated tofu and nutty lime aftertaste. She even ignored her glass of merlot, which spoke volumes for the quality of the Thai, and Gilda had to laugh.

"It's like you've never eaten before," she said, shaking her head and reaching for her own glass.

Roxy tried to smile, her mouth bursting with noodles. Eventually, she said, "Sorry, Max is mad about Indian, so I haven't had Thai for ages. Forgot how much I missed it."

Gilda stared at her sideways. "You don't *have* to eat what he wants to eat all the time, you know. You are your own person."

"I know, but I do almost nothing else he asks, so ..."

"Oh, I see. You're compensating?"

She smiled weakly, picked up her glass. "Something like that. Anyway, let's not go there tonight, what've you got for me?"

Gilda held a hand up as she polished off her wine. "I'll fetch more vino while I get my bag."

She jumped up and strode to the kitchen where the merlot bottle had been left, then brought it back, along with her oversized Oroton handbag that had been dumped by the front door on her arrival. It was late on Tuesday night, and both women had been so famished when Gilda finally got away from work, they couldn't contemplate anything until some food had found its way to their stomachs.

Gilda refilled her glass and topped up Roxy's, then reached into her bag and produced a notepad.

"My colleagues think I'm a pain in the butt, poking around in everyone else's cases, but they're getting used to it," she said, giving Roxy a pointed look, then opened the pad and began to read. "Okay, so according to the Robbery Squad, Robert 'Bob' Brownlow was found deceased outside his residence exactly three weeks ago tomorrow. Suspected mugging as his wallet had been raided, several credit cards missing and no cash found on his premises."

"*On his premises?*" Roxy repeated, laughing. "You mean, in his pockets? On his body?"

"Hey, don't knock 'police speak', it's the only thing that keeps me going—working out clunkier ways to say ordinary things and confuse the crap out of the public. Even better, you should try saying it into a news camera with a straight face. Hilarious! We take bets who's going to crack up first."

"It's just one big barrel of laughs on the police force, eh?"

"It's either that or we're crying all day. I know which one I prefer. Rightio, so the investigator tells me he was beaten pretty badly, even for a mugging."

"Like it was personal, perhaps?"

"Maybe, maybe not. Some junkies can get a bit carried away. Maybe the victim tried to fight back. In any case, there are a few leads, nothing strong, etcetera, etcetera. It's another one of those 'open' cases that seem to be going nowhere fast." She placed her pad down. "So you think this is connected to your Berny Tiles?"

Roxy nodded and got up to retrieve the print she had made of the old photo. She handed it to Gilda, pointing out Brownlow as she did so.

"I went to see Wolfman this arvo, to see if he knew where any of these people might be. He reckons he hasn't seen Brownlow since 1975. Called him Browny; also said he wouldn't amount to much, whatever that means. He certainly wasn't living large and had no family, at least not according to the newspaper reports."

Gilda considered this before glancing at the man on the right. "And that's Berny Tiles?"

"Yep. He's about the only one Wolfman has nice words for, oh, apart from the woman, of course. But then again, I don't think Sir Sleazebag has ever met a woman he didn't like." Roxy pointed out the other man in the picture. "Still tracking down Gordon Reilly. Wolfman says he hasn't seen him in decades either."

"You believe him?"

"No reason not to. Although I got the distinct impression he wasn't happy about my questions."

"Why?"

She squinted slightly behind her thick, black glasses. "Nothing concrete, he was just ... I don't know, not very *forthcoming*. I mean, it was pretty obvious he didn't have much respect for Gordon and Brownlow but he wouldn't elaborate or explain himself. Said they were losers and insisted I leave it at that."

Gilda plucked a bit of corn from her teeth. "So, he's not a gossip."

"No, I think there's more to it than that. He told me some pretty salacious stuff for his book—all about his first wife and his affairs before he met and married Ginny. Reckons he's been faithful ever since and I believe him, she's way too scary to cheat on. So why clamp up over a bunch of guys he has barely seen in thirty-something years? Bit odd, I'd say."

"Hmm. I'll hunt around and see what I can find, although I'm still not quite sure what this is all about."

Roxy leaned back on the sofa, patting her stomach, which now felt the size of a bar fridge, and sighed. "Tell me about it. Sondra has hired me to do a job but I'm very confused exactly what that job is. I do think there are some odd connections and coincidences, but I'm not a hundred percent convinced any of them add up to much."

"Let's spread it out and see, shall we?"

Roxy nodded and they cleared the coffee table of the takeaway containers then placed the seemingly benign looking photo in the centre. As Gilda sat staring at it, Roxy ducked into her bedroom to find the treat she had bought earlier.

"Nourishment for the little grey cells," she announced, dropping the large block of dark chocolate into Gilda's lap.

"And *that's* why you're my favourite person," Gilda said, wrestling with the packaging and breaking them both off a large chunk. They chewed away as they continued to stare at the photo.

"Okay, so as far as we know, it all starts with this simple group shot." Roxy nodded. "Right, so, just to be clear, you wrote a book about *this* man." Gilda tapped a long silver nail on Wolfgang's head. "*This* man," now she tapped on Clive, "died innocently enough of cancer about ten, fifteen years ago. Nothing too suspicious there. This man," tap tap on Berny Tiles, "only recently died, most likely deliberately killed in a hit and run, and *this* man," she indicated Browny, "similar thing, but switch 'hit and run' with 'mugging'. And this man is nowhere to be found." She kept her nail pointing at Gordon Reilly. "Seems to me that he is the missing link."

"My sentiments exactly. Do you think he might have killed the others?"

She broke off another two squares of chocolate and handed one to Roxy. "I'm not saying that. But with the others either dead or on their sick bed, you've got to wonder where he is and what he's up to."

"And what about her?" It was Roxy's turn to tap on the picture.

"Yes, Betty Reilly, the only woman in the frame. Vely vely interesting."

"Wolfman tells me she was married to Gordon but it's most likely she has since left him, but he says he has no idea where she is now or why she was even in this picture."

"And you don't believe that either?"

Roxy went to speak when a shrill ring caught her off guard and she nearly jumped out of her skin. She flung a hand to her beating chest, shot Gilda an apologetic smile and reached for her landline. It was now almost 11:00 p.m., way too late for polite phone calls, so it could only be one person.

She relaxed considerably and said, "Hi, Oliver."

"You want the good news or the bad news?"

"Just spit it out."

"Okay, well, the bad news is, your week of easy money is over. Needy Woman won't be needing you anymore."

"Really? Why?"

"That's the good news," he told her. "I found the elusive photograph."

CHAPTER 15

Oliver's office was almost as dingy as the scanning agency, but in a more favourable location, at least as far as Roxy was concerned. It was wedged in the heart of the city, just a quick train ride away from her apartment, down a dusty alleyway and up four floors.

Olie's long-suffering assistant, Sharon, had her bony, Lycra-clad butt in the air as Roxy walked through, and was clearly digging away for something under her desk. She swung around with a wide smile when Roxy called out hello.

"How're you doin', Rox? Good?"

"Yes, all good. You?"

"Oh, don't even start me, love. Go on in, His Highness awaits." She waved a scrawny hand towards the inner office and Roxy did as instructed, finding Oliver chowing down on a donor kebab, a giant glob of red sauce on his stubbly chin.

In front of his desk sat a bright blue armchair that looked like it had been taken straight out of the box. There wasn't a stray thread or a dust particle to be found. She raised her eyebrows, impressed as she sank into it.

"Been decorating I see," she said, caressing the smooth, spotless arms.

"Shazza talked me into it." He ripped another bite from his kebab, talking as he chewed. More sauce dripped onto his chin. "Reckons the old one made us look 'cheap'."

"And cheerful! I liked the old one. It suited you perfectly."

"That's why it had to go," Sharon announced from the doorway. "Coffee, darls?"

Roxy nodded and she disappeared again.

"Okay, hand it over," Roxy told Oliver. "I won't believe it 'till I see it."

He quickly finished chewing then he wrapped his kebab back in its foil, dropped it onto the desk and reached for a serviette, which he dabbed at his fingers before lobbing it towards the bin, missing spectacularly.

"And that, ladies and gentleman, is why I never made the NBA."

"That and the fact you're a short, fat, white man," Roxy added, tapping on her chin.

"Huh?"

She tapped again and, comprehending this time, he swiped his chin across the sleeve of his polyester bowling shirt, then began glancing around his desk.

"Now, where did I put it ..."

She groaned. "You have not gone and lost it again."

"Don't get your knickers in a knot, it's here somewhere ... Oh, yeah, here it is."

He pulled an A4-sized photograph out from under some papers and passed it across to Roxy like it was made of egg shells. She took it just as carefully and studied it again, still wondering what on earth all the fuss was about. It was a mirror image to the copy she already had.

"Turn it over," he told her, raising his eyebrows a few times.

She did so and saw a few simple words scrawled in fading lead pencil across the back. It was hard to make out but she was pretty sure it said, *Beautiful Bett.*

"Beautiful Bett?"

"Is that a double T at the end, or is one of those an exclamation mark?" Oliver asked.

She squinted her eyes and studied it more closely, trying to think, then turned it back over. Her eyes widened suddenly.

"Bett! It must mean Betty Reilly. Beautiful Betty Reilly."

She stared at the picture, glancing from Betty to Berny and back again. "Oh my God, why didn't I see that earlier? In this photo, Berny Tiles is looking away from the camera, towards Betty. I didn't think much of it before ... but maybe ... maybe there was something there."

"How so?" he said, just as Sharon returned with two Horowitz mugs in her hands. She plonked them down and gave Oliver the evil eye.

"I'll tell her, I promise!"

"Tell her what?" asked Roxy but Sharon had already slunk away again.

"It'll keep for now. So what are you trying to say? You think Berny and Betty were getting it on? Doing the *naaaasty?*"

Roxy stared at him. "What are you? Twelve?" She looked back at the picture. "Maybe. He is looking towards her fondly and she is quite a catch as Wolfman pointed out. Maybe Berny and Betty had an affair back then. Berny was married, so was Betty, so I guess that would be pretty scandalous stuff."

"Is Berny's wife still around?"

"No, he told me she died in a car accident about six years ago. He's got a new wife on the scene called Renata."

"Okay, but what's that got to do with anything? I mean, why did Berny need the picture? Do you think they were still having an affair when he died?"

"If so, why marry someone else? Besides, Sondra's never heard of Betty. Maybe Berny just wanted the photo for sentimental reasons, was still holding a candle to Betty and it's the only picture he has."

"But he was dying. Why would he want to bring attention to an affair that would only upset his daughter, not to mention this new wife?"

"Yeah, it doesn't really work, does it?" She chewed on her coffee cup for a while, contemplating it all. "Either way, it probably doesn't matter now. Sondra will be relieved we found this photo. Maybe she doesn't need me to track down everyone in it. Maybe it will all make sense to her when she gets it back and, as you so eloquently put it, I'll be out of work again."

"Oh, I can hear the violins playing now."

"Really? I thought that was the scratchy old sofa crying to come home."

He laughed then just as quickly dropped his smile. "Okay, so here's the deal. Shazza wants all our clients to clear their crap out of the office by Friday. We don't have the space to store your shit anymore, it's getting too cramped in here, apparently. Plus it's not a 'good look'."

He did that curly finger thing and Roxy eye rolled him in return then glanced around his office. Cramped was an understatement. It had always been a messy, dusty space, cluttered with client memorabilia and other debris, but lately it was beginning to resemble an episode of *Help me, I'm a Hoarder!*

"I didn't think you guys went in for interior design."

"Yeah, well, Shazza's on a bloody mission. Did some feng shui course and reckons ours is stuffed. After last year and all the grief I went through, she reckons it was my own fault and I need to clear my bad energy or some bloody nonsense."

Roxy smirked. "Starting with this fab new chair?"

"And the old boxes. They've gotta go, Rox."

"I hear you, Olie. I'll bring my car in on Friday and collect them. I didn't even realise I had much stuff here."

"Well, you do. It's mostly just leftovers from past books—old research papers, manuals, photos, that kind of thing."

"Is that how you found this?" She indicated the photo in her hands.

"Kind of." He took a sip of his coffee. "Johnno, the Bergman publisher from Book It, rang me. They had to do an inventory of all the crap that got nicked last weekend, and they discovered from their files that they'd sent this picture off—"

"Yes, I know, it went to the scanners."

"No, it was *supposed* to go to the scanners but then it got cut at the last minute."

"Cut? What do you mean?"

"Remember you said it wasn't in the layout of the Bergman book that you saw? Well, it was in the original, apparently, but then they were told to remove it from the book, so they did as instructed, and then, because the picture was no use to them, packaged it up and posted it to me. One of their interns sent it so they forgot all about it for a moment there. Thank God they keep records." He paused to scratch his double chin. "Anyway, they were going to return it to Berny Tiles directly but didn't have his address so they sent it to you, courtesy of me. Shazza got it a few weeks ago with a stack of other stuff from the publisher and chucked it in your box. Didn't look at it properly, didn't think anything of it, to be honest. She found it again while going through the boxes last night."

Roxy sat forward. "So let me get this straight. You've had the original picture sitting here all along? While I've been chasing my tail, it's been sitting quietly in your office?"

"Oh get off your high horse, Rox. You've been paid to chase your tail, don't complain."

She stared at the picture again. "So Wolfman wanted this picture removed, eh?"

"Not Wolfman, no."

"Then who?"

"Johnno says the word came in from Wolfman's wife."

Her eyes shot up. "Ginny?"

"He calls her Imelda Marcos. Says Imelda took one look at the pic and demanded it be removed. Immediately. Gave no explanation, just wanted it out. Was very firm about it."

The plot thickens, thought Roxy, staring hard at Beautiful Bett again.

CHAPTER 16

Roxy knew she should be heading straight for Sondra's house to hand the precious photo over, but there was one avenue she still wanted to go down first. She had been hired to track down the people in the photo and she really wanted to come through with at least one of them, preferably alive.

Already in the city, she strode the few blocks it took to reach Sydney's main library on Macquarie Street, just down from the Town Hall. She wanted to see if she could get some more information on Betty Reilly first. If she knew Sondra, and she was only just starting to, she had a hunch she would want to know who the woman was and why her father seemed to have such a crush on her.

The State Library is a grandiose, sandstone structure in the heart of Sydney with towering Roman columns, expansive reading rooms, and a vast collection of reference material—over five million items, in fact—so Roxy headed straight for the information desk when she arrived and let the librarian do the hard work for her. After telling her what she needed, the woman tapped away at a computer for several minutes, then jotted something down on a white card and pointed Roxy towards a wide staircase that led down into the bowels of the library. Roxy made her way and promptly handed the card to another librarian at the bottom who then pointed her in the direction of an aisle titled Asia. She followed it along to the Indonesian section then used the card to locate the correct reference number.

Within minutes Roxy had hold *of Indo-Surveyors: how Australians helped map a foreign land.* She tugged the heavy tome from the shelf and took it over to a side table where several student types were tapping away at laptops and tablets, not a book in sight. A scrawny, light-haired man with a poor attempt at a beard looked up as she sat down and gave her a smouldering smile (or what he thought passed for one) and she returned the smile with a look that read "In your dreams" before opening the book up. She flipped straight to the back and began scanning the index. Within minutes, Roxy had found several "Reilly" references, including a T, an E and two Gs. She started with those and immediately found information on Gordon Reilly, although not a great deal. According to the book, he was a small-time surveyor who once worked for Samsara Surveys out of Sumatra. Originally from Sydney, it said that he returned after two years and was last seen working for Henry Mapping Consultants in Chatswood.

Well that was promising.

Delighted, Roxy pulled the smartphone out of her bag, created a fresh "memo" and tapped in the relevant information then turned her attention to the other Reillys in the index. She already had a hunch that E stood for Elizabeth (shortened to Betty) but when she located the relevant page, her spirits dropped. Elvin Reilly was a Dutch chainman who worked in Lombok and seemed to bear no relation to either Gordon or Betty. T. Reilly was actually Timothy O'Reilly, an early patrol officer on the Irian Jaya/Papua New Guinea border and, again, no relation.

Roxy was about to give up when, flipping through the pages, she spotted a photo that caught her by surprise. She spread the page out and stared at it. It was almost identical to the copy in her hand—a black and white photograph taken at the 1975 Survey Congress. This one, however, had only four people in the image; both Wolfgang and Betty Reilly were nowhere to be seen, and the four other men were not smiling as they were in hers. In this one, they looked sternly towards the camera, all serious and business like.

She wasn't sure what exactly it meant and why Wolfgang and Betty were not in this shot, but she also wasn't sure it was relevant, so she eventually shut the book and returned it to the shelf, noticing as she went that Beard Boy was now ogling the young woman on his right.

Goodness me, she thought. *There's got to be better pickup joints.*

Back at the front desk, Roxy smiled at the librarian and asked, "Have you got a Yellow Pages handy? I need to look up H for Henry."

****

Henry Mapping Consultants was a small business, housed with several others on the sixth floor of a sparkling office block in the heart of Chatswood. When Roxy stepped through the elevator towards the front desk, the receptionist, a nuggety forty-something with a blond crew cut and a crooked nose, was all smiles until she mentioned the name Gordon Reilly, then he turned surprisingly combative.

"What do you want him for?" he demanded, his mouth slanted down into a scowl.

"I'm chasing him up for a book I'm writing," she said, stretching the truth considerably.

He stared at her as though weighing this up and then shrugged. "We have no one by that name here."

Now she was confused; a second ago it had sounded as though he knew the guy. She said, "Well, he wouldn't be here *now*. He'd be well into his seventies. But I believe he worked here once. Probably from the late 1970s until about the '90s. I just need to track down a contact number or address for him, and then I'll be out of your hair."

"You're not in my hair but I can't help you. We don't give out employees' details, current or ex. To anyone."

"So you *are* saying he did used to work here?"

"I'm saying nothing of the sort. What is it you want with him, again?" The scowling lips almost reached the bottom of his chin and that, coupled with the wonky nose, made him look a lot like an amateur boxer. Not the friendliest face to have on your front desk.

"I just need to speak to him."

"And I just need to show you where the exit is."

He pointed a stubby finger towards the elevators, his lips now twisted upwards into the fakest of smiles and she wanted to smack him where it hurt, but she had a feeling he'd smack her right back. She tried a different tack.

"Can I see Mr Henry then?"

He studied her carefully. "Which one?"

"Whichever one's available," she replied and his eyes squinted a little as he thought about this.

"I will see if Mr Henry—Mr Beau Henry—is available. Your name?"

"Roxy Parker."

He picked up his phone, tapped a number in and said, "Hi there, sorry to disturb you. I have a woman out here, a Rossy Parlour, wanting to see Mr Henry." He gave Roxy the once over. "She has no appointment and I've already told her it's out of the question so ... Huh? ... Oh, well, here's the thing, she's trying to track down ..." He lowered his voice considerably, "Gordon Reilly, but I've already told her she's wasting her—" He stopped. "I have no idea." He glanced at Roxy. "Yeees ... I suppose so, but ..." He glanced away from her and to the side. "Are you *sure?*" He took a deep breath. "Okay then, I'll send her in." He turned back to Roxy. "It's your lucky day. Take the corridor all the way to the end. Through the glass doors. Mr Henry's assistant will meet you there."

Roxy did a silent whoop of joy as she gave him a smug smile and made her way down the corridor as instructed. She didn't know what the guy's problem was but, like the receptionist at Scott's Scanners, she decided he was better suited for a trendy nightclub. He had the door bitch vibe down pat.

When Roxy got to the end of the corridor, an elderly woman was already swinging the glass doors open, ushering her through. She was well into her sixties, with white, shaggy short hair, bright green spectacles and a beaming smile that made her look twenty years younger. She was wearing a red woollen jacket over black trousers, and a colourful scarf around her neck, dangly Indian style earrings on her ears. Her friendly demeanour could not be more different to Door Bitch and she seemed more than eager to help her out, leading Roxy straight to a lounge area on one side and offering her a seat.

"You're here about Gordon Reilly?" she said, eyes wide behind her specs.

"That's right. Did you know him?"

"Know him?" The woman laughed. "I was married to the man!"

By the time Roxy had picked her jaw up off the floor, Betty Reilly was offering her tea or coffee. Roxy managed to ask for coffee and then waited with bated breath while the executive assistant got busy in a small kitchenette at the back.

She returned with two cups and placed them on the table in front of them, eagerly asking, "So how is Gordon? Have you seen him?"

Roxy's elation evaporated. "No, I was hoping you had. I'm trying to track him down."

The woman sank into her chair, also looking deflated. "Oh dear, I thought you might have had some good news. We lost him, you see. Some time ago."

"Lost him?"

Betty looked at Roxy, her eyes narrowing a little. "Perhaps you'd better tell me who you are and why you're here before we go any further."

"Yes, of course." Roxy pulled out the picture of the 1975 Survey Congress and handed it to Betty.

Betty looked a little shocked and blinked rapidly a few times. "Goodness! That's a blast from the past. Where did you find this?"

"It was sent to me by Berny Tiles for a book I've just written." She paused. "You obviously remember Berny Tiles?"

Betty nodded. "Of course, although I haven't seen him in years. I did read about his death. That was very sad. He was a lovely fellow."

Roxy studied the older woman's face but she didn't look like a grief-stricken lover so she had to assume their dalliance, if there was one, was in the past. She proceeded to fill Betty in on the Wolfgang Bergman biography and the series of unfortunate incidents that had happened since, including Brownlow's mugging and Berny's final words, asking for Roxy Parker.

"His daughter, Sondra, seems to think there's some important message in all of this and has asked me to hunt down the people in this photo. She thinks maybe you might have some idea why this picture was so important to her father. Do you?"

Betty looked bemused. "Not at all."

"Can you tell me about that day, the day the picture was taken?"

She placed the photo back on the table and Roxy noticed her hand was shaking a little. She wondered if that was from old age, or something else.

"It was obviously the Survey Congress."

"Yes, can you tell me about the Congress?"

"Well, they were all much the same. Lots of drinking, lots of partying, not a lot of congressing going on. They'd have official meetings at the start of the day, but then it would all sort of ... *deteriorate* from there. It was a bit like the Wild West, I guess you could say." Her earlier smile had disappeared and she looked a little shaken as she said, "Not much to tell."

Roxy recalled Wolfgang saying a similar thing, and wondered just how wild it got.

"So how were you involved? I gathered these congresses were pretty blokey affairs."

"Oh they were. Us wives were dutifully called upon to organise the lavish parties, book the hotels for the visiting 'dignitaries', the likes of Wolfgang Bergman who always flew in from one of his mines to honour us with his presence." *Was that cynicism in her voice?* Roxy wondered. "We didn't take part in any of the official meetings, you understand, were just required to pretty up the cocktail parties and dinners, so to speak. Then after that the women would generally head back to the hotel, exhausted, and the men would hang around the bar, drinking, playing poker, smoking enormous cigars. As I said, not much to tell."

"Yes, but did anything happen at *this* particular Congress?"

Betty began blinking rapidly again and looked like she was about to say something when she had second thoughts. She thrust her lips together then into a forced smile and shook her head, her dangly earrings flying about as she did so. Roxy didn't say a word, hoping her silence would encourage her.

Eventually Betty sighed and said, "I wasn't really part of the Congress, you do understand that, my dear?"

"But you're in this shot."

"Only because they dragged me into it. Same with Wolfgang. He's not a surveyor. We were both on the sidelines watching the official photographer and the lads called us over to jump in at the end. He'd already taken a series of snaps, this isn't the official shot."

"Yes," said Roxy, "I've seen that one."

"I shouldn't have even been there, my toddler was back at the hotel with the sitter and I ... I don't know why I hung around. Stupid really." Her face clouded over and as she raised her cup to her lips, Roxy noticed the shaking had not subsided.

"You have a child?"

Her face brightened as she took a quick sip. "Yes, Brian. Not much of a child now, of course. He turned forty last month—I don't know where the time goes!" She smiled and stared wistfully out the glass doors. "Anyway, I'm surprised this picture ever saw the light of day. I can only guess that Berny wanted it because it was a bit different to the usual stuffy pictures they take at these events."

"And maybe because you were in it?" she asked.

Betty looked back at her surprised and Roxy said, "I know about ... what happened that night."

She didn't really, she was just taking a stab in the dark, but Betty's sudden rapid blinking and the red blush that now crept up her neck were all the confirmation she needed.

"How do you ...? Did *he* tell you that?" She looked mortified.

"No, Betty. I worked it out."

"But how? I don't understand ..." A buzzing sound interrupted them and Betty looked around anxiously, then got up to answer her desk phone. She talked to someone in a hushed voice, darting glances back at Roxy as she spoke, then hung up the phone and returned, still blinking madly.

"Look, I really can't talk about any of this, I'm very busy. Sorry." She still wore her polite smile but could barely look Roxy in the eye now, and Roxy held a hand up.

"No, I'm the one who's sorry, Betty. I'm not here to dredge up the past, I just want to find Gordon."

The blinking slowed down. "Well, good luck with that."

She offered Roxy a conciliatory smile and rounded up the cups. Roxy helped her and they placed them back in the kitchen as she said, "As I told you, we haven't seen poor old Gordon in many years." She turned to look at Roxy. "That's why I was so happy before. I thought maybe you had some word. My son can be a pain in the neck, but I know he's very keen to find out where his dad is, what happened to him."

"It must be very distressing for you both, losing him like that."

"Well, yes, although Gordon was lost to us a long time ago. It was my fault really. We had a very ... *difficult* breakup." The blinking started again. "He didn't take it well at all."

"Do you think your boss, Mr Henry, might know where Gordon is?"

She seemed surprised by the question. "No, he has no idea. Why?"

"I just thought, since he used to work here—"

"Oh, only briefly, dear. Mr Henry, the original Mr Henry, Beau's father, was a very old family friend. He kindly gave us both a job when we got back to Australia in '76 but, well, Gordon didn't really settle in. It was me ... he had trouble seeing me every day ... I offered to find another job, he refused, and well, I lost touch with him soon after. We ran into him about ten years back, he didn't look well even then. He doesn't have any family here, so I implored him to return home to Perth, but I don't think he went. Last we heard he was living on the streets."

"The streets? As in homeless?"

She turned away from Roxy's look of surprise and began leading her towards the glass doors. "Yes, sadly, that's what we heard."

"Do you have a more recent picture of him?"

"Not on me, no." She turned back to Roxy. "You really are going to try to find him?"

"Yes I am."

"Good," she said and then added, "just a second." She retraced her steps back to her desk and retrieved a business card. "Please, if you do find Gordon, tell him we're okay, tell him to get in touch. With *me*. He should call my mobile." She leant down, grabbed a pen and circled the number. "Not the office, you understand? He should call me, directly."

Roxy agreed, handing one of her own business cards over. "And if you can think of anything else related to this picture or those days, will you give me a ring?"

"Of course. Anything to help. Now, I'm sorry, I really must get on."

She held the glass doors open for Roxy. "I'll walk you out."

She then led Roxy through the glass doors and back down the corridor, forcing the smile back onto her face. When they reached the front desk, the surly receptionist was sweeping glances between them and Roxy tried not to look too smug as she thanked Betty and made her way out, the elderly woman blinking wildly behind her.

CHAPTER 17

That evening, tucked snugly under a mohair blanket on the lounge, Nick Drake singing a moody tune on the stereo, Roxy went through the day's progress in her head. She was glad she had found Betty alive and well, but she was no closer to finding Gordon, nor to confirming why that picture was so special to Berny Tiles. Betty's reaction seemed to validate her theory that the two were having an affair, but she hadn't quite come out and said as much. In fact, the older woman had turned quite evasive when Roxy pressed her on that 1975 Survey Congress, much like Wolfgang had.

She thought about this. Something definitely happened that night, but no one seemed to want to elaborate. She shrugged. Perhaps they were just protecting the memory of Berny Tiles and his first wife.

Or were they?

A ringing noise broke through the wistful sounds of *Pink Moon* and Roxy jumped up to answer her mobile, hoping it was Sondra. She had been unavailable all afternoon and Roxy was keen to get her up to speed and get the photo back to her. If someone really was breaking into places to get their paws on it, she wanted it out of hers, pronto.

She smiled when she heard Sondra's voice.

"I'm so sorry it's taken ages to call you back," the other woman said down the line. "I don't know what's worse, a bride on her wedding day, or a bride three days *before* her wedding day."

Roxy laughed. "And people wonder why I don't want to get married."

"Don't do it! If only to spare the poor florist the grief." She laughed, too. "Okay, so how did it all go?"

Despite groaning about brides, Sondra was clearly in a good mood, less nervy than past conversations, and Roxy took this as a positive sign. She wasn't looking forward to breaking the news that Sondra's beloved dad might have been unfaithful to her mum, but it had to be said. First, though, she told her about Brownlow, and his mysterious fatal mugging, then of her meeting with Betty and learning of Gordon's disappearance, before getting to the brightest note of all.

"I have your father's photo and I'm happy to drop it off to you now if you like."

In truth, Roxy didn't feel like going anywhere. The Chinese restaurant downstairs was currently whipping up her dinner (beef in black bean sauce) and she was looking forward to a slothful night catching up on the news. Yet she owed it to Sondra—and her own sense of security—to get the picture back.

"No, no, don't trouble yourself," Sondra was saying. "I'll send a courier now, if that's okay?"

"It's more than okay, it'll be a relief. If all these break-ins have been related to this photo, I'll be glad to see the back end of it."

She was also half hoping to see the back end of the case. While Roxy knew there were many unanswered questions, she had a hunch this would be her first and last progress report. Sondra would agree the picture was related to an illicit affair and want to drop it like a hot potato. Roxy couldn't have been more wrong.

"Oh no, I want you to stick with it, you're making great inroads," Sondra said.

"Really?"

"Oh yes, I mean, those words on the back are very ... *telling*." She paused. "So they're the only words you could see, 'Beautiful Bett'?"

"Yep, scrawled on the back."

"And you think my father had an affair with this Betty woman?"

Roxy hesitated as well. "I'm not trying to cause trouble here, Sondra, or damage his memory, but yes I do."

"Did Betty admit that?"

"Not in so many words, but she didn't exactly contradict it, either. Something obviously happened that night. Just mentioning it made her visibly uncomfortable."

"Right, well, I still think it's worth tracking down her ex-husband, that Gordon fellow. He might know more."

"More about the affair?"

"Yes ... and what it all means."

It means your Dad was an unfaithful rat, Roxy wanted to say but said, instead, "Do you really want to know? You think it's worth all this?"

There was a very long pause before Sondra spoke, and when she did, her voice sounded jittery again. "I know what you think and maybe you're right. Maybe my father and this Betty woman ..." She let the thought drop. "But what if you're wrong? What if there was another reason he wanted the picture back? We can't just let it go, we need to find Gordon Reilly. We need to find out once and for all."

"Betty has no idea where he is, Sondra. Thinks he might be homeless."

"Can't *you* find him?"

Roxy thought about this. "I could try."

"Good, then try. Please Roxy. I want you to stick with it. But I also want you to keep me in the loop. Just call me re e-mail me as you find more information."

"Okay, if you think it will help."

"Oh I know it will. You're close, Roxy, I can sense it."

Close to what? Roxy thought as she hung up. She wished her own senses were sending positive signals; all she was getting was a growing sense that she was poking her nose where it didn't belong. Judging from Wolfgang and Betty's reactions, the photograph only reminded everyone of a night they'd all rather forget. And perhaps it was a night that a grieving Daddy's Girl shouldn't be hearing about.

Roxy spread the mohair blanket over her legs again, picked up the remote control and began scanning through the channels for the seven o'clock news. As she did so, her mind wandered to her own love life. Since Max had left for Melbourne they had barely spoken, instead playing phone ping pong, missing each other's calls and returning them without success. She checked her smartphone and saw he had left her another message, just letting her know the advertorial was going well and he'd call later. Ping! She picked up her phone and tried to return his call, but it went straight to voice mail. He probably had a camera lens focused deep inside a shiny new Mercedes at that very minute. She left a quick cheerio then hung up—Pong!— wishing, for the first time in months, that he was here with her now, stealing the blanket and settling in for the night.

She sighed, ramped up the volume and began to watch the news.

****

Across town, in a very different part of the world, another woman was staring at her television set, too, but she wasn't really taking anything in. Instead, she was tapping her foot maniacally, her mind darting about in all directions.

"Why can't she just mind her own bloody business?" she said to the man beside her. "What's it got to do with her, anyway?"

He ignored this and continued watching the program so she snatched the remote control and stabbed the mute button. That got his attention. He slowly looked around, his eyebrows raised wearily.

"This had better not catch up with us."

He smiled. "Stop stressing so much. It does your beautiful face no favours."

"Oh fuck my beautiful face," she railed. "What are you going to do about all of this? You promised me it would be simple. There would be no problems."

"And there won't be, I promise you that. Again."

She glared at him then continued tapping away while he simply smiled again and ramped up the volume.

CHAPTER 18

Thursday morning dawned crisp and cold and while the rest of Sydney bemoaned the late start to spring, Roxy smiled. She liked the chill, and she *loved* the clothes—the luscious coats, the long boots, the bright and cheerful scarves—but she was struggling to find just the right outfit today. She certainly didn't want to look bright and cheerful. That would not do at all. Instead she needed to be inconspicuous with a little trustworthiness thrown in for good measure. How you dressed "trustworthy" was beyond her, but she'd give it a red-hot go.

Roxy reached for a grey sweater, cargo pants, and black Converse sneakers, then pulled a baggy black beanie over her hair and retrieved a few strands that had got caught up inside. She then took her ID, Betty's business card and some cash from her purse and placed them in a small backpack that securely zipped on one side.

She was heading for the mean streets of Sydney and she didn't want to stand out, nor attract prying hands. She knew Max would have a fit if he knew what she was doing, but she didn't care. Pre-Max she'd do it in a heartbeat, so why should things change just because she had a boyfriend?

Then she thought of her mother. She couldn't even begin to think what her mother would say about all of this.

Roxy braced for the cold and headed out, through her shabby but dignified suburb, Elizabeth Bay, and up into the neighbouring Kings Cross with its brothels and strip clubs, junkies and outlaw motorcyclists, and amongst them all, wide-eyed backpackers and tourists, ogling this red-light district as though it were pure entertainment. Roxy could never understand the allure, and tried to keep a low profile as she strode through, the picture of Gordon in one hand, the other balled in a fist by her side.

She knew it was like looking for a needle and all that, but she had to try. She was being paid to try.

Being paid to waste my time, more like, she thought gloomily as she studied the faces around her looking for a craggier version of the man in the black and white photograph. She wandered the streets for a good hour, peering into doorways and down alleyways but didn't see anyone who fit the description. Most of the homeless types she spotted were much younger, more like street kids, but that didn't lessen her resolve and she kept trawling the streets and scrutinising faces as she methodically made her way to a twenty-four-hour crisis centre she knew was tucked away in neighbouring Potts Point.

At Macleay Street she took a detour down Hughes Street to an old brick building with bars on the windows, bright red doors and a yellow sign that read Wayside Chapel. A haven for street youth, the homeless and other troubled souls, Roxy had walked past it many times in the past but never had the need to step inside. She did so a little warily now, but was greeted warmly by an elderly man wearing a Bulldogs cap, a red apron and a trimmed grey beard.

"Can I help you?" he asked, placing aside a garbage bag of old clothes he'd been sorting.

"Yes, I hope so. I'm looking for a man in his seventies by the name of Gordon Reilly, known as Gordo. I think he might be homeless and I'm just wondering whether you've seen him around."

"Gordo Reilly," the man repeated and then shook his head slowly. "A lot of the folks who come through here don't give their names, of course, at least not their real names that we know of, got anymore for me?"

She produced the photo—a copy of the original which a courier had collected from a very relieved Roxy Parker the evening before—and he took it off her and studied it for some time before saying, "Anything more recent?"

"Unfortunately, no."

He shook his head again. "Try Matthew Talbot's Hostel down near the wharf."

Hearing her stomach rumble and not liking the look of any of the grotty cafes on this side of town, Roxy decided to take a quick detour back to Elizabeth Bay to get something to eat at Peepers. On the way there, she dropped into the newsagency to fetch her *Herald* so she'd have reading material while she fuelled up. Both Costa and Rocco were nowhere to be seen today and there was a young Asian girl behind the till.

"I just want to grab my paper," she told her.

"Name?"

"Roxy Parker."

She reached below the counter and began shuffling through until she found the one she was looking for. "Just the one today?"

"Yes thanks."

She paid for it and continued on to Peepers where she ordered a warm poppy seed muffin and a latté, and sat down to devour the day's news. It had been a slow news week and there weren't many stories that would make Roxy's Crime Catalogue. The front page seemed to be captivated by a federal government power tussle and some mining company's latest gold find up in Irian Jaya. Her thoughts instantly went to Sir Wolfgang Bergman and she wondered if it was one of his. Funny how the rich just kept getting richer. She briefly wished she had taken up Caroline's offer and invested in mining stock. She was never going to make her fortune accepting obscure, odd jobs like this one, she thought, polishing off the muffin and then ordering another two.

On the way out, she paid for and pocketed the muffins, then began to stride back through what Oliver called "the arse-end of Kings Cross", through Potts Point to the super steep McElhone steps which provided a short cut down to the wharf-side suburb of Woolloomooloo. At the top, she soaked in the stunning Sydney skyline, the Harbour Bridge in the distance, and the old navy docks that were now home to the rich and famous, their gleaming yachts and cruisers bobbing about. And tucked away incongruously nearby, several public housing blocks, boisterous pubs and a halfway house for men called the Matthew Talbot Hostel.

Roxy waited while several joggers puffed their way up the 113 stone steps and then began her descent, grateful she was heading downwards and conveniently forgetting she would have to puff her own way back up at the end.

At the bottom, she checked her bag then walked away from the trendy wharves towards the slummier side of the suburb, under a rail bridge, past a police station and down an alleyway to a shabby, three-storey brick building with a fenced roof terrace on top. On one side, below the words Matthew Talbot Hostel, was a large white cross that spoke volumes for the poor souls inside.

Just like the Wayside Chapel, Roxy had walked past this hostel many times before, always affording it a wide berth, not so much to avoid the old men who loitered nearby, but because it always seemed to smell like a public urinal. The road was freshly washed today and there wasn't a soul about, so she made her way straight to the front door where a white van was parked and a young Aboriginal man, barely out of his teens, was loading what looked like ratty old blankets into the back.

Roxy stepped up to him and produced the picture. He shook his head and pointed inside. She went in and found a weary looking middle-aged man behind the front counter. He, too, shook his head.

"Jeeze, sweetheart, we get a few people in here from time to time, trying to locate loved ones. Most our blokes don't want to be found so you've got Buckley's chance."

"And you haven't seen anyone who might look like an older version of this?"

"Everyone here's an older version of that," he said, glancing around. "But, no, can't say I have."

She, too, looked around and sighed. There were various elderly men in the room and he was right, any one of them could be Gordon, thirty-seven years later.

"Oi, anyone know a Gordon Reilly?!" the older man yelled out and various faces turned to look at her and then away. No one said a word. He shrugged at her again and she thanked him, returning to the street.

This was going to be even harder than she thought.

The hostel van was just pulling out as she made her way back onto the main road, and she noticed it turn down a side street towards what looked like a small park at the other end. Roxy decided to follow it and watched as it parked in a loading zone and the young man jumped out and stepped around to the back. He opened the van and dragged out a few of the blankets and then secured the van again before heading into the park.

Roxy reclaimed the photo and then secured her bag before crossing the street and entering the park behind him. It was barely a park, just a grotty patch of dirt and some scratchy grass where half a dozen homeless guys were now lying on old sleeping bags, or sprawled under trees with makeshift cardboard canopies overhead.

The teen was handing out the blankets to several of the men, and she stood back and watched for a few minutes, assessing the situation. Everyone seemed fairly sedate—she regularly encountered homeless types in Elizabeth Bay and they were sometimes aggressive, swearing and spitting and cursing the world at large, and she didn't blame them, but this lot looked relatively relaxed. She took a deep breath and walked up to one elderly man in a jumble of stinky clothes who was just shoving the blanket into his swag. Closer, she realised he was probably more like fifty, but life had taken its toll.

"Hi there," she called out, holding a hand up to show that she meant no harm.

He glanced at her and away again, then dropped back onto his bum beneath a tree.

"I'm looking for Gordon Reilly. Known as Gordo? Do you know anyone by that name?"

She held out the photo but he didn't even look at her this time, so she tried a different tack, reaching into her coat pocket and producing the brown paper bag of muffins.

"Are you hungry?"

This time he stared at her like she'd just offered him poison and turned away, growling something she couldn't quite make out. She knew a bottle of vodka might have been more welcomed but that felt too much like a bribe and it didn't sit comfortably with her.

She glanced around and noticed the hostel worker was already exiting the park and, not comfortable with the idea of being here alone, she considered giving up completely when someone called out, "Oi, lady, whadyawant?!"

Roxy swung around to find a short, fat man staring at her from a dilapidated park bench with colourful graffiti all over it. She walked towards him slowly, realising as she approached that he was actually a she, and a very scary looking she at that. The woman was dressed just like the men around her, in a shabby black coat and boots, and her hair was cropped short, a stream of rings up her ears, and a smudged tattoo down her neck. It looked like someone had taken a bottle of black ink and flung it at her.

"Hi there," Roxy said, trying to pull off a mixture of friendly and confident. "I'm looking for Gordon Reilly."

"Never heard of 'im," the woman replied, her eyes dancing with delight.

"Okay, just through I'd try."

"I'll 'ave the cake though."

Roxy glanced at the muffin bag and back at the woman. She handed one of the muffins over.

"What d'ya want 'im for?" the woman said, taking a large, wolfish bite.

She wondered how to play it and eventually said, "Um, his wife is worried about him, that's all."

The woman cackled. "Then I definitely don't know 'im." She cackled again.

"I just want to speak with him for two minutes. Then I'll leave him alone. I promise."

"Said I don't know 'im."

She had stopped cackling and was already moving away, stuffing the remains of the muffin into her coat, when Roxy said, "I have a picture!"

She held the image out with one hand, her other pointing at Gordon Reilly, and the woman turned back and snuck a quick look at it, then went to look away when something stopped her. She snatched the picture out of Roxy's hand and stared at it.

"Surly the Surveyor? That who you're lookin' for?"

Roxy held her breath. "Yes, I guess so. I know him as—"

"Boring as bat shit is what he is. Always goin' on about his bloody survey days out in bloody wherever. Best years of his bloody life, yada yada yada. Why don't he fug off and go back there then, eh? Got any more food? Grog? Spare a tenner?"

Roxy smiled. She knew how this went, and found the spare cash she'd placed in her pocket for just such an occasion. She held it up for the woman to see.

"Know where I can find him?"

The woman eyed the money hungrily. "Yeah, at Matt's place."

"Matt?"

"Matt Talbot's Hostel. Where else you reckon he is? The Hilton?" She cackled again.

CHAPTER 19

The Surly Surveyor was up on the roof terrace of the hostel, hunched over at a table reading a book when Roxy finally found him. The same weary manager had walked her up and pointed him out.

"Sorry, sweetheart, but he's never used the name Gordon, far as I know. Had no idea."

"Don't worry about it," she said. "Do you mind if I speak to him?"

He shrugged. "It's a free world. This one don't bite, but you'll be lucky to get much out of him. Quiet type. Unless you bring up Indonesia, then you can't shut him up."

She smiled. "So I hear."

"Call out if ya need me," he said, and left her to it.

Gordon Reilly was a gaunt, almost ghostly looking figure, his eyes like hollows in his head, his long, thin neck as scrawny as a plucked chicken's. He had a bald head and a smattering of stubble across his bony chin, and was clad in the homeless uniform: oversized black jacket and trousers and lumpy old boots. He was also wearing a thick, fraying, green scarf flung several times around his neck and, she noticed, a thick, tarnished silver wedding band on his left hand.

She stepped towards him. "Gordon Reilly?"

For a few moments he didn't say a thing and she was wondering how to play it when he finally said, "Who wants to know?"

His voice was soft and well spoken but his eyes did not leave the ratty, yellowing pages of what looked like pulp fiction in front of him.

Roxy pulled the picture from her jacket and placed it beside the book. "Berny Tiles. Or, his daughter, Sondra, to be more precise."

That got his attention and he shot a quick look at her before looking at the picture.

"May I?" Roxy indicated the plastic chair in front of him and when he didn't say anything, she pulled it out and sat down slowly. She didn't want to spook the guy, but she was sick of the wild goose chase and was determined to get some answers, today if possible.

"Is that you?" she said, indicating the G. Reilly in the photo. He still didn't speak so she tapped on Betty's face. "And that's your ex-wife."

"*Wife*," he said, glancing at her quickly and then away. He began playing with his ring, turning it round and round on his bony finger. "We're not divorced."

"She's worried about you."

"She shouldn't be. I'm perfectly fine."

"You call being homeless fine?"

His brow furrowed but he still didn't meet her eyes. "Who says I'm homeless?"

She stammered, "I just thought ..." She waved a hand around the rooftop that was bustling with men of all shapes and sizes, ages and ethnicities hungrily tearing into hot meals or sharing games of chess and dominoes.

"I work here, you know. I've got a job."

"Sorry, I didn't realise."

Still he didn't meet her eyes, just stared down at the table, whether focused on the photo or the book she could not tell. He had stopped playing with the ring.

"I was ... on the streets. Matt's took me in. Cleaned me up. I'm 443 days sober."

"Congratulations."

He didn't acknowledge this. "I do odd jobs now and again, pickups and deliveries mostly, occasionally help out in the kitchen, that sort of thing. It's not survey work but it's honest work. Pays my board up at a bedsit on Challis Avenue. You go back and tell that to Betty and Berny. I'm fine."

Roxy's eyebrows shot up. "Berny? Berny's dead."

She hadn't meant it to sound so blunt, and she couldn't tell if this was news to Gordon or not, but his demeanour did not alter one bit.

Eventually he said, "Oh well, that will happen."

"He was killed in a car accident on Father's Day. Police suspect he was deliberately hit."

That didn't seem to surprise him either and he still didn't look at her. "Is that why you're here?"

He flashed her a very quick glance then before turning his eyes back to his book. Roxy tapped on the picture beside him.

"I'm here to ask about this photo. It seemed to mean something to Berny. He gave it to me for a book I've been writing and was desperate to get it back before he died. His daughter wants to know why."

"Book?"

"Yes, about Sir Wolfgang Bergman."

He hunched over even further towards the table and she couldn't make out his expression at all. He had begun playing with his wedding ring again.

"I'm trying to find out why Berny wanted this picture so badly. Do you have any idea why it was so important to him? If there's anything particularly special about it?"

She was deliberately keeping things vague so as not to scare him off. If Betty really did have an affair with Berny that night, he wasn't going to want to chat about it.

"Can't think why he'd want that photo," he said eventually. "It would just remind him of all that he lost."

"Lost? What do you mean?" Was he referring to Betty, she wondered?

He lapsed into silence again so she tried a fresh angle.

"How well do you remember that Congress? The day that picture was taken?"

His jaw tensed. "Like it's been tattooed to the back of my brain." He paused. "It was the day my life fell apart."

It was a startling statement but his matter-of-fact tone had not changed and he simply pushed the photo back towards Roxy and returned to his book. Throughout this entire exchange he did not meet her eyes once and she wanted to scream, "*Why?! What happened?!*" But she had to play it cool, so she produced the final muffin and placed it on the table.

"Are you hungry? Would you like something to eat?"

He looked at the muffin and then, finally, at her. "No thank you, but I'll have your paper."

He indicated the newspaper that was poking out from her backpack and she pulled it out and handed it over.

He pounced on it, stashing it under his novel. "Nothing decent to read around here."

"Nothing decent to read in there either," she said, nodding at the paper and he smiled suddenly, revealing a mouth full of discoloured teeth. He was obviously a smoker, although she noticed there were no ashtrays or smokers about. It was probably banned up here on the roof, and she couldn't help wondering why. Lung cancer was surely the least of their worries.

Feeling encouraged, Roxy said, "It'd really help me, Gordon, if you could tell me about that Congress, what happened, why everyone's being so secretive?"

He looked down at the table again. "Betty didn't tell you?"

"Not really, no."

"Then I certainly won't. But I will say this. My life fell apart that day, so did Betty's. It was the beginning of the end. A dreadful, dreadful day."

Again, his tone was flat and unemotional, as though he was merely discussing the weather, and she felt like giving him a good shake. Instead, she decided to shake things up.

"Was Berny to blame?" she said, thinking of the words "Beautiful Bett".

He nudged an eyebrow at the photo. "Berny had his own problems that day."

"Such as?"

"Wolfie didn't give you the juicy details for his fancy book, then? Didn't tell you all about it? What a surprise." His voice was now laced with sarcasm and there was an edge she didn't like but she was getting increasingly confused. Were they even discussing the same subject?

"Tell me *what*? I'm not sure what you mean. Gordon, what happened at that Congress?"

He glanced up at her again. "What happened to Berny?"

"Yes!"

He shrugged and said matter of factly, "He got played. Simple as that."

"Played? By whom?"

"Wolfgang, who else?"

Her head was starting to ache and she must have looked as confused as she felt because he added, "It was the oldest scam in the book. Wolfie made Berny look like a fool at that Congress, which is why I'm bloody surprised to hear he wanted the picture. If I was him, I'd burn it." His eyes clouded over. "Wolfie made fools of us all that day, but I was also a coward and that's worse. Much worse."

Then he turned back to his book and continued to read.

Roxy tried several more angles but Gordon Reilly was done and didn't acknowledge any of her questions. "Can you tell me any more?" she pleaded. "It would really help Sondra."

He continued to ignore her as though she wasn't even there and eventually she gave up, taking the photo and getting to her feet. She was just reaching into her backpack when he finally spoke again.

"How is Betty? My boy?" Gordon's hollowed eyes looked up at her imploringly.

She gave him a reassuring smile. "Betty seems good. I haven't met Brian, but she said to tell you they're both doing well. She said they're anxious to find you."

Gordon's eyes brimmed with tears suddenly which surprised her and she stepped towards him, wanting to comfort, but he shook his head firmly as if warning her off, and looked back at his book. She pulled Betty's business card out of her pack and placed it on the table in front of him.

"She asked you to get in touch." She tapped the card. "Call her on her mobile."

He didn't take the card, nor did he look at it, so she took this as her final exit cue and left him there, lost in his thoughts or his hard-boiled mystery or both, the swirl of sad and lonely men around him. Gordon Reilly might have cleaned up his act, but he was still as sad and lonely as the rest of them.

And Roxy was nowhere closer to clarity.

CHAPTER 20

All Roxy wanted was a long, warm bath, but what she needed was to have another little chat to Wolfgang, and soon. She wanted to know what Gordon was talking about. How exactly had Berny been "played" by his old billionaire mate? What was this scam, and could it have something to do with Berny's violent death?

She retraced her steps, back through Woolloomooloo and up the grinding stone steps to Potts Point, cursing her lack of fitness yet again. At the top her phone rang and she answered it, panting hard as she did so.

"Jesus, Parker, you're a hard woman to track down," Max said. "How are you?"

"I'm great."

"You don't sound great."

She gulped in more air. "Just puffing, I've been out power walking," she lied. "How's the advertorial going? Bored yet?"

"No, I'm actually really enjoying this one. In fact, I've got a spare minute and I wanted to talk to you about something—"

A sudden "beep beep" sound could be heard in the background and Roxy groaned. "Sorry, someone must be trying to get through. Just ignore them, what were you going to say?"

"It's just that I have some news." The "beep beep" sounded again.

"What news?" she asked.

"I'd better let you get that. Don't worry, it'll keep. I just wanted you to know I miss you and I'm looking forward to seeing you tomorrow."

That's right, she thought, *I'd better not forget to pick him up.*

"I'll text you the flight deets now, okay?"

"Great, yep, I'll be there." The "beep beep" sound persisted and she said, "Bugger it, I'd better go."

The impatient caller turned out to be Sondra, looking for another update. As Roxy continued walking back to her neighbouring suburb, she filled her in on all she had found, including the phlegmatic Gordon Reilly.

"What did this man mean about my father being played?" Sondra asked. "Do you know? Do you have any idea?"

"Not yet, no. He was a man of few words, but he did say your dad got the raw end of some deal."

"And he knows all the details of this ... *deal*, does he?"

"I suppose so, but he wasn't giving anything away. Everyone is ridiculously secretive about that Congress, which makes me think you are definitely on to something. I mean, why all the secrecy? As soon as people start putting up brick walls, I start wondering what's behind them."

By now Roxy had reached Elizabeth Bay and was leaning against her car, catching her breath. "I'm off to see Sir Wolfgang now, maybe he can help me dismantle a few of the bricks."

Not if Ginny Bergman had anything to do with it. Wolfgang's wife was clearly not happy to see Roxy again so soon and told her as much.

"Look, Roxanne, I do not like all these visits, you are not welcome to just drop in whenever you please! Who do you think you are? The Queen?!" She bat her thick black eyelashes at Roxy and folded her arms across her ample breasts, pushing them up and out of the skin-tight, black Lycra jacket she was wearing over leopard print leggings. "I told you before, he is very, very sick!"

Roxy apologised. "But I wouldn't be interrupting him, Ginny, if it wasn't extremely important. I won't take more than a few minutes. I promise." She tried batting her own eyelids innocently and when that didn't work she added somewhat cryptically, "I've got some questions that absolutely need answering. If Sir Wolfgang can't or won't answer them, I'll have to find someone who will."

That did the trick. Ginny's eyes narrowed and she sighed dramatically before leading Roxy through the house and, this time, out the back into the sprawling back yard. Roxy had interviewed Wolfgang out here several times before, but it still took her breath away each time she saw it. It was a truly stunning garden, much like an English country estate, transplanted to the Australian landscape. There were immaculately clipped hedges, one in the shape of a dove, another looked a little like a turtle. There were numerous pebble pathways winding through pretty clusters of lavender and camellias, violets and rose bushes, a spouting fountain against a rock wall at one end, a lacy pergola at the other. And right in the middle, surrounded in fresh green lawn sat a towering weeping willow under which several wrought iron chairs and a table had been placed.

It was late afternoon and the sun was beginning to lose its shine. Roxy spotted Wolfgang sitting just beyond the shade of the willow tree in a recliner, a blanket over his legs and what looked like a dark hat on his head.

Ginny took the pebbled pathway towards the tree and then held a hand up halfway along to indicate that Roxy was to remain put. Ginny continued on, bent over and had a word with her husband before waving a hand to usher Roxy on.

Roxy walked up slowly, giving him enough time to gather himself, then smiled as she approached. He was wearing another velour tracksuit and had a fisherman's cap over his scaly bald head. Beside him was a small, wicker table on which had been placed a newspaper, a jug of water and an empty glass. *Things must be grim*, Roxy thought. *He's off the scotch.*

"You're becoming my stalker," he said croakily, his watery eyes meeting hers. Today they were more lacklustre than lecherous and she preferred them that way.

He waved at one of the chairs under the tree and she pulled it closer and sat down. Ginny remained standing behind her husband, her arms still crossed, her eyebrows nudged together fiercely.

"I'm really sorry to disturb you again, Sir Wolfgang, but I need to ask you another question regarding Berny Tiles."

"I hope Sondra is paying you well for chasing your own pretty little tail."

She ignored this and said, "I spoke to Gordon Reilly today."

His eyes widened slightly. "Gordo, eh? So you tracked him down."

"Yes, he's here in Sydney, and he's now off the grog." She decided not to mention his living status; she had a feeling Wolfgang would relish the information and didn't want to give him the satisfaction.

"Good for him."

"I asked him about that 1975 Survey Congress. Gordon tells me it was a dreadful day. Can you tell me a bit more about that?"

He coughed violently and his wife reached down to pour him some water. "Is this really necessary?" she asked, handing him the glass.

Bergman took a large gulp before saying, "It's all right, Ginny." He glanced across at Roxy and his expression was now one of amusement. "'Course that night was dreadful for Gordo. It was the day the stupid bugger realised he was no match for his beautiful wife."

"I know all about Betty's affair with Berny." She didn't really, she was bluffing and the look of surprise that now entered his eyes wasn't what she expected.

"Betty and Berny, eh?"

She nodded, unconvincingly. "Anyway, that's not what I'm here to talk about."

"Then why are you here, Roxanne?" Ginny demanded, placing a hand on her husband's shoulder. "Just get on with it, will you. Let's have it done with!"

"Gordon told me something else much more portent than that." She looked at Wolfgang. "He said you ripped Berny off that day. Something about a scam?"

"Oh for goodness sake!" Ginny began and Wolfgang held a hand up to mollify her. She tsked several times and looked away.

"What else did Gordon tell you?"

"He told me that Berny got played that night. That he lost 'big time'. I just want to know what he meant. Then I'll leave you in peace."

Wolfman scoffed and a sliver of a smile found its way to his dry, scaly lips. "*Lost?* Berny didn't lose anything. The way I remember it, Berny was the winner that night, not me."

"Winner? So why did Gordon say you ripped him off?"

Ginny stepped forward now, long, glittering fingernails splayed across her hips, a look of outrage on her face. "Bernard Tiles did not get ripped off! It was all completely above—"

"Ginny, please, go back inside. I'll deal with this."

"I won't stand around and let this woman—"

"Ginny."

Wolfgang's wife leaned in close to Roxy's face, her own screwed up so tightly, she looked like she might snap. When she spoke, her voice was like a screech. "You tell that Sondra woman, her father got our best housekeeper; what more does he—"

"Virginia!" The boom had returned to Wolfgang's voice and she glanced at her husband and then back at Roxy, before tsking again and striding off down the pebbled pathway back towards the house, her voluptuous bum waggling behind her.

Roxy wondered what she was talking about. As far as she knew, Berny didn't have the income to hire a housekeeper. Meanwhile Wolfgang, who was watching his wife walk away, turned his shrewd eyes upon Roxy.

"You're taking the word of a deranged man who's living in a halfway shelter, still brooding over his ex-wife?"

"How do you know where—"

"I know everything," he said simply, his trademark arrogance in full throttle. "And I know for a fact that what Gordo is talking about has nothing to do with you, or Sondra for that matter. It's history, ancient bloody history, and if she'd actually spent some time with her father in the months before he died, she'd know that. All she's trying to do now is play catch-up out of some misguided sense of guilt or greed. I don't know and I don't give a damn. It's too late. You go back and tell her, it's ... too ... late."

He said those last three words very slowly, drumming the point home.

"Too late for what?" she asked, knowing she was treading on very thin ice now but he didn't reply, instead he began coughing violently again. She tried to help him to a glass of water but he brushed her off and reached a shaky hand towards his glass, taking several loud mouthfuls. His fisherman's hat toppled to one side as he drank.

Roxy said, "I'm sorry, Sir Wolfgang, I'm not trying to upset you. I'm just trying to find out what happened at that Congress. Something happened that night, you've all admitted it, but no one seems to want to talk about it."

"There's nothing to talk about."

"So why cut the picture from the book?"

"What?" He slammed the glass back onto the table, spilling water everywhere.

"That picture I showed you, of the 1975 Survey Congress, was in your book. It was in the original layout. The publisher says your wife had it removed. Can you tell me why?"

He stared hard at her as though not quite sure how to play it. He straightened his hat and then brushed the blanket down.

Eventually he said, "You're talking about a shitty old black and white photo. It was insignificant, it wasn't worth the space. It's certainly not worth your time now. It's irrelevant to anything."

"It's relevant to Sondra."

"Why? Does she think it has something to do with Berny's death?" When Roxy didn't say anything, his eyes widened again and he looked almost amused. "Good God, she thinks I had something to do with that?! She thinks I got up out of my sick bed and ran over her father—my old mate?"

"No, no, not at all—"

"But you clearly do."

"No, I—"

"Didn't you just tell me that Berny had an affair with Betty that night?" She nodded slowly. "Yet you're here, interrogating *me*?" He leaned forward in his chair as best he could. "It seems to me that if anyone had a beef with old Berny, perhaps it was Betty's husband."

"But he's—"

"What? Homeless? Doesn't mean he can't drive. I recall him getting about in a rattly old truck back in his day."

"Yes, but he doesn't have access to a—" she began and then stopped as the image of a white van flashed before her eyes.

Oh my God, he was right. The police suspected a white van had hit Berny, and she knew there was a white van at the Matt Talbot Hostel where Gordon Reilly worked. She now recalled Gordon's words, "I do a bit of driving, pickups and deliveries". She could feel the blush rising in her face and Wolfgang could clearly see it because he was no longer smiling.

In a very slow, measured tone, he said, "You go back and tell Sondra she is barking up the wrong bloody tree." He cleared his throat. "I've had enough of this bullshit and I will be speaking to the publisher. How dare you come into my home and accuse me of murder."

Roxy recoiled. "I didn't mean to—"

"All you're doing, young lady, is dredging up old wounds. You think reminding Gordo of that night made him feel any better?" She shrank back. "You think any of this is helping anyone?" He paused, coughed again then had a change of tack: "Is my book done? I was under the impression my book was finished."

"It is, yes."

"And are there any more questions you need to ask me for my book?"

She shook her head and he stared at her with hard, cold eyes. "Then get the hell off my property before I have you thrown off."

CHAPTER 21

It was a very shaky Roxy Parker who returned to her car that evening and made her way home. She had not meant to upset Sir Wolfgang, had already warned herself not to get in his bad books, and now she was so far in, she was practically at the Index. Roxy didn't really believe he could hurt her, but still, it was a terrible way to end a business relationship and she realised that she had better alert her agent. No doubt there would be complaints coming in from the publisher, if not the man himself. This would really make the marketing department happy.

Back at home, Roxy ripped her gear off and stood under the shower for many minutes, trying to let the day's grime wash off her. But it was going to take more than some soap and a scrubbing brush.

She eventually got out, dried herself off and changed into comfy trousers, sweater and bed socks, then made her way to her kitchen to retrieve a fresh bottle of merlot and a glass. Only after several good long sips, did she find the energy to call Oliver.

"I've already heard," he said, sounding blasé. "Don't worry about it. It's not the first time you've pissed off a client."

She conceded the point. "Still, I went in accusing the man of God knows what, on the word of an alcoholic. What was I thinking?"

"Obviously not much. Look, let it go, Rox. I managed to calm Ginny down."

"Oh my God, Ginny's already called you?! What about the publisher?"

"Nah, haven't heard from them but she tells me you've set her husband's recovery back a month."

"Bloody hell."

"Listen, don't sweat it. We're talking about Wolfgang Bergman here; you think he made his billions by playing nice? You just gave him some of his own medicine as far as I can tell. Besides, I hardly think a little tiff with you will leave a blip on his radar. They're just bluffing, trying to put you back in your box."

"Well it worked. I'm about to ring Sondra and tell her enough is enough. I'm fishing around like a blind woman and I have no idea what it is I'm trying to catch. Or even if I've got any bait on my hook."

"Nice metaphor there, Rox. That's why you're my favourite writer."

"Might be an unemployed writer if word gets out about me harassing the client."

"Nah, don't worry about it. Listen, pour yourself a steady drink and chill out."

"I'm already onto it. It's got me thinking though."

"Uh-oh."

"Maybe he's right about Gordon. I mean, the guy is clearly still carrying a torch for his estranged wife. I wonder why they never divorced? And he does have access to a white van. Maybe I am barking up the wrong tree? Maybe Gordon ran over Berny."

"What? Revenge, thirty-something years later?!"

"Don't they say revenge is a dish best served cold?"

"Cold? It's turned positively mouldy. Surely, if he was holding a grudge against Berny, he would have acted decades ago? That's a long-held grudge, Rox. And do people really kill because their wife had a fling?"

He was right, of course, and she sighed with exasperation. "It's so bloody frustrating! I think there's much more to this than a simple fling. Something obviously happened that night. Something so bad that no one wants to talk about it. I just wish it made a little more sense."

"Hey, don't sweat it. This is Sondra's problem, not yours. Let it go."

"I'll try," she said, knowing only too well she would not succeed.

Roxy hung up then stared at the phone for some time before placing two more phone calls, both unsuccessful. Sondra was not answering her mobile, nor was Max. He was probably working late again, she decided, and penned him a quick text message, telling him that she missed him and would pick him up tomorrow. She wasn't one for platitudes, but she had a feeling she needed to make more effort. She also wondered what it was he seemed so eager to tell her. She hoped it wasn't bad news, but ever since he had called, an unsettling lump had formed in the pit of her stomach.

Roxy then turned to her computer and constructed a long e-mail to Sondra, giving her the full rundown of the day's events, being sure to include everything that Gordon and Wolfgang had said. After she sent it, she reread Gordon's words again, carefully:

My life fell apart that day, so did Betty's. It was the beginning of the end. A dreadful, dreadful day.

Berny had his own problems. He got played. The oldest scam in the book. Wolfie made him look like a fool at that Congress, which is why I'm surprised to hear he wanted the photo. If I was him, I'd burn it.

She thought about that. Whatever happened, Berny obviously had a very different perspective of that Congress than Gordon. Not only had he *not* burnt the photo, he had kept it all these years and then called for it with his dying breath.

But why? Was this really all to do with a simple affair? Or was there something darker and more sinister at play?

Feeling increasingly frustrated, Roxy checked the time— 8:55 p.m.—then grappled through her handbag for Betty Reilly's mobile phone number. She placed the call and after many rings was about to give up when a male voice answered. It sounded strangely familiar.

"Oh, hello," Roxy said, surprised. "I hope I've got the right number. I'm looking for Betty Reilly."

"Betty Jones now," the man snapped. "It's really not a good time."

"Oh, sorry, I thought she'd be at home. I don't mean to interrupt—"

"We are at home. What's this about?"

Roxy hesitated. "Um, my name's Roxy Parker. Who am I speaking to, please?"

There was hesitation on the other end, too, and it felt like a full minute before the man spoke. "I'm Betty's son, Brian."

"Oh, Brian, hello. I spoke to your mother yesterday. I've been trying to find your dad." There was silence again and she realised this might have come as a shock to him, so she quickly added, "Listen, I'd really like to speak to your mum, if that's all right."

She didn't know whether he lived with his mother or was just visiting, but considering he was now forty, she had to assume the latter. Still, this guy sounded very protective and she was trying hard to place his voice when Betty came on the line.

"Oh hello, Roxy, I didn't expect to hear from you so soon." She sounded upbeat.

"I didn't expect to find your husband so soon either, but—"

"My goodness, you found him?! That's fantastic! Oh, hang on a minute." Her voice lowered considerably. "I'll just shut the door." There was a pause while Roxy heard footsteps and a creaking sound. "So how is Gordon? *Where* is he?"

"I found him at the Matt Talbot Hostel in Woolloomooloo, it's down—"

"Yes, I know where Matt Talbot's is." There was another pause and when she spoke again, she was no longer upbeat. "Oh dear, so it's bad as we thought."

"No, Betty. Gordon tells me he just works there, he has a bedsit somewhere on Challis Avenue. That's in Potts Point."

"A bedsit? Okay, well, that's better I guess."

"I gave him your card. I asked him to call. I'm not sure if he will."

"No, well, at least you tried. Oh, this is such overwhelming news, Roxy! And such a surprise. We've both looked down at Matt Talbot's before and had no luck, you see."

"Well, he's not using his old name. They call him the Surly Surveyor."

She half laughed. "The Surly Surveyor, that fits the bill. Oh, I am so glad he's okay. He is okay, isn't he?" Uncertainty now.

"Yes, he seems fine, Betty. Says he's given up drinking."

"Really? Good ... good."

"He asked about both of you and said to tell you he's well. Not to worry."

There was another strangled pause. "How can I not?" she said eventually, her voice trembling with emotion.

"Betty, he's okay. I can assure you of that." She took a deep breath. "Listen, it's late so I won't take much time, I just wanted to ask you again about that night, the night of thre Survey Congress."

"Oh dear, not now, please." Her voice had turned hushed again. "It's not the time ..."

"Then can I come back and see you? Maybe at work tomorrow?"

"Not at work, no ... um ... I can meet you for lunch, say around 12:30? Just out on the street, in front of my office? I really must go."

"Of course. Thanks, Betty, I'll see you tomorrow."

Roxy hung up and put the phone aside. She felt a little better. If there was one good thing that had come from all of this, it was the chance she had just given one family to reunite.

She just hoped it wasn't too late.

CHAPTER 22

The man glanced at his watch, hoping he wouldn't be late. It was early, even for him, and he wouldn't normally be up and out at this hour, but the call had sounded important. They needed him in at work, and he was happy to oblige.

He needed the extra money now, was going to turn his life around. Was going to reach out and make a difference at last.

But he couldn't think about that now, he had promised to be in by daybreak and the sun was already starting to peek out from behind the cluttered apartment blocks that shadowed this end of the Cross. He hurried up, reaching the stone steps and taking a few deep breaths before heading down. He wasn't fit like the old days, those endless hours in the bush, lugging Theodolites and chains, not to mention hammer, axe, fly tent, food, lamp, the works. They were the good days. The strong days. The days of hope.

He had withered away now in every sense of the word, he knew that, but things were going to change. He would see to it. It was his time.

A few steps down, he heard a voice call out. He stopped and looked back, startled at first and then, after several long seconds, surprised.

It couldn't be, could it?

He wasn't expecting this. Not at all. But he felt joy for the first time in a long time, and relief. He took one step up, anxious, not daring to believe, and held out his hand, hoping against hope.

But the hope was short-lived.

When he saw the flicker of raw hatred in those familiar eyes and felt the fierce, determined push, he knew it was too late. His legs fell out from under him but he understood completely, and he forgave everything, every lie and brutal deceit, as he tumbled with resignation towards his inevitable demise.

CHAPTER 23

The early morning call nearly sent Roxy falling out of the bed as she grappled for the phone, half asleep in the dark. She glanced at her clock radio. It was 6:45 a.m. and she half expected it to be Max, so when a woman's voice came on the other end, she took a few seconds to register who it was.

"Sorry, I know it's an obscene time to call, but I've been waiting a while."

"Gilda?"

"'Fraid so. We need to talk. Now. Can you come meet me?"

Roxy rubbed the sleep from her eyes and stared at the clock again. "What are you doing up at this disgusting hour?"

"I've told you before, Roxy, crime has a really bad case of insomnia."

"Crime? What crime?"

"Homicide, hence the reason I'm calling. We found a body, not far from you."

"And?"

"And it's got your name written all over it."

Roxy sat up on one elbow. "Huh?"

"Just pull some gear on and meet me at Peepers." She hung up and Roxy stared at the receiver bewildered. Then she shook herself out and did as instructed.

Fifteen minutes later, after throwing on jeans, her warmest jumper and fleece-lined jacket, Roxy swung a scarf around her neck and a beret on her head, and stepped out onto the cold, wet pavement beside her building. It was now starting to get light but there were very few people about, just a few joggers looking miserable and several equally miserable suits heading into work. Nothing else was open, so she was surprised to find Gilda seated at a table inside Peepers, a giant plate of greasy bacon and eggs in front of her. Roxy didn't even realise the café served breakfast this early.

"See the things you discover when you get up before noon," Gilda told her. "Want some?"

Roxy shook her head and ordered a latté from the bleary eyed waiter hovering nearby. He looked as bad as she felt and she slunk into the seat beside Gilda, one eyebrow raised.

"This is a new one for you."

"Nah, I often stop by if I'm in this part of the world."

"I mean, dragging me out of bed at this hour. Normally it's about the time you're getting me home."

Gilda laughed. "Yeah, well, suck it up, lady. I've been up since 5:30 a.m. trying to identify a body."

"And you called me because ...?"

"Because of this," Gilda said, swooping down to pick up a plastic bag beside her handbag. She flung the bag across to Roxy who caught it with one hand, surprised her reflexes were so good so early. It looked like a newspaper, indeed it was a newspaper, yesterday's, judging by the date.

"So?"

"So, if you turn it over, you'll see your name scribbled in bright red ink on one side. Care to tell me how your newspaper ends up in the hands of a dead homeless guy?"

Roxy's heart sank. "Oh my God. Gordon Reilly! It's not Gordo, is it?"

"Dunno, but that's a start. He had no ID on him."

She sighed heavily. "I think this is the paper I gave Gordon Reilly yesterday, when I went to see him at the Matt Talbot Hostel. You remember, he's one of the guys from the old photo I showed you."

"Oh right. You tracked him down pretty quickly."

"In the nick of time, by the sound of it."

Gilda stopped eating and reached back into her bag for a notepad and pen. She jotted down a few things then returned to her meal, waving her fork around as an indication for Roxy to continue. And so she did, filling her friend in on all that had happened since last they met. She told her about the original photograph and how it had the words *'Beautiful Bett'* scribbled on the back, and how she had tracked down first Betty and then her ex.

"Although Gordon said they weren't actually divorced, so I guess you'd better get in touch with Betty pretty fast. She says she hadn't seen him in years, but she seemed to care for the guy, so she'll probably be cut up. They have a son, Brian, so he'll be devastated, too."

She paused while the coffee appeared in front of her and, judging from the lack of steam, took a long, hearty sip. It was exactly as good coffee should be: strong, warm, steadying.

"So what happened to Gordon? How did he ...?"

"Still working it all out and the coroner will have more this afternoon. Some teenage revellers found his body early this morning, at the bottom of the McElhone steps, at Woolloomooloo."

"Bloody hell, I just walked up and down those stairs yesterday." She shivered and tightened her scarf around her neck.

Gilda finished chewing and said, "Look, I'm not the lead on this, it's a guy called Brent Wiles, a good bloke. He'll be calling on you to question you later this morning, and because I know you, I'm not allowed to be present, but I wanted to give you the heads-up and find out what the hell is going on. So, this Gordon Reilly fellow had digs at Matt Talbot's, you reckon?"

"Not digs. Said he boarded at a bedsit on Challis Avenue, but worked at the hostel, driving, cooking, that kind of stuff. They called him The Surly Surveyor."

"The Dead Surveyor now," Gilda said, stating the obvious.

"Did anyone see anything? Any witnesses?"

"Not exactly. The revellers only saw the end of it—the deceased crashing to the bottom of the steps—and rendered assistance, or tried to. They dialled Triple 0 but he was dead by the time the paramedics got there. Reckon they didn't see anyone around, but it would have been hard to tell at that hour. Still pretty dark."

"And do we know if he fell or ...?"

"Was pushed?" Gilda shrugged. "We suspect he was pushed, but who knows? He could have just been drinking and stumbled, wouldn't be the first time, but as I say, we'll know more this arvo. I'm not even supposed to be talking to you. They could have my badge for this. But, well, I had to see the paper for myself and once I did, I offered to drop this off at Forensics, mostly so I could have a quick word with you."

Roxy was shaking her head. "You know, Gordon used to be an alcoholic but told me he'd been sober for over a year."

"Wouldn't be the first alco to lie about it. Or fall off the wagon."

"Hmm, maybe, but I don't think so. I didn't take him for an alcoholic. He was pretty low, but he was very articulate and I didn't smell anything on his breath. Besides, I doubt the hostel would let him drive their van if he was a risk." She took a gulp of her coffee. "In fact, I was starting to wonder whether he was involved in Berny Tiles's death but ... well, now ..."

"Oh?"

Roxy told Gilda about her suspicion that Betty and Berny had had an affair all those years ago and that Gordon had access to a white van.

Gilda looked at her sideways. "So you thought Gordon Reilly had borrowed the van from the hostel and run over Berny? Why, to avenge a thirty-seven-year-old affair?"

She scrunched up her face. "Sounds silly now you put it like that."

"Sounds absurd, but I've heard worse. I'll pass your thoughts on to Leary. They may as well check out that van at Matt Talbot's. Of course, now Gordon Reilly has shown up deceased, it kinda deflates that theory."

"It also puts Wolfgang Bergman in the frame."

"How do you figure that?"

Roxy repeated the conversation she had had with Gordon the day before and her subsequent conversation with Bergman. "When I told Wolfman that Gordon was alive and was pointing the finger at him for some supposed scam back in 1975, he tried to play it cool but then he started getting tetchy, like I was poking at some wound that he wanted me to stay well away from. His wife went ballistic, he had to send her back inside."

Gilda considered this. "What was it about, do you think?"

Roxy shook her head. "I have no idea, that's what makes it all so frustrating. But it seems too much of a coincidence to me. Gordon Reilly's been missing for a decade. I find him yesterday, confront his old acquaintance about something he said and next thing you know, he's dead."

"Did you tell anybody else about Gordon? About where he was living or working?"

"Well, yes, I told Sondra, she had asked me to track him down, and I told Betty, his estranged wife."

"Really?" Gilda looked interested but Roxy was shaking her head.

"No way, Gilda. Betty was *relieved* to hear he was alive and well, there's no way she did this."

Gilda shrugged. "She is one of the few people left alive from that photo of yours."

Roxy sat forward. "Jesus, you don't suppose someone is knocking off everyone from that Congress? Maybe you'd better get some protection for Betty."

"Protection? I was thinking she might be the culprit."

Roxy laughed. "She's sixty-five, Gilda."

"So, you think little old ladies can't push little old men down flights of stairs? Pretty easy if they've got their back turned to you."

"So, what, you think Betty tracks him down, arranges the rendezvous and gives him a shove? Why would she want to kill her estranged hubby?"

Gilda shrugged. "'Cause he left her all alone to raise their son?" She clicked her fingers. "No, maybe she believes Gordon killed her old lover, Berny, and she wants revenge!"

Roxy stared at Gilda and she laughed. "I don't really buy it either, Roxy, I'm just letting my imagination run wild."

"No, no, this is good. Let's say you're right and Gordon did kill Berny as payback for wrecking his marriage. It's a crazy theory but let's run with it. So then Betty hears about Berny's murder and is distraught, maybe she's been seeing him all along, or she just can't ever get past their great love affair. So, I show up and pretty much hand Gordon to her on a platter. She then arranges to meet Gordon and kills him as payback for killing her one great love."

"Forget biographies, you should write romance," Gilda said, laughing again.

"Yeah, yeah, but where does all this leave Bob Brownlow? Why was he killed? And how does an elderly man, let alone a woman, manage to beat another man to death on a public street?"

Gilda wiped her mouth with her serviette and sighed. "They don't. That's where it falls apart. That and the lack of motive. The other person, of course, who's still alive from that Survey Congress is Wolfgang Bergman."

"That's why I reckon he did it! He's a scammer, Gordon told me that. He's obviously hiding something."

"Maybe, but if you're wrong about him, he could be next. Perhaps he's the one who needs police protection."

"Oh, I think he can look after himself. He's got Ginny the Doberman by his side."

Gilda finished off the last of her bacon, then pushed the plate away and signalled for the bill. "All this theorising is good fun, Roxy, but I've got to get back to the real world, get this bag to Forensics—honestly, my policing skills have gone AWOL since I met you."

"So what are you going to do about Betty? Lock her up or get her some protection?"

She shrugged. "Sorry, Roxy, but I'm not sure I can make a case for either."

"But you have to protect her! Can't you see, four out of the six people in that photo are now dead, three probably murdered. Surely Betty could be in danger."

Gilda sighed. "E-mail me the shot, and I'll look into it. That's all I can promise. Oh, and it'd be good to get Betty's contact details. I'll pass them on to Wiles. He'll probably want me to go with him to break the bad news."

"She works at a consulting firm called Henry Mapping something or other, in Chatswood. Just be wary of the beefy, blond receptionist. I don't know what his problem is, but he makes Ginny the Doberman look like a pussy cat."

"Duly noted," Gilda said, scribbling the name down in her pad. She then stared at her friend, one eyebrow raised sky high. "This is the murkiest brew you've ever landed me in, and that's saying something."

"Me?"

"Yes you! It seems wherever there's a corpse, you're not far behind."

"God, you sound like my mother."

Gilda paid the bill then walked Roxy back to her building. "Thanks for meeting me. And for identifying the deceased, at least giving us an idea who it might be. I'll let Wiles know and I guess he'll ask Betty to do the official honours."

They said their goodbyes and Roxy returned to her apartment, her heart low, her head buzzing with questions.

Yesterday Gordon Reilly had been alive and well. Okay, he was living in a bedsit and working at a homeless men's shelter, but he was *alive*. Then she had gone and spoken to him, even half suspected him of murder, and now he was dead.

What the hell had she done? And who, she wondered, *would be next?*

CHAPTER 24

It didn't take long for Detective Inspector Brent Wiles to come knocking at Roxy's door. He was a sharply dressed thirty-something with a clipped goatee and piercing blue eyes, and had a female detective with him, a relatively plain woman called Doreen Oliver who wore a drab grey suit and her hair in a tight ponytail. As they began questioning Roxy, it was clear they had already spoken with Gilda because they cut straight to the chase.

"We just need to confirm, in your own words, please, how your *Sydney Morning Herald* happened to be in the hands of the deceased, please," Wiles said.

Roxy nodded and repeated the story she had told Gilda.

"So a Ms Sondra Lane asked you to locate the deceased?"

"Yes, she was trying to track down the people in an old photo of her father's."

Roxy showed them a copy of the picture on her laptop and they studied it. "I can e-mail it to you," she said but Doreen was already holding out a thumb drive.

"Now, if you don't mind."

Roxy took it from her and downloaded a copy of the image onto the thumb drive, then handed it back.

"And where were you this morning, around 5:20 a.m.?" Wiles was asking.

Roxy felt a wave of anxiety as she replied, "In bed asleep and alone, I'm afraid."

This didn't seem to bother him and he simply nodded and then double checked Betty Reilly's office address before departing, Roxy guessed, to break the terrible news.

She didn't really believe that Betty was the culprit and she wondered how the poor woman would take it. Sure, she had been estranged from her husband for years, but did that make the news easier to bear, or much, much worse?

After fixing herself another coffee, Roxy tried Sondra's number again but it went straight to voice mail and she groaned aloud. Sondra had warned her she was busy, something about three weddings and a flower expo, but Roxy was anxious to talk to her. The week was almost up and she had done exactly as she had been asked, she had located the original photograph, and everyone in it.

Of course, nothing had turned out as she'd expected, and the picture was even cloudier than before. It was now indisputable that Sondra was onto something big. Something had happened at that Survey Congress and no one wanted to talk about it, yet their silence spoke volumes—as did all these suspicious deaths—and Roxy's curiosity was on red alert.

There was no turning back now. She was no longer searching for answers for a grieving daughter; she was hunting for a killer. She tapped her screen again to stare at the seemingly boring old photo, and then sighed.

What really happened in 1975? Why had Browny, Berny and Gordon met such sad and violent ends? And why now, after all this time?

Roxy knew *that* was the crucial question. Why was it happening thirty-seven years down the track? She glanced at her mantelpiece clock and stood up. It was time to get some straight answers from one of only two people still left alive from that fateful day.

As Roxy made her way back to Chatswood to see Betty Reilly, she hoped that Wiles had had the chance to break the awful news about Gordon, and she wondered if she would even find her at work. When she did spot Betty, standing in the outdoor car park below her office block, it was clear the deed was done. The older woman looked puffy eyed and a little dazed as she stood beside a small, silver hatchback, keys in her hand, not moving, and Roxy felt dreadful for even considering that Betty could have done this awful thing.

"Betty?" Roxy called out.

Betty looked up at her and for one moment didn't seem to know who she was, then it must have dawned on her and she tried for a smile but couldn't quite pull it off.

"Mr Henry told me to take the day off ... I just can't seem to find the energy to leave. I'm not sure where I would go."

"How about a cup of tea?"

She glanced around furtively. "I don't know ... Brian said I should go straight home ..."

"Come on," Roxy said. "It'll do you wonders."

She took her by the arm, leading her back through the car park and towards a small street-side café she'd noticed earlier. She helped Betty into a seat, then ordered two pots of English Breakfast tea and sat down to join her.

"They said he had your newspaper with him," Betty said and Roxy nodded.

"He asked me for it when I saw him. Wanted something decent to read."

"He always was a voracious reader." Her eyes brimmed with tears.

"Betty, I'm so sorry. I feel so responsible."

Betty stared at her aghast. "But why, my dear?"

"Well, it's just that he was perfectly fine until I showed up. I just wonder if I'd left him alone, if—"

"He fell down a flight of stairs, Roxy, it had nothing to do with you. Nothing! As Brian says, he could have fallen at any time. He was getting old ... I'm just glad that you got to see him before he died. That he got to hear that we were well and thinking of him. Besides, the police told me he had no identification on him. They may never have worked out who it was, or at least not for some time, if it wasn't for your newspaper." She shook her head firmly. "Oh no, no, my dear you mustn't blame yourself. I don't know what happened last night or why, but Gordon was lost many years ago. He gave up on life long before now, and if anyone's to blame for that, it's me." The tears spilled over now and she brought a crumpled hankie to her nose and gave it a long blow.

"Betty," Roxy began and she shook her head.

"Don't try to tell me it's not my fault. It's *all* my fault. He was happy until we ... until I ... It was one night! One night. But it destroyed him. And it destroyed me, and it destroyed my son."

Roxy thought about this. "It didn't need to, you know? I'm sorry, I don't mean to sound harsh, but affairs happen every day, most people pull themselves together and dust themselves off, they get on—"

"Affair?" Betty said, staring at her as though she were speaking in tongues.

"Yes, you and Berny ...?"

Betty held her palms out. "Me and Berny? There was no 'me and Berny'."

The tea arrived and Roxy took it as an opportunity to collect her thoughts. She didn't think she could be any more confused, but clearly she was wrong.

"I ... I thought you had an affair with Berny at the Congress."

Betty was just starting to pour her tea when she clunked the pot back down and looked at Roxy, stunned. "Berny Tiles? And me? No, dear, not at all."

"So who ...?"

Betty looked away but Roxy could see she had started her frantic blinking again and she decided she was not going to let that stop her this time. She took one of Betty's hands and gave it a reassuring squeeze.

"Please, Betty. It's time to tell the truth. If you weren't with Berny that night, then who were you with?"

After a long, agonising pause, Betty whispered the word, "Wolfgang." Then began to sob quietly into her hankie, her head buckled over.

Roxy was stunned. She'd read that one completely wrong. She reached across and tried to console the weeping woman. "I'm sorry, Betty, I seem to have everything completely muddled up. I thought you and Berny had had an affair."

Betty pulled off her glasses and wiped her eyes. "No, dear, Berny wasn't my type at all. A lovely chap, but far too dull for me, I'm afraid." She sighed, placing her glasses back on. "Back then, I preferred them wild, like ..."

She trailed off and Roxy said, "Like Wolfgang."

She nodded. "I was such a fool."

So was I, thought Roxy. Wolfgang was the sleaziest man she'd ever met, Berny one of the most boring. It seemed so obvious now. "So how long did you and Wolfgang ...?"

"Oh, just the once." Betty glanced up at her and there was pain in every crevice of her face. She no longer looked youthful. She looked old and a little haggard, her bright green glasses doing little to cheer up her now glum face. "It wasn't an affair, Roxy. It was ... a mistake. A very stupid, brutal mistake, and Gordon never got over it." She picked her cup back up with shaking hands and took a sip, her eyelids continuing to blink away. "Gordon just couldn't get past it. And I don't blame him, I don't. It killed Indonesia for us, we moved to Sydney soon after, Mr Henry gave us the jobs ... well, you know the rest."

Roxy gave her hand another squeeze. "Did you ever see Wolfgang again?"

"God no, never!" She looked horrified by the thought.

"And Berny?"

The blinking stopped. "From time to time. I was better friends with his wife, Deandra, to be honest, but even then we were never best chums. You know how it is when expatriates are thrown together in foreign lands? Once we all returned home, we drifted apart. Berny and Dee kept in touch occasionally, Christmas cards every other year, that kind of thing, but I hadn't seen either of them until Dee's funeral a few years ago. Only had a few words with Berny. He was still so fond of Wolfgang, you see, so *admiring* of him ... I ... well, I couldn't relate." She sipped her tea quietly as though lost now in a long, distant past.

Roxy tried to get her thoughts together. She realised she had made a terrible assumption. She had thrown out the idea of the affair and Betty had agreed, Gordon had agreed, even Wolfgang had not disputed this, and so she had connected the wrong dots. There had been an affair but it wasn't between Betty and Berny.

And yet Wolfgang had let her believe that.

"Then why did Berny write your name on the back of that photo?" she asked. "Why was that photo so special to him?"

"I don't understand."

Roxy explained about the original picture, and finding those words scrawled in faded pencil on the back.

The blinking had subsided and Betty shrugged. "It's all very flattering but ... Oh hang on, did he write *Beautiful Betty* or bet?"

"Beautiful Bett."

She waved her palms in the air. "Then he wasn't referring to me, my dear."

"Really? Who was he referring to?"

"The bet, of course."

"Bet?"

"Yes, I'd say he was talking about the beautiful bet he made that night with Wolfgang, except, of course, it didn't turn out so beautiful in the end."

"But he wrote the word 'bett' with a double T. Unless ..."

Roxy thought about the faded scrawl on the back of the photograph and realised she had made another stupid assumption. The second T could easily be an exclamation mark as Oliver had suggested. She'd been so intent on her theory she'd ignored the bleeding obvious. He had written *Beautiful Bet!*

Roxy chided herself silently. She had been so successful over the past few years, solving several brutal murders that had seemed unsolvable, that she had let ego get in the way of evidence this time. She had not listened properly and she had jumped to foolish conclusions.

She sighed heavily, pushed her teacup away and said, "Okay, I'm now well and truly confused. You're going to have to start at the beginning and tell me exactly what happened that night of the Congress."

And so Betty did. Between sips of tea and the occasional wistful tear, Betty took Roxy back to 1975 when the whole sorry saga began.

It was Jakarta, August 24, and the annual Indonesia Survey Congress was in full swing. Cocktails had been drunk in copious quantities, dinner had been served and largely ignored, and the weary wives had made their way back to their hotels, some of them to their sleeping children.

"Although I wasn't smart enough for that," Betty told Roxy, her voice loaded with regret. "I hung around at the bar waiting for the poker game to finish."

"Poker game?"

"Yes, several of the men—the ones in your photo actually—all sat down to a game of poker in the hotel bar. All except for Gordon, of course, he'd already drunk far too much and was passed out in a corner somewhere. I wasn't surprised. That was standard procedure for my husband in those days. I found it so dull, and I guess he was. More interested in his bottle than me." There was no bitterness in her tone as she spoke, just a resigned sadness. "Anyway, the poker game dragged on and Wolfgang was losing, apparently. I don't know the details as I had left the room by then, I was out by the swimming pool waiting ..." She blinked a few times. "I heard about it the next day, I heard that Wolfgang was losing badly and had bet an old mine of his which he then lost to Berny Tiles."

"Really?" Roxy said.

"Yes, apparently Wolfgang had run out of cash and had said something like, you can have $5,000 cash next week or you can have the deeds to the mine now. So, completely out of character for Berny, he took the mine. But the joke was on him, because it was a dud. The mine hadn't produced anything of value for two or three years, I believe. The other men at the table knew that, but obviously Berny didn't. Or if he did he thought it would come good one day. Berny, bless him, wasn't very business savvy. He made the wrong choice. I don't think Dee ever forgave him, and as far as I can tell they never mentioned it again, at least not to me. We were all pretty broke in those days, especially when we returned to Australia and the work dried up. Five grand would have been very useful. Oh well ..." She took a gulp of her tea. "I can't believe Wolfgang didn't tell you about all this for the book you've just written. I thought it'd make a very interesting chapter."

Roxy wasn't surprised. Wolfgang's whole spiel had been about what a winner he was, about all the successful gambles he'd taken in his life. Why tell her about a poker game that he lost? Even if the mine was a dud.

"Of course I'm not at all sure how legitimate it all was. Whether he ever signed a proper deed. The whole thing kind of got forgotten after that, so ..."

"What was this mine called, can you remember?"

Betty sat back and considered this. "Oh, it's all very rusty now ... um, Bellu or Boyo or something—"

"Byou?"

"Oh yes, that was it. Buy you. The men all teased Berny the next day, said, he bought you, that's for sure."

Roxy's skin prickled suddenly. "Was it a gold mine?"

She shook her head. "Don't think so. I think it was copper, something like that. I remember it wasn't very glamorous and I just wondered why he accepted the bet. Anyway ..."

Roxy recognised the name Byou, but she had a feeling it was related to gold, not copper, and couldn't think where she'd heard of it. Perhaps Wolfgang had mentioned it in the book. If he had, he certainly hadn't said anything about losing it in a poker game. She'd remember that. Roxy made a mental note to look up the transcripts again. All she recalled was Wolfgang waxing lyrical about what a brilliant businessman he had been. Yet that wasn't exactly good business—betting away your copper mine, even one as defunct as Byou.

CHAPTER 25

"The Byou mine's not defunct," Caroline stated a few hours later and Roxy was so surprised she nearly drove into a median strip, swerving at the last minute, her heart racing a million miles per second as she straightened the vehicle and refocused on the road.

Earlier, she had returned Betty safely back to her car, the older woman still looking a little stunned, and had then done a mad dash home to shower and change before collecting Caroline at Darlinghurst. They were *en route* to Sydney's domestic airport to collect Max from his Melbourne flight, and she had been filling Caroline in on her latest "adventure". It was Caroline's word, not Roxy's, and it was typical of Max's sister. She made everything out to be a game, a lark, a barrel of laughs, but Roxy wasn't laughing. Not today. The memory of Gordon Reilly was still so fresh in her mind, and she still felt somehow complicit in his death, especially when she considered the silly assumptions she had made.

She shook the thought away and stared at the road ahead. After a few settling minutes, she asked, "What do you mean it's not defunct? Betty says it was a depleted copper mine, and that Berny got ripped off."

"Well, I don't know anything about that, but there's been a lot of buzz lately about one of Wolfgang Bergman's *gold* mines up in Irian Jaya that's just come good and I'm sure it's called Byou. It's been all over the news for the past three weeks. Haven't you noticed anything?"

"Yes, I remember reading something about a gold mine, but Betty says the Byou is a copper mine. Besides, crime's more my shtick, you know that. I don't really retain financial info."

"Hence your poverty level," Caroline replied, eyeing her old car pointedly.

"Oi, it beats the bus which is what you'd be taking if it wasn't for my beautiful V-dub." Roxy caressed the steering well as though soothing the vehicle's feelings. "So what's the story with this gold mine, then?"

"Oh, the story is fabulous!" Caroline curled her long legs up underneath her and turned to face Roxy. "They found gold up near Bergman's old mine a few months ago, he reported it to the stock exchange about a month back. Stocks in Wolfgang's Indonesian operations have gone through the roof. I've even put some money on it for my stock market course. So the mighty Sir Wolfgang didn't mention anything to you, not even for the book?"

Roxy shook her head. "We did finish up the interviews several months ago, so maybe it all happened after that."

"Still, you'd think he'd want to add an extra chapter on that. He's set to make a fortune!"

"Yes, except if Betty's story is true, that mine's not strictly Wolfgang's mine, he lost it in a bet with Berny, back in 1975."

The women caught each other's eyes and gasped in unison.

"My God," said Roxy. "No wonder Wolfgang didn't mention it, and no wonder Berny wanted that picture back. That was the night he won that mine."

"And no wonder he got run over," added Caroline. "A gold mine is *definitely* worth killing for."

An hour later, the two women were seated with Max at his favourite Indian restaurant at Taylor Square and Roxy was still having difficulty focussing, this time on her returned boyfriend, now that she had just stumbled on a genuine motive for murder. It was a tricky balancing act, and she knew from Max's clenched jaw and occasional sighs that she was not pulling it off. Unfortunately, Caroline was not reading the signals, nor was she making it any easier, and kept steering the conversation back to Wolfgang and his mine. *Her* interest, however, was mostly self-motivated.

"So let me get this straight," Caroline said, shoving a thin slice of lime into her bottle of Corona. "If Wolfman doesn't strictly own that mine," she paused to lick her fingers, "if he did sign it over to Berny Tiles all those years ago, then me investing in Wolfgang's mining company isn't exactly going to reap rewards. It's not his mine."

"Boo-hoo for you," Max said, pouring red wine into a glass for Roxy.

She thanked him and said, "But do we know if Wolfman really *did* sign it over to Berny? I mean, according to Betty he signed over a copper mine, not a gold mine."

"Could be the same thing," Max said and they both stared at him. "What!? Didn't you guys do Geology in high school? They often find gold deposits in copper mines. The two go together."

Roxy gave him a light tap on the shoulder. "That makes a little more sense then." She quickly added, "So how did your trip go?"

His jaw loosened a little. "Really good, actually. In fact, I wanted to talk to you about something—"

"And how *dodgy* is that?" Caroline interrupted. "I mean, if he really did sign it over to someone, why is *his* name still connected to it and isn't that fraud?!"

Max glared at his sister, wishing she hadn't come along. Roxy gave his knee a squeeze under the table. "What did you want to say, Max?"

"Nothing, it'll keep." He flashed his sister another scowl.

"Oh, you'll get her all to yourself soon enough, chill out, Grumpy Bum. So is there any actual proof that Wolfgang gave the mine away? I mean, does a drunken poker game back in 1975 count for anything?"

Roxy shrugged. "I guess if there are witnesses to it."

"But didn't you say all the witnesses are dead?"

She felt a small shiver run down her back. Caroline was right. If Betty's recall was correct, every single person who was present during that poker game was now dead. Except for Wolfgang Bergman.

"It *has* to be Wolfgang," she said. "He's the only one who's left and he's the only one who stands to lose if the truth about that bet ever came to light. Although ..." She shook her head. "I still don't get why he had to kill Gordon."

"Because he was there," said Caroline.

"Well, yes, but according to Betty he was passed out in a corner during the whole thing. So he's hardly a viable witness. Besides, I don't think Gordon knew that this mine had come good." She took a sip of her wine. "He told me Berny was a loser, had been scammed by Wolfgang, why would he say that if he knew about the gold find?"

Caroline scoffed. "It was all over the papers yesterday. How could he *not* know? I mean, really, it was front page news."

"Yeah, but life gets pretty small when you're living hand to mouth—" She stopped. "Oh God."

"What?" said Caroline as Max sighed impatiently again.

"My newspaper! That's it. He must have read about it in the paper I gave him. Maybe he then contacted Wolfgang and ..."

"And Wolfgang got rid of the final witness?" Caroline said, her own lips wide.

Max groaned. "Could you guys just take a chill pill for one second and tell me what you want to order?" He waved the menu in front of them.

"You can do the ordering, Max. I always seem to get it wrong at this place."

"Yeah, I'll have what you're having," Caroline concurred, turning back to Roxy. "So where does all this leave that Betty woman? The one Wolfgang had the affair with?"

"It wasn't much of an affair, more like a really bad one night stand from the sound of it. Anyway, she says she wasn't in the room at the time, only heard about the bet second hand; so that would be hearsay. Her word against Wolfman's and I know what he's like. She wouldn't stand a chance up against him."

"Yeah, if I was Berny's daughter, I'd want a signed deed. Especially after all this time, anything less wouldn't stand up in a court of law."

Roxy considered this. "Betty said something about a deed but she's not sure how legit it was. I've left a message for Sondra to see if she knows anything about all of this, but from what Gilda told me, there wasn't much of an inheritance, so I have a hunch she knows nothing about it and is going to be pleasantly surprised."

"She'll be over the bloody moon," Caroline said, blowing a blonde lock from her face. "Call her now, tell her!"

Roxy glanced around to see Max by the counter talking through his order with the waitress. She bit her lower lip and pulled out her smartphone, noticing two missed calls from Sondra.

"Her ears must be burning, excuse me a second, Caroline."

Roxy made her way out to a side balcony, which she knew would be quieter, and returned the call.

"I got your message," Sondra said, sounding a little breathless. "It didn't make a lot of sense."

"Sorry, Sondra. It's hard to explain everything in a text. I've now located everyone from that photo but there's some bad news."

"Oh?"

"Gordon Reilly—the man with the pork chop sideburns—"

"Yes?!"

"He was found dead this morning, I'm not sure if you heard."

There was a long pause. "My God. Do you think it's related to my father? To that photo?"

"I don't know for sure, but yes I do. Listen, that's what I need to talk to you about. I think I know why your father wanted that picture so badly."

"Really? What did you find?"

A burst of laughter came from an outdoor table and Roxy placed a finger in her other ear, trying to diffuse the sound. "Listen, I can hardly hear you, it's really noisy here. Can we meet in the morning? For brunch? I'll tell you everything then."

"Can't we meet now?"

Roxy glanced back into the restaurant and spotted Max who had returned to the table and was now looking around trying to find her. It was the last thing their relationship needed. "No, I'm really sorry, I can't get away. Can we meet around 10:00 a.m. tomorrow?"

"That's too late for me, it's going to be another manic one. How about earlier? Say, seven-ish?" Roxy grimaced at the thought but agreed. "Where do you want to meet?" Sondra asked.

"Where did your dad keep all his old files and papers, legal documents, that sort of thing?"

There was a hesitation on the other end. "At home. Why?"

"Can we meet there then?"

"Oh ... Um ..."

The table laughed loudly again and Roxy had to yell to hear herself. "I think it will be really helpful!"

"Fine. I'm actually here now, so I'll just stay over and put some breakfast on for us. You're sounding very cryptic, Roxy. Can't you tell me more now? What's this about?"

"Do you know if your father has a deed or any papers regarding an old mine up in Indonesia?"

"Mine? What kind of mine?"

"A copper mine originally, but it may also have gold."

There was another pause. "Well, no. No, not at all. My father was a surveyor, Roxy, not a prospector, why?"

"Just do me a favour and take a look through your father's things tonight if you can. Maybe ask his wife. See if you can find anything with the words Byou on it."

"What did you say?"

"By-you!"

"Hmm, that sounds familiar."

"It should."

"What's going on, Roxy?"

Max had now spotted her and was holding an open palm in the air as if to say, "What the hell are you doing?"

"Listen, I'll explain everything tomorrow, I promise. Just text me the address and I'll see you at seven."

They hung up and Roxy returned to the table and to a relieved-looking Max.

"We really have to talk," he said, and when Caroline went to open her mouth, he held a hand up. "Caro, shut it."

Caroline looked offended and scrunched her glossy lips together sulkily. "Fine! I'm going for a smoke."

She pulled out a packet of cigarettes with a gruesome looking foot deformity on the front, and made her way to the balcony from where Roxy had just come.

"When is she going to give up those cancer sticks?" Roxy said, but Max ignored this.

"I've been offered a job with Mercedes."

Roxy's eyes widened. "Oh, right. Great. Another lucrative ad, eh?"

"No, you don't get it. Not for Mercedes, *with* Mercedes."

"What does that mean?"

Caroline reappeared. "Bloody fascists. I've just been told I can't even smoke out on the balcony. I mean, really?! It blows away, people!"

"There are diners out there, Caro," Max growled.

"So why should they get to rule the world?!" She flung herself back into her chair and rolled her eyes.

"Anyway," Max continued, looking back at Roxy, "Mercedes loved my work on the advertorial so much, they want me in-house for a twelve-month contract, working in their marketing department."

"Oh," said Roxy.

"Wicked!" said Caroline.

Max shifted in his seat and his sister eyed him suspiciously just as a plate of curried vegie samosas arrived. The waitress placed the dish down, handed over three plates and forks, and then left them to it.

"So why do you look so miserable?" Caroline asked and Roxy wondered that herself. She had a funny feeling in the pit of her stomach again. She knew Max. He loved his freedom as much as she did, why would he take a full-time job, especially one with such a commercial brand?

"It's in Berlin," he blurted, and sat back, broad shoulders hunched as if waiting for the fallout. His floppy fringe fell into his brown eyes and he could barely look at Roxy.

"Berlin? As in Germany?" asked Caroline, and when he nodded she squealed, catching the attention of everyone in the room. "Oh that really is wicked!" She jumped up and gave her brother a long hug. "I can *not* wait to visit you! When are you going? How much are they *paying* you?"

As Caroline continued to fire questions at her brother, Roxy's heart sank. What did this mean for her? For *them*?

"Berlin?" she managed.

"It's just one year," he said quickly, sitting forward and taking her hand. "It's huge money, I can pay half my mortgage off in one hit and—"

"And what about me?"

"Well, it's just a year, Roxy. I thought—"

"No, you didn't think at all," she said, dropping his hand. "You saw the big dollar sign and you didn't give me a single bloody thought!"

"That's not true. I ... didn't think you'd care."

She gaped at him. "Why wouldn't I care? We're supposed to be going out, Max."

"Really? 'Cause I haven't been getting that vibe lately."

She gaped wider. "You're the one who choofed off to Melbourne and—"

"And you didn't seem to care. You didn't even remember I was going. You probably wouldn't have noticed I was gone if Caroline hadn't mentioned it."

"That's not true! But so what? My memory's crap. That doesn't mean I don't care about you, about *us*."

He stared at her. "Look at you. We've been separated all week and all you care about is some bloody dead guy and his gold mine."

"It's work, Max."

"It's always work with you." He sighed. "I just wish I could get a tenth of the passion you show your 'work'—"

He did the finger squiggle and she wanted to rip those fingers from their sockets, except the waitress had reappeared with a steaming bowl of rice and a spicy beef dish.

"Oh yummy!" Caroline said, glancing uneasily between Max and Roxy, a forced smile on her lips.

Max took a deep breath and spoke a little more calmly now. "You don't want to move in together."

"That doesn't mean anything."

"Exactly my point. There's nothing there from you, Parker. It's like you're treading water, like you don't really want to be in this relationship but you don't want to be out of it either. You're in a kind of limbo. I'm the one who's always calling you. Always suggesting you come over. You never want to stay at my place but you never invite me to stay at yours—"

"I like my space, you know that."

He sighed again. "It's just one year, Roxy. You can always come out and visit."

"*I'll* be there!" Caroline chimed in again and when they both glared at her, she quickly turned back to the food, helping herself to the curry.

Now Roxy tried to calm herself down. She took a good sip of her wine and some deep breaths, too. "Just tell me this, Max, are you taking the Berlin job because you want to take the job, or because you want to have a break from me?"

He shook his head. "Jesus, Parker, you think the whole world revolves around you, don't you?"

She grabbed her bag and stood up. He stood up, too.

"Sorry, I didn't mean that," he said. "Come *on*, don't be like this."

She held a hand up. "Look, you're right. It's not about me. It's about you and your career, and I'm happy for you. It's a great opportunity. Besides, as you so eloquently put it, it's not like we're living together or even married, so why shouldn't you go."

"Married? I didn't think you wanted to get—"

"You'll love Berlin. You really will."

She then turned on her heel and left them there, Max shaking his head angrily while Caroline pretended to be deeply interested in her creamy Tika Masala.

CHAPTER 26

All Roxy wanted to do was stay in bed and mope. She knew she was being childish. She knew she was being ridiculous. But she was furious with Max and she wasn't about to admit why. It wasn't that he had sold out and taken a full-time job, or that he was travelling halfway across the world to some glamorous European city without her. It was the fact that he'd beaten her to it. She had always assumed he'd needed her more than she needed him, but here was the proof that she was wrong. He didn't need her at all.

And *Berlin*? Why couldn't they post him to Baghdad or out the back of Bourke? She flashed a glance at the clock. It was 6:30 a.m. The alarm clock had been screaming at her for fifteen minutes and she needed to stop wallowing in self-pity and get going. She had to be at Sondra's place in half an hour; there was a murder mystery to solve. For Roxy Parker, it would be the perfect distraction.

She found her way to the shower, then into a pair of dark, skinny jeans, high-heeled brown suede boots and baggy cream jumper. She flung some jangly beads around her neck and smudged some rosy lip gloss on her lips. If she was going to be miserable, she might as well look good while she was at it.

She stared at her reflection, at her tussle of black locks and her oversized Rayban glasses and she scowled. "You are such a fool," she told herself before scooping up her handbag and heading for the door.

Bernard Tiles's house was a modest two-storey brick number, just one street down from busy Military Road, Cremorne on Sydney's lower North Shore. There was a tiny, neglected garden at the front with little more than a few nondescript hedges and an old deck chair that had seen better days. Roxy assumed from this, and her conversation with Gilda, that the Tiles weren't exactly loaded, so when the Bergman housekeeper opened the front door with her bashful, brown eyes and meek smile, Roxy was taken by surprise. So Ginny wasn't lying after all.

Today, though, the housekeeper didn't have her usual white slip dress and apron on. Instead, she was wearing high-waisted denim jeans and a baggy sweater with the number 49 on the front. Her ponytail was out and she had small gold rings in her ears, and a diamante stub on her nose. She was a plain looking woman but there was beauty there, too, in the creamy brown skin and the wide, dark eyes.

"Oh ... hello! Do you work here now?"

The woman's smile deflated. "I no *work* here," she said, her tiny shoulders rising considerably. "This my home."

"Oh, God, sorry ... I was looking for Sondra."

Roxy took another peek at the address in her hand, wondering how she could have got it so wrong when Sondra appeared.

"Thanks, Renata," she said briskly. "I've got it."

Renata slunk backwards, disappearing into what looked like a lounge room at one side, while Sondra led the way past the lounge room, down a dark hallway and through into a pokey looking kitchen.

"My new stepmum," she explained as she went.

"I know her. Wasn't she—"

Sondra stopped; her back appeared to stiffen a little. "The Bergman's housekeeper, yes. They met at one of Wolfgang's soirees, I believe. Dad couldn't seem to shake her after that and ... well ..." She shuddered as though the rest were too horrible to contemplate, then continued to lead Roxy through to a small, bright sunroom at the back of the house. This, in turn, opened out to a patio overflowing with potplants. The interior of the house was also modest for the upmarket North Shore with fraying beige carpet and '70s style furnishings that looked like they had been recently prettied up with bright cushions and assorted knickknacks.

"Are you living here, too?"

"Good God, no. I've just been here on and off, sorting through Dad's things and ... well, I feel closer to him here."

"Of course you do."

They had reached a round wooden table where a platter of pastries and jams had been placed. "Please, take a seat and help yourself. Would you like a tea or coffee? There's no juice here, I'm afraid."

"A coffee with milk and two would be perfect, thank you."

Sondra nodded and returned to the kitchen while Roxy placed a flaky, piping hot croissant on a bread plate. As she broke it open and began slathering on jam, she wondered about Renata and Berny and what an odd couple they made. Renata had to be at least thirty-five years his junior, and from quite a different world, although, glancing around the room now, Roxy could see what their connection was. This room was totally devoted to all things Indonesian. There was a large Ikat cloth hanging on one wall and a grotesque mask with enormous eyes and protruding tongue on another. Several Balinese-style statues decorated a mantelpiece, and all around that, a dozen variously framed photographs, each one featuring images that looked like they'd been taken in Indonesia.

They were all happy snaps, mostly of Berny and a pretty young woman in a short, '60s-style dress who must have been his wife, Deandra. In one they were standing in front of an ornate building, in another a rice paddy, and a third picture showed Deandra holding a baby with several local women looking on. There was a very blurry shot of Berny on a boat with Deandra and a young girl who must have been Sondra, aged about five and dwarfed by an oversized life jacket. Roxy wondered how secure Renata felt and if she had ever wanted to remove these reminders of the first wife. Then she spotted a few blank spaces on the wall where pictures had clearly once hung, and guessed she already had. They were probably the wedding photos, Roxy thought just as Sondra reappeared with a plunger of coffee in one hand and a chipped white mug and small milk jug in the other.

Taking the cup and jug from her, Roxy asked, "So what's going to happen with the house? Will Renata stay on?"

"Not if I can help it. We really need to sell the place, we need the capital, but well, Wolfgang's been in her ear and—"

"Wolfgang? What's he got to do with it?"

"Exactly! It's none of his ruddy business but he obviously feels responsible for the woman and I guess you would if you'd palmed her off to someone who then goes and dies on you." She paused, sniffed a little. "He's been *advising* Renata and has told her the house should be hers."

"That doesn't seem very fair for you."

"It's an absolute joke, is what it is! She's a Johnny come lately and she can jolly well—" She caught herself and blushed. "I'm sorry, I keep dragging us off the track. It's really not pertinent to this and I shouldn't waste any more of your time than I need to, plus," she glanced at her wristwatch, "I haven't got long."

Sondra pushed the plunger down and poured Roxy's cup before helping herself to a pastry.

"You're not having a coffee?" Roxy asked, looking around for the sugar and not seeing any.

"I've already had plenty. I've been up for hours wondering what you could possibly have discovered."

"Then I'll get straight to it, shall I?"

Roxy took a good sip of her beverage then proceeded to tell Sondra all about her meeting with Wolfgang, and how she had suspected Gordon of running down Berny, until he, too, had shown up dead. She told her about the "Beautiful Bet!" which she had assumed referred to Betty Reilly but which most likely referred to a game of poker and a bet on an old mine that had only recently proved valuable.

"Do you remember him ever mentioning the bet or a mine called Byou?"

"No, never," Sondra said, shaking her head slowly.

"Well, I think that's why your father wanted that picture back. It was a link to that bet, and maybe he was trying to point you in that direction, let you know you have a right to claim it. The problem is, I'm not sure it's enough. It's just a photograph with a few words on the back. Maybe he was telling you to track down the witnesses to the bet."

"But they're all dead!"

"Yes, except for Betty and she's not really a witness, never saw any deed and has no idea if one exists. Did you find anything here?"

Sondra shook her head, emphatically this time. "I've looked everywhere. Turned Dad's place upside down and it hasn't been easy with what's her name and her son watching on all the time, wondering what I'm doing." She nodded her head towards the inner sanctum where a booming television revealed Renata's whereabouts.

"She has a son?"

"Yes, Timothy is here so often he might as well just move in."

"How old is he?"

She shrugged. "I don't know. Nineteen? Twenty?" She sighed. "He's a nice enough kid, it's not his fault his mother's a—" She caught herself again. "Sorry." She placed her hand on the table, her fingers wide. "Back to the subject.

It seems to me that we need to find that deed, if there is one. But where on earth could it be? This is all so exasperating!"

Roxy had to agree. "And potentially dangerous."

"How so?"

"Well, the way I see it, both your father and Gordon could have been killed to shut them up about the mine, and the 'beautiful bet'. Brownlow could have been a victim, too."

"I thought you said he was killed by an overly zealous mugger."

"That's what the press says, but in the light of all this, you've got to wonder."

Sondra sat forward in her seat and said, "You don't really think that Sir Wolfgang had something to do with these deaths? That he might have ...?"

"It's all I can think," Roxy replied. "I mean, think about what Wolfgang stands to lose if the truth ever came out. Surely, a suddenly lucrative gold mine is a very good motive for murder?"

Sondra's eyes lit up. "Yes," she said. "Yes it is!" She chewed on a fingernail for a few moments giving this considerable thought, then stopped chewing and asked, "What do we do now?"

"We need to go to the police, obviously."

"The police?" She looked dubious.

"Yes, this is getting very serious, Sondra. Most of the people who knew about the bet are now dead, most of them murdered, I suspect. That leaves you, me and Betty."

"You don't honestly think *we're* at risk?" Her eyes narrowed.

"I don't know, I doubt it. I mean, we didn't witness the bet, nor did Betty. But still ..."

Sondra was shaking her head. "I still think we need to find the deed first, prove our case."

Roxy agreed it would help. "But I thought you said you'd looked everywhere."

"I have, which is why I still need your help."

Roxy scrunched her lips to one side. "I'm not sure what more—"

"My father said you had it. I thought he meant the photo, but maybe he meant the deed. Did he give you anything else?"

"Sondra, we've been through all this. I promise you he didn't. All I got was that old photograph which you now have. The answer must lie in those words on the back."

"But they don't prove anything!" She stood up and began pacing the room. "It's not a legal document. It's useless to me. And, as you say, the people who can help prove it are now all gone. Probably thanks to Wolfgang."

There was bitterness again in her voice and Roxy had to agree, the mining magnate had plenty of questions to answer. "That's why we need to hand this over to the police; let them deal with it."

Sondra glanced at her watch again and stopped. "I just can't think about that now, I have to get going. I promised Tony I'd be at the stall by now. Damn it!" She turned imploring eyes back on Roxy. "*Please*, Roxy, all I ask is that you keep thinking about this. Try to remember if my father gave you any more clues, if he gave you anything else, anything at all."

Roxy pushed her unsweetened coffee aside and stood up, too. "I have been thinking constantly about this, but I'm sorry, I keep hitting a blank wall."

She gathered her cup and helped Sondra take the plates to the kitchen before returning to the sunroom to retrieve her handbag. As she did so, she glanced again at the photos on the wall and that's when it hit her.

"Speaking of blank walls," she said aloud, then called out to Sondra who was still in the kitchen cleaning away the plates. "Can you come here for a second?" Sondra reappeared, her eyes wide. "What was in that spot, can you remember?"

Sondra followed Roxy's finger, which was pointed at an empty space where a nail sat idle, an A4-sized patch of wall below it, the paint brighter where it hadn't had a chance to fade. She raised one shoulder.

"I can't remember. I haven't spent a lot of time at this house in the past few years, to be honest. Do you think it might—"

"Was it a wedding photo?"

"Maybe." She stepped closer. "No, no it wouldn't have been. Dad called this room his "Indonesian haven". He kept all his artefacts and photos here. Besides, Mum and Dad got married in Sydney." She stopped. "You don't think ...?"

Roxy grabbed her handbag, her emerald eyes sparkling with anticipation. "I have to get to Oliver's office. I have a hunch I know where that deed might be."

CHAPTER 27

And so the wild goose chase continued. After being escorted out of the house to her car, Roxy put a call through to Oliver who was just waking up and not exactly chatty.

"You need to meet me at your office in half an hour. Can you manage that?"

There was a grunt on the other end and he hung up. She took that for a yes and opened her car door, explaining herself to Sondra as she took her seat.

"I didn't really think about it," she said, "because I never actually got the photo. But what if it was sent in a frame? What if it had been hanging on the wall of your dad's sunroom and he took it off and sent the whole shebang to my agent's office, not just the print?"

"Then where's the frame?"

"Probably still at the office. If I know Sharon—that's my agent's assistant—she would have taken the photo out of the frame before she sent it on to the publisher. I mean, it'd be cheaper postage that way and more practical, too."

"So the frame could be at your agent's office? And the deed could be in there?!"

"Yes ... but ..." She broke off. "I'm not quite sure how you hide a deed in a frame, but it's worth checking out."

For her part, Sondra promised to keep looking through her father's belongings when she finished work that day to see she if could find any papers or information relating to the old mine. "But you're right, Roxy, it's in that frame, I just know it!"

"Yes, but *where?*" Roxy persisted, starting her engine. "How do you hide an entire deed in a skinny photo frame?"

"I don't know, maybe there's a clue in there."

"This isn't *The Da Vinci Code*, Sondra, people don't just hide clues in clever spots."

Sondra wasn't about to be deflated. She was soaring now and her lively eyes and blushing cheeks were proof of it. "It *has* to be the key, don't you see? Please, Roxy, track it down and get back to me the second you do."

"And the police?"

"Find the deed and we'll get them up to speed then. I mean, you're right to be sceptical, it may not be there and we'll both look like a couple of fools, but it's a start."

It better be the bloody end, Roxy thought as she drove back along the Harbour Bridge towards Oliver's office. She didn't normally like to park in the city, mainly because if it didn't send her mad trying to find a spare spot, the exorbitant parking metres would do the trick, but she was in luck today and found a space fairly swiftly, and right outside his office block.

Oliver was just moping towards the building as she got out, and she waved to grab his attention. He scowled as soon as he saw her.

"I thought you promised to get your boxes yesterday. Shazza was not a happy woman when she left."

"Sorry, I have been pretty busy tracking down a killer, you know." She slipped several gold coins in the parking metre.

"Story of your life," he said, keying a code into the security box at the front. It buzzed loudly and he pushed the door and led the way inside and up the stairs.

Within minutes they were standing in the middle of Oliver's office staring down at a pile of boxes clearly marked "Roxy Parker" with a few smiley faces added for effect.

"I had no idea I had this much crap here," she said.

"Now multiply that by fifteen clients and you can see why Shazza's stressed out. Okay, you take that one and I'll start with this. Tell me again what I'm looking for."

"Not sure exactly. I never saw the frame but my guess is Sharon took the photo out and placed the empty frame in one of these boxes, with all my other crap."

"Except you're hoping it's not an empty frame."

"I know it's a stretch, but I've got to try."

Oliver picked up the phone on his desk. "Why don't I try Shazza first and see if she has any idea. Might save us some time."

"Great idea, although if she tells you she threw it out I will leave these boxes here to torment her forever."

Roxy began looking through the first of the boxes while Oliver spoke to his assistant at her home. Sharon had no recall of the picture or the frame but insisted she would never have thrown it out, nor would she have sent the frame on to the publisher.

"Says she's being paid to save me money and why would she send a bulky frame when it'd cost twice the postage," he told Roxy after he'd hung up.

"And she can't remember what it might have looked like?"

He shook his head and then kneeled down as best he could next to another box, groaning as his legs buckled underneath him.

As they slowly and methodically went through the inventory, Roxy got Oliver up to speed on the case so far. He agreed that Wolfgang Bergman had guilt written all over him.

"He certainly has motive up to his eyeballs," she explained, "but opportunity is a bit scarce. I just can't see him getting out of the house these days, let alone ramming a car into someone or shoving them down some stairs. His heart would be in it, but not sure he'd have the grunt force."

"And the wife?"

"Oh she has plenty of grunt, but ... I don't know, not sure I can see either of them doing it, to be honest. No, my money's on a hit and hire. If there's one thing Wolfgang has, it's means. He's got the money and he probably has some dodgy contacts from his days in Indonesia. Everyone tells me the men were pretty rough in those days, maybe he called on one of these rough types to do him a favour."

Oliver nodded, conceding the potential in this theory.

"So you reckon Wolfman learns that the old mine, the one he bet away, is now worth a motza, so he hires someone to take out Berny before Berny stakes his claim?"

"Yep, and I wouldn't be surprised if he also hired a hit on the only two witnesses to the bet—Browny and Gordo—to shut them up."

"That's a lot of corpses for an old gold mine. Doesn't this Wolfgang fellow have mines and money coming out his ears? Why would he kill for one little gold mine in Irian Jaya?"

"Because he's a greedy, arrogant bastard?"

Oliver shrugged. "Yeah, works for me ... Oh, is this it?" He pulled out an empty black frame and Roxy glanced across eagerly then shook her head.

"Too small. Remember the picture? It was A4-size, so the frame needs to be at least A4. Of course, it could have been larger."

They continued wading through old diaries, books and photos with little success. Oliver shoved his box to one side and turned towards another, and Roxy did the same, and for the next ten minutes they didn't say a word, just methodically made their way through the contents.

"I'm gonna need a coffee," Roxy said just as her hand brought out an empty, peach-coloured frame. It could easily fit an A4 photo. "Ooh, this looks promising."

She brushed the dust off the front of the frame, which still had its glass casing and white cardboard backing, and took a deep, steadying breath. Despite what she said to Sondra, it really did feel like she was caught up in a scene from *The Da Vinci Code* as she carefully turned the frame over, unlatching the small hooks at the back that kept the glass in place.

Oliver watched on, his own heart beating rapidly, as she slowly lifted out the glass and then the cardboard, and let out a small gasp.

"Bingo," she said, beaming.

There, taped to the inside of the cardboard, was a thin slip of yellowing paper. She hesitated for a second before slowly working the tape off, careful not to rip the paper at the corners. It was facing towards the cardboard so she could not immediately see what it said, but she already knew this had to be it. This had to be the changed deed to the Byou mine.

"Oh get a move on!" Oliver wailed, crouched beside her awkwardly, and she flicked him a scowl.

"This could be a legal document, Olie. I have to be careful."

Soon she had the paper free, and she took another deep breath as she turned it over and began to read.

In scrawly blue ink that was slightly smudged on one side, someone had handwritten the words: *"August 25, 1975. In this Deed, I hereby transfer ownership and all mineral rights to the Byou Copper Mine, Irian Jaya, Indonesia, to Bernard John Tiles, formerly of Sydney, Australia."*

It was then signed and dated in four different hands. She recognised Sir Wolfgang's signature instantly, she had seen it before, and she could make out Berny's name and Brownlow's, under the word "Witness". The fourth signature was impossible to decipher and she assumed it was Clive Holderson's. It didn't look anything like Gordon Reilly.

They both stared at the page for many minutes, Roxy holding it by the tips of her fingers as though she were holding a winning lottery ticket, and she felt a similar kind of jubilation, too, even though the winnings had nothing to do with her.

Eventually she said, "Sondra is going to love me."

"Bloody oath," Oliver said, and then added, "You should have charged her more."

"Ever the agent." Roxy giggled to let off the pent-up excitement. She was about to place the old scrap of paper back where she'd found it when she had a thought.

"Can I use your photocopier?"

"Sure, but I'll need to warm it up. Just a sec."

He struggled to his feet, his belly bulging out of the Hawaiian shirt he had on, and then made his way out to the bulky contraption behind Sharon's desk and switched it on. As it whirred to life, he also popped on the kettle and began to make them coffee.

Roxy found her way to the new chair in front of his desk and sank into it, still holding the paper carefully, and still staring at it as though it might suddenly disappear. Her first instinct was to call Sondra, but before she could, her mobile announced an incoming call. It was Gilda.

"Hi there, got a sec?"

"Sure," Roxy said, her voice breathless from all the excitement.

"You won't be surprised to hear this, but I'm now running the Bernard Tiles case."

"Fantastic! So they finally decided it was a serious crime, eh?"

"Well, that and the fact that Leary's been forced to take sick leave. Having trouble with blood pressure or something. Really, the man should be retired by now, he's not in good shape. Anyway, Eddie Calhoun's not up for it, way too green around the gills, so they've pushed it onto us. We're putting together a task force to look into all three suspicious deaths, including reopening the Brownlow mugging case. Your photo has got everyone very excited. The chief agrees there could be a connection, but before I get started I've got some questions for you. Can you come in?"

"Oh yes," said Roxy. "Because I think I've just solved your case for you."

Gilda groaned. "Oh God, I only just got the bloody thing."

Twenty minutes later Roxy was sitting across from her friend in Sydney's Crime Squad headquarters, watching as Gilda studied the handwritten deed very carefully, Eddie Calhoun leaning across her to have a look, his baby blue eyes batting wildly. She had already placed it in a plastic evidence bag and, after a few minutes, she handed it to Calhoun and asked him to make a copy.

"You mean, like on the photocopier?" he said.

Gilda stared at him. "Yeees, hence the word photo*copier*."

He blushed beetroot red and scurried away while Gilda shook her head behind him. "Nice enough kid," she told Roxy, "but as thick as three bricks. Still, the chief wants to keep him on the case because he was there from the beginning so he's been seconded to us for the interim. I'm mentoring him apparently." Her twisted top lip told Roxy what she thought of that idea. "Anyway, tell me about this mysterious deed. Hidden inside an old photo frame, you say?" Roxy nodded. "How bizarre. Why hide it? And even more importantly, why send it off in the mail—the notoriously dodgy mail, I might add—to *you*? That's a very valuable document."

"It wasn't at the time, you have to remember. Until about three weeks ago, the gold find at Byou wasn't public knowledge. Berny probably put that deed in the frame with the picture many, many years ago, thinking it wasn't worth the paper it was written on. It was probably just a keepsake to go with the photo. He probably forgot all about it. Then, a few months ago, I asked him to send me a picture of his days with Sir Wolfgang and he probably just saw this photo hanging on his wall and sent it. Didn't give it much thought. He'd probably forgotten the deed was even there."

"But as he lay dying, it occurred to him?"

Roxy nodded. "Maybe he saw the face of his killer and put two and two together, or maybe he saw a news item about the mine before he got struck by the car. Who knows, but he suddenly realises the old mine is viable, and remembers where he's put the deed—that it's in the frame he sent me."

"So he tells his family to find you, except he doesn't live long enough to explain why."

Roxy nodded again. "It has to be Wolfgang who did this, or someone related to him."

"Doesn't Wolfgang have some grown-up sons?"

"Yes, now you mention it! He has two sons, although ..." She looked disappointed. "They're in Indonesia. I had to interview them over the phone for the book." She paused. "Maybe you should check that out. See if they've visited the country lately. I hadn't thought about them, but it's in their interests as much as Wolfman's to shut this story up."

Gilda scribbled something down on her desk diary and nodded. "Back to Berny Tiles, though. You said there's a new wife on the scene; I think I better have a chat to her."

Roxy's eyes squinted. "Yeah, she seems sweet enough, but Sondra calls her a 'Johnny come lately' and you have to wonder about her motive, too."

"Oh?"

"Well, why is a pretty, thirty-something woman suddenly attracted to a crusty old surveyor with very little to his name? I mean, it all happened very fast."

"So what's her motive? She wasn't even written into the will and no one knew about this mine," said Gilda, and Roxy shook her head.

"Maybe Renata did!" Her eyes squinted further. "Think about it. She'd been working at the Bergman house. The

Bergmans would have learned about the mine long before it became public knowledge. They probably discussed it at home amongst themselves. Well, guess who was also in that home? Renata! She was their housekeeper until two months ago. What if she overheard them discussing it, saying how it really belonged to Berny Tiles and got the idea to lure Berny in, marry him and thus claim her share of the lucrative mine?"

"Except, like Sondra, she wouldn't have had a clue where the deed was, or she would have claimed it by now."

"That's true," said Roxy. "But maybe she hoped to get her mitts on the deed. Sondra said that Renata's been watching her like a hawk. Maybe she's also been going through Berny's stuff trying to find it. Her son's practically moved in, too, maybe he's helping."

Roxy suddenly had a flash of a tall, faceless man rushing her in her apartment. Could that have been Renata's son, searching for the deed?

"Okay, but here's the thing I don't get. Why kill Bernard Tiles *before* the deed is found? Wouldn't it make more sense for Renata to woo it out of her husband, then, after he's claimed the mine, bump him off for her share? Or, more sensibly, wait for him to die—he was no spring chicken, after all—then cash in?"

Roxy sighed and sat back, pulling her glasses off and giving them a wipe on her cream jumper. "I know, that's the bit I keep getting stuck on. The only person who had a reason to kill Berny *before* the deed was found was Wolfgang Bergman and/or his wife and sons. Everybody else— Sondra, her hubby, Renata, her son, whoever you want to point the finger at—would be absolute idiots to bump him off before the deed was located." She shoved her glasses back on. "And what if I had never looked in that frame? What if Sharon had chucked the frame out? It's too risky. Berny was more valuable to everyone alive than dead. Everyone that is, except Wolfgang Bergman."

Gilda stood up and stretched. "So we're back to square one. To Sir Wolfgang himself. Fan-bloody-tastic. I'm gonna have to bring him in and the chief is not going to like this one bit."

"Neither will Ginny. Wolfman's been battling pneumonia for the past month so you might have to go to him."

She nodded begrudgingly. "What are you going to do?"

"I'm going to go to him, too. He's got a lot of explaining to do."

"Hang on, Missy, this is a homicide investigation now—"

"Don't even try!" Roxy said, holding one hand high. "You guys would have nothing if it wasn't for me, and who's to say I wasn't chatting to Wolfgang just as you showed up?" She jumped up and grabbed her handbag. "I'll beat you there!"

Roxy raced out the door just as Calhoun was opening it, a photocopy in his hand.

"Good copying, Constable! We'll make a detective out of you yet," she told him while Gilda bellowed loudly behind her.

CHAPTER 28

Ginny Bergman had given up being annoyed with Roxy and simply sighed dramatically when she arrived and showed her through, bum wiggling, beehive hairdo bobbing up and down on top of her head.

"He's getting better," she snapped, "and he wants to have a word with you anyway."

Roxy's eyebrows shot skyward. This was one for the books! She followed Ginny through the house and back out to the garden, which came as a relief to Roxy. The weather was still chilly but she didn't like the idea of being cooped up in the library with a potential killer, even one as frail as old Bergman.

The sun poked out of the clouds as Roxy peered across the freshly mowed lawn and spotted Wolfgang in his recliner, his head tilted to one side awkwardly.

"Go ahead," Ginny said, not following. "He's just dozing."

Roxy walked towards the aging mining magnate and coughed as she got closer, hoping to wake him up, but when she got there, his eyes were still shut, and for one dreadful moment she thought he was dead. She reached a hand out to touch him when he suddenly stirred and stared straight at her. She jumped back, startled.

"Not gone yet, Roxanne," he croaked and she smiled nervously.

"No, 'course not."

He straightened up and waved a rough hand towards the seat beside him. She brushed a few leaves off, sat down and waited as he took a good gulp of his water and straightened the checkered blanket that was across his legs.

"Old age is crap, Roxanne, and don't let anyone tell you differently."

"Oh I won't. I've already suspected as much."

He chuckled, coughing again as he did so. "You're a little too clever for your own boots, you know, even if they are very sexy boots."

He was ogling her high-heeled, brown suede boots and she tucked them underneath her, thinking, "Sir Sleazebag is back. He must be on the mend."

"So, you've come to harass me again?" he said.

"Actually, your wife said *you* wanted to see *me*."

He nodded. "I did want to have a word with you, come clean so to speak. But perhaps we had better wait for the coppers, eh?"

Roxy followed his eyes back towards the house where Ginny was showing Gilda and Calhoun down the pebbled pathway towards them.

"You called them, I assume?" She shrugged, not giving anything away. "I didn't kill Berny Tiles, Roxanne, or Gordo for that matter."

"You're the only one with clear motive," she said and his eyes flickered across to her.

"Now that's where you start to disappoint me. You've been led down the garden path, my dear, and I'm not talking about my garden here."

"I don't understand."

"Clearly," he said and then glanced back at the approaching officers.

Gilda flashed Roxy a quick, "I'm not happy with you" glance, then stepped towards Wolfgang and held out her badge.

"Chief Detective Inspector Gilda Maltin," she told him, "and this is Detective Edward Calhoun."

"Eddie," the younger officer said, stepping forward with a beaming smile, while Gilda tried not to roll her eyes. He had a lot of learning to do.

"My, my, look at *you*," Wolfgang was saying, ignoring Eddie and devouring Gilda's sexy black dress with his wet, cold eyes. "You must have the criminals lining up to be frisked by you."

She gave him a straight, humourless stare. "I only frisk the young, good looking ones, so you're off the hook." She smiled serenely. "We'd like to have a word. In private, if you don't mind."

Wolfgang laughed at her response and then waved a hand in the air. "That won't be necessary, Detective. In fact, I think it might help get this stalker off my back. Roxanne can stay. I'd introduce you but I have a hunch you've already met."

Both detectives now stared at Roxy and for a moment it looked as though Gilda was going to push the point, but she didn't. Instead, she indicated for Calhoun to help her and they dragged another two seats out from under the weeping willow, and sat down in front of Wolfgang. Gilda produced her notepad and he chuckled again.

"Should I have my solicitor present?"

She shrugged. "If you think it's necessary."

"Bugger it," he said, his eyes full of mischief. "Let's live dangerously, shall we?"

"As you like. We're following up a few enquiries regarding the suspicious deaths of Mr Bernard Tiles and Mr Gordon Reilly. Are you familiar with the deceased?"

"You know I am."

"Have you seen or spoken with either man in the past ten days?"

"No I have not. I last saw Berny about two months before he died. Haven't seen Gordo in decades."

"Do you own a white van or have you had access to a white van in the past ten days?"

"There are no white vans in my life, Detective. Not really my style. I do have a very sporty red Alpha Romeo I'm quite fond of, a green Jaguar sedan that's been causing me a few headaches lately, and a vintage Harley that hasn't seen the light of day for some time. You can check them for yourself, they're in the garage." He coughed. "Now, can we just cut to the chase, please, my time is pretty precious these days, as you'll appreciate?" Before she had a chance to respond, he said, "You suspect I had something to do with their deaths and I'd like to categorically deny that. As I just told Roxanne here, you're barking up the wrong tree ... although I think I might have used a garden path metaphor instead."

"We need to verify your whereabouts and the whereabouts of your wife on the nights of ..." She paused to glance down at her pad.

"Home, sick, both times. It's been a boring couple of weeks. And my wife was right beside me."

"And your sons?"

His eyes widened. "My sons?" He chuckled. "Goodness, you really are reaching for straws. My sons are both in Jakarta minding their own business, or, rather, minding my business and not botching it up too badly, I have to say." He had stopped chuckling and his tone was now stern. "Leave them out of it. They've got nothing to do with this."

Gilda stared at him for a few seconds. "Is there anyone who can verify that you and your wife were here the whole time?"

"You have my word, Detective Maltin."

She smiled. "I'm sorry to say that won't quite cut it."

"Oh what a shame, and I was getting quite fond of you." He licked his lips. "Then you have my CCTV footage." It was his turn to smile. "You will have noticed on your way in, I have a pretty sophisticated security system installed at the front gate. There's also one at a side gate, the only two exits from my property and I'm certainly not capable of scrambling over my high rock walls—although I could have leapt over them in my heyday." His cheeky glint returned momentarily. "Both cameras record all incoming and outgoing traffic, cars and pedestrians, and will show that I haven't left my property for weeks. My wife, of course, is another story. She does rather like her shopping, especially when there are shoes involved, but I think if you speak with my security guys—ask Ginny for the number—they'll have the digital files and will show you that neither of us left the premises on the occasions in question."

He was an old pro at this, Roxy realised, and had probably already prepared his answers long before either of them had shown up. He had also left Gilda momentarily speechless, which worried Roxy because Gilda was never speechless, and Calhoun was no help to anyone, so she took this as her opportunity to speak up.

"Who's to say you didn't organise the hits? Get someone from outside to do it for you?"

Wolfgang turned to her with a wry smile. "My, my, look who's been watching too many gangster movies."

"It's a valid question," Gilda said now. "You certainly have the means to pay for a hit man."

"I did not pay for anyone to 'hit' anyone. What you seem to be missing is a motive. Why, pray tell, would I want to kill my old mate, Berny? I mean, sure, Gordo was a bit of a tosser and he won't be missed, but Berny was a good bloke. I liked him. Either way, I did not harm or order the harm of either man. And I had no reason to."

"Oh come *on*, Sir Wolfgang," Roxy said, getting a little sick of his smarmy banter. "We know all about the bet, back in 1975. And you know we know."

He shrugged lazily. "So, there was a bet."

"A bet that you lost to Berny Tiles. A copper mine that now has gold. It belongs to Berny and his family now, and yet—"

"No, in fact, it does not."

"I have the deed," Roxy told him, pulling her copy from her bag.

"Ah, it's shown up at last." He took it from her and began to read it over while Gilda glared at Roxy.

"Perhaps you can leave it to me to do the questioning," she told her in a lowered tone and Roxy smiled and mouthed, "Sorry."

"Jesus H Christ, we were sloshed that night, I can barely read me own bloody writing," Wolfgang was saying. He handed the paper back to Roxy. "Still, it's not worth shit."

"A lawyer might just dispute that," Gilda said and he shook his head.

"You lovely ladies have no idea. Berny was not interested in the mine. He decided not to claim the bet."

Roxy scoffed. "As if!" And then, when Gilda glared at her again, shut her lips.

Gilda coughed and said, "I find that hard to believe, Sir Wolfgang. Please explain."

"It's very simple, Detective. No great mystery. No great *conspiracy*." He waved his fingers in the air. "I learned, about three months ago, that gold deposits had been discovered close to the old Byou copper mine, which we'd had shut down and forgotten about back in '73."

"Two years before you handed it to Berny in a poker game?" Roxy said and he glanced at her wearily.

"Yes, well, it *was* a poker game, you don't need to get on your high moral horse, Roxanne. Everyone knew I had closed that mine down, including Berny I might add, but he decided to take the gamble. He chose to take the mine instead of the cash and I understand why. Sure, his wife was frickin' furious, his friends all thought he was a joke, but I got it. I knew what he was doing. Berny just wanted to own a little piece of Indonesia, as simple as that. He adored that country and an old copper mine, however worthless, was a lovely memento. That's all that mattered to him."

"Except it wasn't worthless was it, Sir Wolfgang?" Gilda said. "The mine came good a few months ago."

"Yes, as I was trying to say, we heard that some local lads had found gold deposits up near Byou, so I got my boys to look into it. They did some exploration work and discovered that the old mine was still viable. We have much more sophisticated equipment now, you understand, and we're able to penetrate much deeper than we'd gone before. There is a vast deposit, some dozen meters below the surface, below where the copper was found. Bit of a shock to all of us."

"But you kept that shocking find from Berny, right?"

"I did not," he said, coughing a little before helping himself to more water. "I called Berny straight away, had him over for dinner and we talked about it. Berny decided he didn't want the mine."

"Oh come *on*," Roxy said again and he turned to her.

"Ever owned a gold mine, Roxanne?"

She held her head to one side. "What do you think?"

"I think you haven't got a bloody clue what you're talking about!" His patience was wearing thin again. "Discovering gold is not as straight forward as you seem to think. You don't just find gold and suddenly become rich. There was an *indication* of gold, but it required enormous resources to start digging. Berny doesn't have those resources or the expertise to do it. I do. And that's just the start. The politics are enough to send you barking mad. You have to acquire a patent for the mineral, licences need to be lodged with the Indonesian government, and they play hardball these days, much harder than before. Bribes have to be paid, local staff assembled. You can't employ expats willy-nilly like the old days. It's not for the faint hearted."

"And Berny was faint of heart?" Gilda asked.

"Not an entrepreneurial bone in his body. Just ask his Sondra. She'll tell you. It was one of the many things she hated about her dad, apparently."

"What would you know about Sondra?" Roxy said, rising to her client's defence.

"I know she didn't give a shit about Berny when he was alive. Said he barely ever saw her, she never came to the house, always busy with her work. Couldn't even be bothered to give him a grandson. He was a lonely old bugger." He waved another hand in the air. "Anyway, that's a whole other story. Fact is, we found out about the gold deposits and I got Berny over for dinner—I don't know when, Ginny will have the date. We discussed it in great detail. In the end, after some consideration, he said, and I quote, 'It was a drunken gamble anyway, and I would never hold you to a drunken gamble, mate.' End of quote. He loved the idea of owning a piece of Paradise but he didn't want any of the headaches that the mine would bring. Plus, I don't think he ever took the bet very seriously. It's probably the reason he couldn't even remember where the bloody deed was. He took it as a joke."

Roxy scoffed aloud. "You can't honestly expect us to believe all that? That Berny would give up his rights to a lucrative gold mine for absolutely nothing?"

"Of course not! I paid him compensation, if that's what you mean. I'm sure our sexy detective here has already investigated the $200,000 placed in Berny's account two months back. That came from me."

Gilda gave Roxy a quick, rueful nod and said, "But why pay him in cash, Sir Wolfgang? Why be so clandestine about it?"

He shrugged. "Why not?"

"I still don't believe you," Roxy persisted and he sighed.

"I don't give a shit if you believe me or not, Roxanne. Facts are facts and you can check all of this with my wife. If you don't believe her, try Renata."

"Renata?"

"Yes, Renata worked for us then, you must know that. That was the night she and Berny ... got together." He smiled almost wistfully. "It seems love was more important to my old mate than money." He chuckled. "Wish I could say the same about my first wife."

"So let me get this straight," said Gilda, handing her notepad to Eddie and indicating for him to take this down. He fumbled with the pen, managing to drop it while Gilda sighed. He quickly picked it up and she turned back to Wolfgang. "You're saying, you discovered the old Byou mine was now valuable, you promptly alerted its rightful owner, Bernard Tiles, who told you he didn't care, he didn't want it. So what happened then? It reverted back to you? Did he sign anything to that effect? Get legal papers drawn up? Where's the proof of this rather remarkable story?"

He shook his head again as if it didn't matter.

"Forgive me, Sir Wolfgang, I'm no business expert like yourself, but I am an expert on the law and if nothing was put on paper to void this handwritten deed, then it must still stand. I have a hunch this paper document will trump your alleged verbal agreement in any court of law. In any case, the family has every right to challenge it."

"And let them try. The fact remains that Berny Tiles did not want that mine and he was going to sign it back to me. That is, until he showed up dead." Wolfgang's watery eyes swept across to Roxy. "I had every reason—twenty million dollars worth of reasons—to keep Berny Tiles alive until he'd signed it back to me. He was killed, sadly, before he got a chance. And that is why you are barking up the wrong tree."

They all stared at him mutely. "You need to ask yourselves, if what I say is true, then who might want to kill Berny before he got a chance to rip up the deed?"

Two names flashed in front of Roxy's eyes but she wasn't prepared to go there, yet.

"I'm sorry, Sir Wolfgang, but you've lied to me all along, so I am having big trouble believing you now."

Wolfgang looked genuinely hurt. "I have lied to you about nothing! I've refused to tell you things that are none of your Goddamn business, but lies? No, I think you'll find I have not said a single one."

Roxy thought back over this and begrudgingly had to agree. She had never actually come out and asked Wolfgang about the bet or the mine, so he had not had the opportunity to lie about them. He'd simply evaded the questions.

"You lied to me about Betty," she said, grasping for straws. "You said she had an affair with Berny when it was you all along."

He scoffed. "No, Roxanne, you were the one who suggested the affair with Berny. What happened between Betty and me is, once again, none of your Goddamn business and has nothing to do with this." His tone was brusque and impatient again.

"It doesn't change the fact that Sondra has every right to demand that you honour that bet with her dad," Roxy told him. "Berny's not around to refuse anything now, so it means diddly squat."

He smiled. "Exactly my point. Why would I kill Berny when he was more valuable to me alive than dead?"

Gilda wasn't buying it. "Tell me then, why didn't Mr Tiles explain all of this to his daughter? Why keep her in the dark? And why send her on a hunt for this document if he was going to rip it up, as you allege?"

"I can't answer that, but I do know he *was* going to tell his daughter. He was waiting for just the right occasion to break the news. I asked him how she'd take it and he admitted she'd blow up, but he said he'd break it to her gently, over dinner one night."

"Dinner?"

"Yeah, he had some new restaurant in mind, I don't know the details."

Roxy thought then of the night Berny died, of the dinner he was supposed to attend with his daughter on Father's Day and how he had cancelled at the last minute.

"Well, isn't it lucky for you that he never made that dinner?" she said. "That he never did get a chance to tell

Sondra? After all, maybe if he had, she might have talked him out of it. Might have insisted he keep the mine."

Wolfgang's watery eyes turned icy. "So now you think I ran him down to stop him from telling Sondra about our agreement?" She didn't answer and he looked back to Gilda, his tone suddenly weary and even a little bored. "Just check out the security footage, Detective. You'll find I have been nowhere near the wheel of a car in the past few weeks." His eyes flickered across to Roxy. "But I wonder, can you say the same for Sondra?"

CHAPTER 29

As Roxy and the two detectives left a weary looking Wolfgang perched in his chair, and returned to the house, Gilda pulled Calhoun aside.

"Eddie, follow up that security footage. Ginny will have the security company details. I want to see every single car, person, dog, rodent that has come and gone from this house over the past fourteen days. I also want you to take statements from Mrs Bergman regarding all that her husband has just said. Also, get in touch with Renata Tiles. I want her down at headquarters pronto to give her statement. I want to know what happened at that dinner he mentioned and I want to sort this mess out once and for all. We're also going to need to check flights from Indonesia, check out the sons' whereabouts, but we'll do that at a later stage."

Eddie's freckled brow furrowed considerably and he looked more than a little confused but didn't say a word as he dashed off before she could throw anything else at him. Gilda then turned to Roxy who braced herself.

"You are unbelievable," she said.

"I'm sorry—"

"No, no, you did well. I couldn't let it *look* like you were running the show, but you know more about it all than me, so I had to let you get a few in. He's a slippery character, that Bergman." They both looked back out to the garden where Wolfgang appeared to be asleep again, his head dropped precariously to one side.

"You don't believe him, surely?"

"About Mr Tiles happily surrendering the mine? Sounds so ludicrous it could almost be true."

Roxy considered this. "Both Sondra and Betty have told me how devoted Berny was to Sir Wolfgang, but to give up a *gold mine*? I just can't buy it."

"Well, I guess we'll have to see what the new Mrs Tiles says about it all. Seems to me, she's someone who stands to lose if the story's true, so if she says it is, well, we might just have to believe it."

"Still, Sondra could challenge that."

"And she should!" They began walking back around the side of the house towards their vehicles. "Wolfgang seems to be suggesting that Sondra played a part in all this." Gilda stopped and faced Roxy. "You don't think she could have found out what her dad was up to and killed him before he ripped that deed up?"

"No way! Sondra didn't know anything about it."

"Are you sure?"

"Yes I'm sure. She didn't even know there was a deed or a mine or anything. She's just paid me to find out what all this is about. Why would she do that if she already knew? She's been as clueless as me, I swear. If not, she's a bloody good actress. Listen, Wolfman is playing us just like he played Berny. He's a very dangerous, greedy slimeball who's trying to deflect attention elsewhere. He might not have lied to me but he kept a lot of truths to himself."

"That story about the compensation is true, though. We did source that money back to Bergman and it could well have been compensation for the mine. And I guess he's got a point. What does an old Sydney retiree want with a mine up in Indonesia? It might have been a romantic idea thirty-seven years ago, but he'd grown up a lot since then. He probably didn't want the hassle. He's newly married, maybe he just wanted the cash so he and Renata could be comfortable in his last few years."

"But two hundred grand? He could have asked for ten times that amount."

She shrugged. "I guess not everyone's as greedy as Bergman."

"Or as business savvy," said Roxy, feeling suddenly very sorry for Sondra.

"Come on," Gilda said, "we better get out of here. It's time for me to have a chat with this mysterious new wife."

CHAPTER 30

As Gilda returned to the police station, Roxy decided it was high time she got the original photo frame and its precious cargo back to Sondra. She no longer had the original deed—Gilda insisted on keeping that as evidence—but she had her copy and she knew that this time, the copy would suffice. Sondra would not only be over the moon, there might even be a bonus in it for her.

After trying Sondra several times unsuccessfully over the phone, Roxy decided to head straight to Berny's old house, just in case she was there, but as she drove up, she couldn't see Sondra's red hatchback anywhere.

Instead, there was an unfamiliar, egg-shell yellow station wagon with rust marks parked out the front. Roxy strode up and pressed the front doorbell. After a minute she pressed it again and was just about to give up when the door opened and a tall, Eurasian man with stunning black eyes and thick dreadlocks hanging down to his shoulders looked out.

"Yes?"

"Oh, hello, I'm looking for Sondra. I just need to drop something off."

"She's not here."

"And Renata?"

"Mum's down at the station, eh? Coppers had some questions. About Berny."

"Oh, right," she said and then, "Hi, I'm Roxy Parker, you must be Timothy?"

He nodded, looking at her warily. "You wanna leave Sondra a message or what?" He glanced down at the frame in her hand then back up at her.

She closed her arms around it and asked, "You don't know where she is, do you?"

He shrugged. "Wedding, I think."

"*Still?*" thought Roxy. She really was having a busy weekend.

"Wanna leave that with me?" He stared pointedly at the frame now and she quickly shook her head.

"I'll just try her on her mobile again. Thanks."

Roxy returned to her car, putting yet another call through to Sondra on the way. At last, it picked up.

"Huge apologies," Sondra said with a rush at the other end. "I've been working on a wedding all day and we've had quite a few nightmares. The Singapore lilies have been a complete disaster. I told them it was the wrong time of the year."

"No worries, Sondra. I've been trying to tell you the good news."

"You found it?!"

"Yes, I did."

There was a loud gasp. "How? Where?!"

"It was in one of your dad's old frames, as I suspected. He obviously just sent the entire package, frame and all, and my agent's assistant didn't notice it when she took the photo out to send on to the publisher. Luckily she kept the frame and put it in storage, otherwise it might have got lost forever."

"Oh, that is lucky! Hang on a minute ..." There was a muffled sound on the other end and then Sondra returned sounding even more breathless. "Oh God, I have to go.

They're about to descend on the reception room and I haven't even finished the centrepiece."

"Listen, I'm at your dad's house now, should I leave it here—"

"God, no! Um, can you hold onto it for now? It's going to be a late one, then another manic day tomorrow. Um ... I'll try and get it off you in the afternoon. Are you around?"

"Yes, absolutely. Just call me when you're done. I'll keep this safe."

"Great, and thanks so very much, Roxy."

"You're welcome," she said and let the harried florist go.

Glancing back at the house, Roxy noticed that Renata's son had remained by the door the whole time and was watching Roxy closely, so she gave him a quick wave and then got into her car. She wasn't sure how much he overheard or even how much he would have understood. But she was working for Sondra and she was looking forward to handing the precious deed over in the morning, even if it was just a poor photocopy.

As she started the engine and began to manoeuvre her vehicle back onto the main road, Roxy glanced in her rear vision mirror again and saw Timothy swing around and step inside the house, his dreadlocks flapping around his ears as he went.

A sudden chill raced down her spine. *Could they be the bunny ears she saw in her apartment last Friday night?* She gulped a few times and thought about his light coloured station wagon. *Could a blind, old neighbour mistake it for a white van on a dark night?*

She shivered a little and accelerated away.

CHAPTER 31

The screaming telephone broke through Roxy's sleep and she awoke with a start and stared at it for several seconds trying to work out what it was and why the hell it didn't just shut up and go away. Eventually she realised it was her phone, and she grappled for the receiver. The clock radio said it was 7:35 a.m. and she knew this meant only one of two people. It had better not be her mum.

"Hello," she groaned.

"I'm really sorry, Rox, I keep doing this to you."

"Hey, Gilda." She scrunched her eyes shut. "Please don't tell me you've found another dead body." Her eyes flew open. "Oh, God, Betty's okay, isn't she?"

"Betty? Well, funny you should mention her ..."

"Gilda, it's way too early for riddles, what's happened to Betty?"

"Betty's fine. We've got a burglary this time. You will never guess who we just busted attempting to break into Sir Wolfgang Bergman's house early this morning."

"Renata's son?"

There was a pause. "Who? What? I don't know what you're on about there but no, we just nabbed the receptionist who works at Betty Reilly's office. You know, the blond pit bull at the front desk."

Roxy swung her legs out of the bed and sat up. "*Really*?!"

"Yep, bizarre, eh? Busted him at 3:45 this morning, or at least their security guy did. He's been in lockup since then, refusing to say a word. It's just lucky I recognised him from my visit to Betty's office yesterday. I'm about to go in and have a little chat, but you don't happen to know why Betty's receptionist would be trying to break his way into Wolfgang's abode, do you?"

"No, I don't." She thought about it for a second. "I mean, he seemed very protective of his colleague, but what he's got to do with any of this is beyond me."

"Didn't you say Betty and Wolfgang had an affair?"

"Yes, but that's got nothing to do with him."

Or did it? Roxy had a sudden thought as a swirl of images came rushing through her brain—there seemed to be several overly protective, middle-aged men in Betty's life. But maybe she had that wrong. Maybe there was just one.

"Listen, before I go," Gilda was saying, "I wanted to tell you something that Renata said last night."

"Renata?" Her head was in a whole different space suddenly.

"Yes, we brought her in for questioning. Another woman of few words and I can't decide whether it's because she doesn't speak English very well or she's got something to hide. Anyhoo, it turns out she *was* at that dinner the night Mr Tiles allegedly rejected ownership of the mine, but she swears she didn't hear anything. Says she presented dinner and returned to the kitchen to clean up. It wasn't until later that evening, after Tiles left, that Bergman brought her into the library and asked if she was interested in marrying Tiles."

Roxy nearly dropped the phone. "You're kidding, right?"

"Afraid not."

"Were they even going out?"

"Don't quite know, but she clamped right up on me when she realised what she'd said."

"Oh my God. You don't think Wolfman exchanged his housekeeper for a gold mine? Was that all part of the deal? Two hundred grand and Renata? Sounds very unethical."

"Sounds like human trafficking to me but, well, I don't know all the details. It may just be a scam to keep her in the country, something to do with visa issues. I'm still trying to get to the bottom of it all. " She sighed again. "This has become a right royal mess. Anyway, the thing I wanted to tell you."

"Yes?"

"Renata swears that Berny *did* catch up with his daughter on Father's Day—the night he died."

Roxy had sat down again and was now shaking her head at the phone. "No, no, he was *supposed* to but Sondra says he cancelled at the last minute."

"Not according to Renata, he didn't. She was out that night with her son at some Indonesian cultural thing, we've already checked her alibi and there's a dozen witnesses to prove it. But Renata swears Berny called her on her mobile that night from dinner and said it wasn't going so well and he would be home late."

Roxy could feel a headache coming on. "Really?"

"Really."

"So one of them's lying."

"Yep. Or maybe Berny lied to his wife. Who knows? I'm not sure Renata can be trusted but I really can't think why she'd lie about this."

"Unless she's trying to put Sondra in the frame, throw the guilt her way. Like Wolfman did."

They considered this for a few seconds before Roxy asked, "Did Renata say *where* Berny and Sondra were supposedly having dinner that Father's Day? I mean, can't you just check that out?"

"Tried that. Renata can't recall which restaurant he'd booked. Just some newbie that he'd found."

"Can't we ask Sondra?"

"Tried that one, too. She's not answering. You don't happen to know how we can track her down, do you?"

"Oh, she's hard at it this weekend, a bunch of weddings apparently. I'm scheduled to see her this arvo so I'll tell her to get in touch. In the meantime, just keep trying her. She's a bit flustered but she'll eventually pick up."

"Speaking of flustered, I've really got to go. Drop in later if you like and I'll get you up to speed. Renata had a few other interesting things to say, especially about your friend Sondra."

"Will do," Roxy said, not sure she wanted to hear any of it.

Wide awake now and with a thumping headache, Roxy threw on a tracksuit and some trainers and headed outdoors for a speed walk. This time it wasn't fitness she had on her mind, it was Betty and Wolfgang, Sondra and Berny, and the wary blond receptionist from Betty's office. She now had a pretty good idea who that was and what his motives were, but it still didn't make a great deal of sense, and she wanted to kick-start her brain as she walked, and maybe clear the headache at the same time.

There were plenty of other fitness fanatics up at this hour but she barely noticed them as she padded the pavement down to Rushcutters Bay Park, a million thought bubbles popping inside her brain. And in amongst them all, confusing the picture completely, was Max Farrell, his puppy dog brown eyes looking up at her, sad and confused.

It was now two days since their fight and he hadn't called. *Of course* he hadn't called. Why would he? She'd been a complete brat and she didn't deserve his phone call. She should have congratulated him, she should have been supportive, instead she had done exactly what he'd accused her of—she had thought only of herself. Oliver, too, had accused her of believing that the world revolved around her, and Roxy's heart was swamped with regret and shame.

When was she going to grow up?

There had been a message from Caroline last night, however, asking if she was okay, and Roxy had texted back with the words, "I will be. Thank you".

She didn't know what exactly that meant but she couldn't let this get her down today, or distract her. Instead, she tried to focus on the case at hand, and what on earth Betty's so-called "receptionist" was doing trying to break into Wolfgang Bergman's house.

She sighed. The receptionist had to be Betty's son, Brian. It fit perfectly. Both men were in their forties, both overly protective, and both with the same sounding voice. They must be one and the same.

So why didn't Betty introduce him as her son when they first met at the office? Why all the secrecy? she wondered.

And, more importantly now, why was he breaking into Wolfgang's house? Surely, the only beef Brian had with the old miner was the fact that he had slept with his mother and broken up an already unhappy marriage.

Was that reason enough? she wondered. Do sons really care whether their mother had a fling thirty-seven years ago?

Roxy stopped in her tracks. She recalled something Betty had said to her when they last met and she gasped aloud, startling another woman who was jogging past her. The woman swept a glance at her and then picked up her pace.

"That wasn't a fling!" she said aloud, then turned around and retraced her steps, back through the park towards home.

The bubbles had suddenly burst in Roxy's brain, leaving one clear thought remaining. It was time to get the truth out of Betty Reilly—the *whole* truth—and she knew exactly where she would be at this early hour.

CHAPTER 32

Betty was hunched over in the waiting room of the Serious Crime Squad when Roxy arrived and she looked distraught behind her bright green spectacles. She didn't seem too surprised to see Roxy, though.

"Your son, Brian?" Roxy said, nodding a head towards the interrogation room, and Betty offered her a small nod.

Roxy sat down on the stiff plastic chair beside her. "How's it going so far?"

Betty sat up straighter and shrugged. "They're not telling me anything."

"Did they give you any idea when they'll be finished?" She shrugged again, blinking a few times. "Come on, let's go and get a cuppa, hey? These things can take hours."

Betty looked warily towards the office and then back at Roxy. Eventually she struggled to her feet, her whole body shaking as she stood up. The once youthful looking woman now appeared all of her sixty-five years and then some, her seemingly cheerful demeanour long dissipated. She was jittery and she was on the verge of tears, blinking rapidly as she always did when stressed, and Roxy took her arm to help her outside. She felt for the woman, she really did, but she also needed to hear the truth and she wasn't going to let jitters get in the way this time.

Spring was still refusing to show up and the day was turning gloomier by the minute. They found a narrow, grimy milk bar two blocks down from the police station and settled into an indoor booth with a small jukebox on one side with the words "out of order" taped across it. She ordered two mugs of tea—coffee was never a wise choice in dumps like this one—and then waited until they arrived before speaking.

Eventually, very gently, she said, "Why didn't you tell me your son was the receptionist at your office?"

"Oh, I'm never allowed to, my dear! Brian makes such a fuss about it, you see. Doesn't like people to know we're related, feels it's unprofessional, even though he did get the job because of me ..." She pulled off her glasses and gave her eyes a rub.

"And does he live with you, too?"

She stopped rubbing and placed the glasses back on. "Always has. He's never been very good at relationships and, well, he just loves his mum, doesn't he? Says I need looking after." She glanced at Roxy with pride then, but there were traces of something else, too, something resembling anxiety.

"Is that why he was breaking into Wolfgang's house?"

Betty looked away and took a small sip of her tea, so Roxy tried a different angle.

"This is all to do with that Survey Congress isn't it? You told me you and Wolfgang had one night, that night of the Congress. You didn't call it a fling or an affair. You called it brutal and I didn't take that literally. But it *was* brutal, wasn't it?"

Betty began blinking rapidly again and wouldn't meet Roxy's eyes.

"You said you were stupid and naïve. You called it a 'mistake'. What did he do to you, Betty? Did he—"

"Force himself on me?" Betty interrupted, staring at Roxy now, her eyes brimming with tears and anguish. "I told myself for years that he didn't. That I had gone willingly because, you see, I *had*. I looked up to Wolfgang Bergman, we all did—hell, Gordon did too, more than anyone, except perhaps Berny Tiles. So, yes, I did go willingly. I flirted with him all night. He was the big man around town, he had all the money, all the power. He was even charming back then, would you believe?" She smiled weakly. "So after my husband passed out on a lounge, yet again, I was angry with him and bored, and I was far too drunk so ... well, I waited for Wolfgang out by the pool, waited for him to finish his poker game and romance me." Her eyes were brimming over with fat, wet tears. "But there was no romance, Roxy. He was aggressive, he was angry, I suppose, after the bet and he ... well, I didn't like it. I told him that. I told him to *stop*."

She put a hand to her mouth and choked back a sob.

"But he didn't stop."

She shook her head quickly. "You young ladies call it date rape these days. Back in my day it was my own goddamn fault."

"No, Betty—"

"Oh yes, my dear. That's what Wolfgang told me. That's what Browny and Clive told me ... Not in so many words of course, but that was the general gist. I'd flirted with him, I'd cheated on my husband, I deserved everything I got. I was an outcast the next day. None of them would talk to me. Except Berny, of course. I'm not sure he even knew. He'd left the bar by then, taken his 'beautiful bet' and gone back to his wife."

"But the others knew?"

"Of course they knew! How could they not? Browny and Clive were still playing poker when it happened. We were out by the pool. I was screaming. I had bruises the next day."

"And no one did anything?!" Now it was Roxy's turn to blink rapidly.

"He was Mr Powerful, Roxy. Of course no one did anything."

"And Berny didn't suspect? From the bruises?"

She shook her head firmly. "Berny wasn't the brightest matchstick in the box. I don't know if he ever knew. Perhaps that's why he still idolised Wolfgang to the end."

"And what about your husband?"

She sobbed. "Oh, Gordon knew, all right. He saw it in my face and in the bruises and in the way I couldn't look at him for days afterwards. Maybe one of the other men told him, too, I don't know, but he wanted to kill Wolfgang, he wanted to rip his head off, but of course he didn't. I loved my husband, deep down Roxy, I know that's hard to understand after what I did to him. But he was weak. He wasn't a strong man. In some ways I wish he had ripped into Wolfgang. Instead he ripped our marriage apart and he slowly died within. You see, he felt responsible. It was *my* fault, I had flirted with that hideous man, but Gordon took the pain and made it his own. He said he should have protected me and he didn't. He didn't feel worthy of me after that."

"And your son ...?"

"Brian was just three then."

"But you told him recently, right?"

She sniffed and didn't speak, so Roxy said, "He wasn't breaking in to Wolfgang's house last night to steal the silverware, was he?"

She choked, flung a hand to her mouth. "He was so angry! I should never have told him. Yet again I was so stupid." She blew her nose. "When he turned forty, I thought it was time. He could never understand why his father had left us, you see, it had been eating him alive, too. I think it was the reason he could never form proper relationships. He just didn't trust love, you see? So I thought if Brian understood how hard that time was, what had happened, maybe he could forgive his father at last, and get on with his own life."

"But he didn't forgive him, did he?"

She shook her head. "He couldn't forgive any of them. He said they were all culpable and they all needed to ... pay."

She began blinking rapidly again and Roxy placed a hand on hers, trying to coax her on. "So he tracked down Brownlow?"

She nodded. "He didn't mean for him to die! He was just trying to teach him a lesson, show him what it's like to be brutalised, he felt he was as guilty as Wolfgang for not stopping it. But then Brownlow started taunting him, calling me a whore, and my son ... my beautiful, protective son ... he saw red ..."

"So he stole Brownlow's wallet and other stuff to make it look like a mugging gone wrong."

She shrugged. "I suppose so. I don't know."

"And Gordon?"

She sniffed. "My fault again. After you rang, I didn't tell him the details, I knew that he was angry with his dad. I didn't want him to track Gordon down. But, well, he must have listened in on our phone call and heard you say his dad was at the hostel in Woolloomooloo, so I can only guess he found him. I don't know what happened. He didn't tell me. I didn't ask ... I don't want to know ..."

"But why kill his dad?"

"I don't know, I don't know!" She sobbed. "Maybe because he didn't protect me. When I told Brian about that brutal night, I was expecting him to forgive his dad, but instead he was angrier than ever. It didn't matter that Gordon was drunk at the time, unconscious. Brian was enraged to hear that he had just let it happen. He said he should have looked out for me, got me back to the hotel, that he was never worthy of me in the first place."

She doubled over and continued to sob while Roxy reached over and patted her softly on the back. A couple who were just sitting down at a neighbouring booth looked at Roxy alarmed but she held a hand up to let them know it was okay.

She gave Betty a few minutes to collect herself before she said, very gently again, "What about Berny?"

Betty looked up, expression aghast. "No!" She shook her head fiercely. "He knew Berny had nothing to do with all of this. I told him that. Berny wasn't there when it happened. He didn't blame Berny, he didn't kill him. I can promise you that!"

"But don't you see, it makes sense? He killed Brownlow. He killed Gordon. It's too much of a coincidence."

"No! No, he's told me everything, he's confessing everything to the police now. But he didn't kill Berny, I promise you that. Why admit to two murders and not a third? He wouldn't lie. He didn't do it."

Roxy sat back and thought about this as Betty continued sobbing into her hands.

"What I don't understand, Betty, is why your son didn't go straight to Wolfgang first. Why kill the others and leave Wolfgang alive? He was the guiltiest of all."

"Oh, don't think he didn't try. Have you seen Wolfgang's house?" She frowned. "Of course you have. You've been there, interviewed him. Then you'll know it's like Fort Knox. It's not his precious money he's protecting. It's his life. I'm sure my son and I are not the only enemies *Sir* Wolfgang has made in his long, horrendous life." She sniffed loudly. "The morning after I told Brian about the ... about what Wolfgang had done to me, he went straight to Wolfgang's house, he wanted to beat him to a pulp, but he told me he couldn't get in. Wolfgang was bed bound so he couldn't get close. I was so relieved. I can't tell you how relieved I was. Oh, I'll always hate Wolfgang, but I didn't want him dead, or any of them. I thought it was over. I didn't know that Brian was biding his time, waiting for Wolfgang to get better. That in the meantime, he would start tracking down the others. But he must have found Browny quite quickly."

Roxy nodded. She too had tracked him down the easiest. He was the only oldie in the group who had bothered to get connected, set up a Facebook page and pour his life details out for all to see. For a vengeful son to find.

"So Brian took his anger out on Brownie instead?"

She nodded and started weeping again while Roxy continued patting her gently on the back, knowing it was insufficient support and there was little else she could do. It was all such a horrendous tragedy, such a bleak, awful time for Betty who had been the original victim and was continuing to pay even now, while Wolfgang slept quietly in his bed, oblivious to all their pain.

Roxy thought about Berny, too. If Betty was right and Brian didn't kill him, then who did? And why?

"Come on," she said to Betty eventually. "Let's get you back to the station. Maybe they'll let you see your son now."

Betty blew her nose again and looked up at her with wet, blinking eyes. "Will you wait with me?"

"I'd like to Betty, but I can't. I have something I need to chase up, and I need to do it now. Before anyone else gets hurt."

CHAPTER 33

The Sydney Flower Markets are located in an enormous warehouse down at Homebush Bay, fifteen kilometres west of the CBD, and as Roxy pulled into the public parking lot, she was surprised to see plenty of empty spaces. She credited the late hour. It was now almost 11:00 a.m. and most florists had probably come and gone.

As she walked towards the front entrance, she counted five vehicles with the name *Blooming Bros* spray painted across the side, including a truck, two vans and a moped, and she was surprised. Sondra's husband's business was not just blooming, it was positively booming.

The inside of the warehouse was like a living, breathing Monet painting with splashes of vivid colours and extraordinary perfumes pummelling the senses. There were around 170 stalls where local and regional growers supplied city florists as well as the general public, and everywhere people were running about and calling out under bright hanging lights. Buyers were wandering the aisles checking out the buds and haggling for prices, and Roxy had no idea where to start. She spotted what looked like an information desk on one side but there was no one at it. She crossed to it and glanced down to find a map of the warehouse with the names of the stalls handwritten in. She had difficulty reading the writing and was about to give up when a voice behind her said, "Need some help?"

Roxy swung around to find a short, plump woman in a bright pink parka staring at her.

"Yes, hi, I'm looking for the *Blooming Brothers* stall."

"Oh, Tony's shop? Sure, just head down aisle nine, take a left and go right to the back towards the corner. You can't miss it, it's in front of the freezer."

Roxy did as instructed and soon found her way to one of the biggest stalls where dozens of buckets were set up with a wide variety of fresh flowers, mostly roses in every colour imaginable. It was cold inside the warehouse, obviously to keep the flowers fresh, and she noticed most of the workers were rugged up, but Tony's corner was colder still, and she thrust her hands into her jacket pockets as she approached.

She couldn't see Sondra anywhere, nor could she see anyone who resembled a tiny "gnome", as Sondra had described her husband a few days ago. She did spot a fairly large, Italian man wearing a thick, black jacket and a woolly, Russian-style Ushanka on his head. He was issuing instructions to a younger man beside him and glanced up when she approached, raising his eyebrows as if to say, "Can I help you?"

"Hi, I'm looking for Sondra Lane."

"Sonnie's out at the moment, I'm her husband, Tony, can I help?"

"Oh," she said, surprised. "I'm Roxy Parker, I've been—"

The man tugged his hat off quickly and reached a hand out to shake her hand. "Yeah, I know who you are." He turned back to his worker and said something that saw him walk away, bucket of yellow roses in his hands. "Sonnie told me she'd hired you. To find her dad's stuff. How's that working out?"

"That's what I wanted to talk to her about. She's not around?"

He shook his head. "You can talk to me."

She considered this and wondered how much he knew. She usually tried to maintain a certain level of confidentiality with her clients, but this was her client's husband, after all. "It's just that ... well, I found what she was after."

"Yeah, the deed. Got it with you?"

So he knew all about that then. "The police are keeping it safe."

He frowned. "The police? What's it got to do with them?"

"Well, they are investigating Berny's murder, as you must know. They think it may be related to the gold mine. It's a possibility, so they've asked to—"

"Yeah but how come they got it in the first place?" His frown had deepened to a scowl that not even the pretty blooms around him could offset. "Sonnie paid you to find it and get it to her."

"I appreciate that. But soon after I found it, the police called and I showed them the deed. They insisted on keeping it as evidence. They also want to talk to Sondra. She hasn't been answering her calls."

"She was working three weddings yesterday, yeah? Plus, it's been a manic weekend down here, got an expo on tomorr'a. She's been run off her feet. Just getting her first break in hours."

He sniffed crudely and reached for his phone, which was attached to his apron. "Hang on, I'll see where she's at."

He moved away as he made the call and he clearly got through because she could see him gesticulating as he spoke. When he finally ended the call and returned to her side, his frown was still firmly in place.

"Sonnie says can you meet her back at her dad's place?"

"Okay. She's there now?"

"Will be."

Roxy nodded, thanked him and was about to walk away when she had a thought. "You don't know where Sondra was supposed to meet her dad for dinner the night he died, do you?"

He stared at her. "Some dive in North Sydney. Why?"

"Oh, I was just wondering. I heard it was one of Berny's faves."

"Can't think why. It's a shitbox where they give you crayons to draw on the tables like you're six."

She wondered how he knew about that but his deepening frown was not encouraging. Instead, she thanked him and walked back through the warehouse towards her car, a growing sense of unease causing her legs to feel increasingly shaky.

Instead of heading to Berny's house, however, Roxy decided to take a detour to North Sydney and the only restaurant she knew of where table drawing was *de rigueur*. There was one other thing they did there that was quite unique, and if her unsettling hunch was correct, it could very well crack the case.

CHAPTER 34

When Sondra Lane walked into the North Sydney restaurant an hour later, it was clear the kite was flat as a tack. She looked as anxious and as frail as she had just a week earlier when she'd first walked into Roxy's life. Her lips were lurid red again today, yet they did little to cheer up her pale and drawn features, and she was wearing a long, tweed skirt with a cream silk blouse over it, her dark hair twisted behind her back in a messy pigtail. Her ears stood out, enhancing the startled appearance.

She glanced around uneasily, first studying a group of diners who were huddled at one table, a wall of cluttered photos behind them, then looking back towards the far end where Roxy was seated, alone. Roxy held one hand up and Sondra nodded then slowly made her way across while Roxy quickly checked her smartphone again. She had left a long message for Gilda asking her to get to Giardineto's restaurant, pronto. So far, no luck.

"I got your text," Sondra said as she approached, a small frown settling on her forehead. "I tried to get back to you but you were not responding. I thought we were going to meet at my father's place."

"Nah, I thought this place might be more appropriate."

"But I'm not really very hungry."

"Good, because we're not really here to eat," Roxy told her and then said, firmly, "Sit down, Sondra."

The frown intensified but she did as instructed, pulling out a chair and slipping into it. She placed her hands on the table in front of her and looked at Roxy with an expectant expression.

"You ever been here before, Sondra?"

She glanced around and shook her head, no.

"Really? That's odd. Your dad loved this place. I'm the one who first brought him here, did you know that?"

Sondra shook her head again.

"I suggested it for our interview. I've only been here a few times myself, mind you. Thai's more my thing, but it was halfway between your dad's house and mine, so, well, it seemed like a good idea at the time. He fell in love with it instantly. Said he was going to make this his new favourite restaurant. You know what he loved most about this place?"

Sondra was now leaning back in her seat, trying to look disinterested but there was wariness in her eyes and she had begun chewing on one of her fingernails. Roxy picked up a stubby, red crayon and started doodling on the white paper tablecloth.

"He adored the way you could draw all over the table. Thought that was hilarious."

The wariness in Sondra's eyes increased and, for just a second, she looked alarmed. Roxy dropped the crayon back onto the table and dusted her hands off.

"Pity they don't keep the tablecloths, though," she continued. "It could have been a really lovely memento of our time together. But I already asked. They chuck them out after each sitting."

Sondra relaxed considerably as a petite waitress appeared with a tall glass of Coke. She placed the glass in front of Roxy and gave her a very short, sharp nod, flashing a quick glance at Sondra and away.

"Do you want anything?" Roxy asked. "A drink? A settling cup of tea perhaps?"

Sondra shook her head firmly, and the waitress looked relieved as she rushed away. Roxy called out to thank her, then took a long sip of her drink and also sat back in her seat.

"Look, what is all this about, Roxy?" Sondra said at last, her hands now fidgeting in her lap. "I've told you before, I'm extremely busy today. I just don't have time for reminiscing about my father."

"Oh, that's a pity. I thought you might like to see the photograph I have of him."

"The photograph? I've already seen that photograph—"

"I'm talking about a different photo, Sondra. A more recent one." Sondra's eyes squinted. "You see, they might throw out the tablecloths here, but they keep the photos, which is handy."

"I'm still not following." She was chewing on one nail again.

Roxy waved a hand around the room. "But surely you've noticed all the Polaroid photos taped to the walls. They take your photo when you come here and, if you look back towards the kitchen there," she waved a hand behind her, "you'll see a photo of your dad and me, grinning from ear to ear. Now *that* is a memento worth keeping. You should ask them if you can have it." Sondra didn't attempt to look around and Roxy took another sip of her drink before asking, "So you've really never been here with your Dad, eh?"

Sondra's eyes squinted again and she seemed to be weighing something up. Eventually she said, "I don't know. Maybe."

"Maybe?"

"I mean, yes, sure, ages ago. I can't remember when."

Roxy blinked several times. "You can't remember having dinner here with your father two weeks ago?" Sondra paled a little then but still managed a nonchalant shrug so Roxy said,

"Perhaps this will jog your memory: it was Father's Day. Oh, and it also happened to be the night your dad got run over."

Sondra stared hard at her. "No, I've already told you. We were *supposed* to meet here that night but he cancelled."

"Really? That's not what Renata says."

"Well Renata is a lying whore." Her tone had turned bitter but there were nerves there, too, and she was clenching and unclenching her jaw, her hands now jittery on the table.

Roxy took a quick glance at the front door. She really hoped Gilda would get here soon.

"Fair enough," she said. "So, if I start wandering around looking at all the photos on the wall here, I won't find one of you and your dad, smiling happily on Father's Day, as though neither of you had a care in the world?"

Sondra stopped clenching and smiled very slightly. "No, you will not."

Roxy smiled back at her. "You're right. I didn't. There isn't a photo of you two because you refused to take a picture that night, didn't you? I just looked. The waitress helped me. You weren't happy that night, you didn't want a picture for posterity."

"I don't know what you're talking about." Sondra's hands were now fists on the table. "This is all very confusing and, I have to say, downright hostile, Roxy. I don't know what you're getting at but I wasn't here that night and you can't prove I was."

"Sadly for you, Sondra, I can. First of all, the waiting staff remembers you very well. Melanie over there," Roxy gave a little wave to the waitress who was watching them with keen eyes from behind the counter, "has just confirmed that she recognises you."

Sondra didn't bother looking around. "So? She remembers me from another time Dad brought me here."

"Nope, no, definitely Father's Day. She says she doesn't remember your dad very well because, well, there were lots of dads in that night, but she remembers *you*. Says you were in a foul mood. Can't recall anyone ever being quite so rude and cranky with their dad. Especially on Father's Day. Says she kept a wide berth and did not expect a tip that night. I don't think she got one, either."

Sondra stared hard at Roxy, her pale face now blushing with anger. "Again, lies, all lies."

"A picture doesn't lie, though, does it?" Roxy said, producing a small Polaroid from her lap. "You might not have posed for a happy snap that night, Sondra—and why would you, there was nothing to be happy about?—but you did get caught in the back of another one, I'm afraid."

Roxy placed the small Polaroid in front of Sondra who didn't appear to want to look at it at first. Eventually, though, she forced her eyes upon it and saw a snapshot of a fat Italian man beaming happily, a chubby woman kissing his right cheek, a chubby boy kissing the other. And just behind them, at a different table, oblivious to the photographer, a surly looking Sondra Lane, glaring towards somebody who was just out of shot. Beside Sondra sat a man who looked a lot like her husband, Tony. He also did not look happy.

"Not your best look, Sondra," Roxy said. "In fact, you look ready to explode. Why is that? Why were you so angry that night, I wonder?"

Sondra's lip twitched slightly. "So, I was here and I was having a bad night. So what? What does it prove?"

"It proves you lied about your whereabouts on the night your dad was killed. It suggests you also knew about your father's gold mine and the fact that he had decided not to claim it. That's why you were angry that night, Sondra. He'd just told you he was going to rip up that deed. I don't blame you, I'd be cranky too!"

Sondra pushed the picture away and went to stand up. "You have no idea what we talked about that night and I have had enough of all of this—"

"Sit down, Sondra, I'm not finished!" Roxy barked. She was starting to feel angry, herself. This woman had led her on a merry chase and she was damned if she was going to let her waltz away without explaining herself. "You sent me off, searching for some photograph, but *this* is the photograph you need to take a good, hard look at."

Sondra had settled back into her seat and was chewing her nails again.

Roxy continued: "Look at your face, Sondra, it says it all. This was the last time you saw your father, and look how angry you were. But regardless of that, Wolfgang has already told me that Berny planned a special dinner to break the news to you. He did it that night, didn't he? He told you on Father's Day."

Sondra rallied suddenly, her face blushing pink with anger. "Father's Day!" she hissed. "What kind of a *father* does that to his daughter? After giving her *nothing* his whole life. Of course I was angry! He was never there for me and Mum, never! He was always away, months at a time, and when he was back, he was sucking up to the likes of Wolfgang and all his disgusting cronies. He finally had a chance to make it up to me, a chance to hand me the deed to a gold mine! And what does he do? He gives it away. Hands it to a billionaire in exchange for a prostitute!"

"Prostitute?"

"What else do you think Renata is? She's certainly no housekeeper."

Roxy blinked several times. "So he did swap the gold mine for Renata?"

She nodded furiously. "Wolfgang bartered her like she was a piece of meat! Like she was *worth* a gold mine!"

"What about the $200,000?"

"What about it?! You think that *compensates*?! We were set to make millions. Instead, Wolfgang has my father over for dinner, gets him blind drunk and sweet talks him into ripping up the deed to the gold mine in exchange for a measly two hundred grand and Renata. Apparently my dad had always had a soft spot for her, so he said, 'Here, she's all yours' like she's a bargaining chip. Like she's worth an entire gold mine!"

"Maybe to your father she was worth it," Roxy said. "Maybe that's all he really wanted? Some company, some intimacy. Maybe he understood that money couldn't buy you that."

"How would he know?! We never had a chance to find out what wealth was like. He was a *loser*. Other men went up there and made their fortunes, set their families up for life. Not my dad. We had to go through all the pain—the long months left alone in a foul, foreign city, third world conditions—but we got none of the benefits. He never made any money, he was *hopeless*. The only clever thing my dad ever did was accept that bet from Wolfgang Bergman back in 1975. My mother thought he was a fool but it turns out he wasn't. It finally came good and what does he go and do? He rejects it! Finally, he'll make money from it, and he says, 'No thanks, I'll take the little cleaning lady!' He could have bought a hundred Renatas if he'd claimed that mine. The fool. The stupid, old fool ...'"

She was shaking violently now and banging her fists on the table. Roxy darted a glance towards the entrance again, wishing Gilda would show. She had already prepped the waitress about what was happening and had asked her to look out for the police, but there was no sign of them and Melanie was now standing with the other patrons at the side table, as if for protection, and they were all staring towards Roxy and Sondra.

Roxy ignored them. She needed to keep going, she had to draw Sondra out, so she asked, "Did you know about the gold mine before Father's Day?"

Sondra took a few deep breaths. "I knew he'd won some mine in some bet all those years ago but he never spoke of it. My mother was furious and never forgave him. I didn't give it much thought. To be honest I began to think of it as a family myth ... until *that* night. *Father's* Day." She spat the words out as if they were repulsive. "First he told me what had happened, how he'd scored the mine and knew it was worthless but didn't care, he just did it for the fun of it. The *fun* of it?! Then he told me how Wolfgang had recently informed him it was now lucrative, and how he had decided not to take it ..."

She was playing with her cutlery now, turning the knife over and over in her hand, and stray strands of hair were flying about her face. "God, I was so furious! Of course I was angry that night. Who wouldn't be?! Tony and I work our guts out just to scrape by, up before dawn, dealing with rude florists and bitchy brides. That's not the life I wanted to lead. Then bloody Tony goes and expands too fast, signs too many contracts, gets too many overheads. We struggled to keep up. But here was our chance! Here was *my* chance to get ahead of our debts, to start again. And Dad was going to give it away ..."

Her fingers were clenched around the knife now and it was pointing towards Roxy. "We tried so hard to change Dad's mind that night. We tried to make him see, but he was adamant. We said, 'You can have the mine and still keep Renata! Wolfgang doesn't *own* her, if she wants to marry you then so be it!' But he said, 'A deal's a deal.' He said, 'Wolfie was drunk at that Survey Congress and he never should have done it.' Like *Sir* Wolfgang needed protecting!" She banged the knife on the table.

Roxy tried not to look at the knife as she asked, "So why, if your father didn't want the mine, did he suddenly tell you where the deed was that night he was dying?"

"Because of what I did—" She stopped suddenly, her face paling again, and looked away.

She had dropped the knife to the table and Roxy felt emboldened. "Because you ran him over?" she prodded. "Because you tried to kill him?"

Sondra's eyes darted back at Roxy and they were glossy with tears. "I didn't mean to! It was an accident."

"Just tell me what happened. Please."

Sondra swallowed hard and brushed the hair back from her face. When she spoke she was a little calmer. "We met

Dad at the restaurant after work, and after that *horrible* dinner, we gave him a lift home."

"In one of your husband's white work vans?"

She nodded. "I could barely talk to Dad, let alone look at him. I was so furious, blind with rage." She sniffed again. "Tony got out to help him into the house and ... well, Dad was just standing there, in front of the van, staring at me with this ridiculous smug smile like I was the fool and one day I would understand. Oh God I was so angry. I just jumped in the driver's seat and rammed the car into him!"

She held a quivering hand up to her mouth, choking back sobs. "I didn't mean to kill him. I wanted to hurt him, that's true. I wanted him to see how much he hurt me. But I didn't *mean* to kill him. You have to believe me!"

She grabbed Roxy's hand and gripped it tightly, her face contorted, her eyes frantic. Roxy glanced back towards the door and noticed that one of the men at the other table was getting to his feet. She shook her head very subtly.

Not yet, she thought, *not quite yet*.

"I do believe you, Sondra. I just don't understand why you left him there. Why didn't—"

"We thought he was already dead! If I had known he was still alive I would never have left him, of course I wouldn't! But Tony said he wasn't breathing. We panicked. Tony jumped in and I drove away. Then, about an hour later we got the call from the hospital. They said he'd been in an accident, was hanging on by a thread but was conscious and wanted to see us. I was never so terrified in my life. When we got there I thought he was going to blow the whistle but he didn't ..."

She swiped a sleeve at her nose and Roxy handed her a tissue which she used to wipe her nose and dab at her waterlogged eyes. She took a few steadying breaths. "Afterwards, when the police spoke to us it was clear they had no idea what had happened and so we pretended we hadn't seen Dad that night, that he'd cancelled dinner."

She shook her head furiously. "We didn't expect to get away with it! Not for one second. We fully expected the police to hear from the restaurant, to hear that we'd been with him that night, and bring us in, but when they didn't, we realised that they didn't know. They really did believe us. They thought somebody else had done it. Some stranger. They didn't even consider us suspects."

"But your father knew."

"Yes," she said, choking back sobs and staring into Roxy's eyes imploringly, "but he forgave me, don't you see?! Before he died, in the hospital, he made it clear it was okay. Why else would he call me in, tell me where the deed was? He finally understood how much it meant to me, how angry I was and he must have regretted that decision. In his dying breath he didn't accuse me of hurting him, he didn't try to tell the police, instead he said your name. He wanted me to track you down and find that deed. He wanted me to have that mine. I know he did."

Whatever makes you feel better, thought Roxy bitterly. Instead she said, "So why didn't you just come to me and tell me the truth? Ask me to help you find the deed to the mine? Why pretend to have no idea what he was talking about? I was chasing my tail for half the week."

"How could I tell you? That gave me a motive for ...""

"Murder?"

"For his *accident*! I didn't mean to kill him!"

She sobbed again as the waitress waved, catching Roxy's attention. She looked up and then across to the front door where Gilda and Calhoun were standing, a look of anticipation on their faces. Roxy held a hand up to stall them. She was close to getting the whole story now but she needed to know one more thing, if only to help her sleep better at night.

"So that's why you broke into my apartment? You were trying to find the deed?"

"That wasn't me!"

"No, it was your goon of a husband. But he didn't find anything, right?"

Sondra looked away and blew her nose again.

"You tried to put me off his scent, didn't you? Told me your husband was tiny, 'the size of a gnome', but you lied, Sondra. I recognised him anyway from that stupid, Russian, floppy eared winter hat he wears, he had it on today and he was wearing it the night he broke into my house. They looked like bunny ears in the dark."

She glanced back at Roxy, chewing on a fingernail again. "I'm so sorry about that. I *told* him I would take care of it. But he didn't listen! He said it was easier if he could just get into your place, look for the deed and go. We didn't know where it was, we didn't realise it was in the photo, but we had to try. Tony said no one needed to get hurt. No one would even know what we were after. But when he couldn't find it there or ..."

"At the publisher's?"

She nodded. "Well, that's when I knew I had to speak to you directly. I thought Dad must have given the deed to you at first, told you about it for Wolfgang's book. But when you had no idea, I figured it must be attached to that photo. That was the only thing he'd given you. That's why I hired you. I'd read how you did a little sleuthing and I honestly thought you'd find it taped to the back of the photo or written on the back or something. I never realised it was in the frame. But you found it. I knew you would."

Yes, thought Roxy, *but you hadn't counted on me finding more than an old handwritten deed.*

"The police are here," Roxy told her gently, leaning back and waiting for the fallout, but she didn't look alarmed. She simply nodded slowly and straightened her hair, pulling it into a tight ponytail again.

"Good," she said eventually. "I've had enough of all of this. It's ... it's nearly killed me. The guilt. The anxiety. It's not worth ..."

She stopped, choked back a sob and Roxy said, "What? All the gold in the world?"

Sondra didn't say a word as she walked her out to where Gilda and Calhoun were waiting, handcuffs at the ready.

CHAPTER 35

Spring had shown up at last and everywhere the sun was shining, the birds were chirping and the first flower buds were beginning to sprout, but none of this was of any interest to Roxy Parker. She was wedged inside the cool, dark confines of Pico's Wine Bar, an oily plate of tapas and a glass of merlot in front of her. To her right sat Gilda, also enjoying tapas on a lunch break from work. She had a glass of cola in her hand and was raising it in a toast to Roxy.

"Are you sure we can't talk you into joining the force?"

Roxy laughed, brushing a strand of hair back with one hand and raising her glass to her lips with the other. "I've told you before, you simply couldn't afford me." She bat her eyelashes playfully.

Gilda placed her glass down and produced her smartphone, glancing at it briefly. "Waiting to hear back from Forensics," she explained. "They've impounded both of Tony Lane's white vans and it looks like one of them has had work done recently, so we suspect that was the one used in the hit and run. They'll find out soon enough."

"And Tony's not telling?"

"Neither is Sondra. We have her confession to you but she's retracted everything, of course, and lawyered up, big time. Berny's neighbour might be some use, and we have the waitress's testimony, too. They're not getting away with this, Roxy, I can assure you."

"They very nearly did."

"That's true. If she hadn't called you in to investigate, if she'd left it all alone, she probably would have got away with manslaughter and be free as a bird right now."

"But she might not have found the deed to the old Byou mine."

Gilda chewed on a calamari ring. "No use to her in jail."

"So what does happen to the gold mine? Where does it end up?"

"With Renata and her son, if they play their cards right." Gilda winced. "Sorry, no pun intended. She's had lawyers lining up to represent her; apparently she's got a good case for ownership so, well, she could end up a very rich woman. You know, I can't help wondering if she's smarter than she looks. Did she marry Berny Tiles for the money or for the visa so she could stay in the country? Or both?"

Roxy shook her head. "I like to think, deep down somewhere, it was love. And if it wasn't love, maybe it was to escape a sexual predator."

Gilda nodded firmly "We already asked if her son was Wolfgang's, but she's not telling. Still, you've got to wonder. The timeline certainly fits. Renata has been working for Wolfgang for almost twenty years, and the son's nineteen. She started as a sixteen-year-old at one of his houses in Jakarta, apparently. He only brought her out here about four years ago. I believe Berny first met her then and, yeah, maybe he gave up the gold mine in exchange for Renata, not so much for himself, but maybe to get her out of Wolfgang's house, save her from that sleazebag."

Roxy grimaced. "I'd like to think so, too, but I have a feeling he died still thinking Wolfgang was a hero. So where does all this leave Sir Sleazebag?"

"Back in his plush mansion, minus one gold mine. Oh, and a wife, apparently. I hear Ginny's filing for divorce. Betty's allegations were the last straw. Hasn't spoken to her husband since Betty made her statement about that night of the Survey Congress. Thanks to Betty, Sir Sleazebag is officially out of the closet."

They clinked their glasses to that. "I'm so glad Betty finally spoke out about him," said Roxy, "told the world what a monster he is."

"Yes, it was very brave, but I'm afraid it won't count for much at this late stage. There is such a thing as a statute of limitations, plus it was in Indonesia and all the witnesses are now deceased. Still, mud sticks and people are already looking sideways at him. You've gotta love that. His reputation is stuffed, but legally he's off the hook and, physically, at least, he's on the mend; I'm told he'll be up and about marketing his autobiography soon. I hear it's brilliantly written."

She winked and Roxy scowled. "I wish I could take that book I wrote and tear into a million pieces. I always knew he was a slimeball, but I had no idea how dangerous he could be."

She shuddered thinking of all the times she had been alone with the man, of all the sleazy comments she had deflected during their interviews, as if they were harmless. But he wasn't harmless at all, at least he wasn't once. Perhaps it was just old age that had saved Roxy Parker. She shuddered again.

"I talked to the publisher and of course they aren't going to mention anything about Betty's rape allegations," Roxy said. "They insist it's all scandals and lies, that she's made it all up to get her son off the hook." Roxy scoffed. "They were quite keen, though, to add a chapter about the Byou gold mine saga. Thought that would make brilliant copy. Not surprisingly, Wolfman has nipped that idea in the bud. He's paying for the book, so well, money always wins in the end.

That's one bio I'm glad I haven't got my name on. Sometimes it's a relief being a ghost."

They munched on their calamari and a fresh plate of Chorizo sausage that had just arrived, and didn't speak for few delicious minutes before Roxy asked about Betty's son. Despite what Brian had promised his mother, he didn't confess to anything when questioned by Gilda but was currently out on bail facing two charges of murder and one of attempted murder and break and enter.

"He's up the proverbial creek," Gilda said, licking her fingers. "Pathology has already connected his DNA to DNA found at the Brownlow crime scene, and we've matched his mobile phone to the call that came in for Gordon Reilly the night before he died."

"The one pretending to be someone from the Matt Talbot Hostel?"

"Yep, Brian must have listened in to your phone call to Betty and found out where his dad was staying. The owner of the bedsit says Gordon got a late phone call that night, saying they needed him in at the hostel, first thing in the morning. Brian obviously wanted to draw his dad out. I don't know if he intended to push him down the steps originally, or if he just cracked, but he'll probably plead manslaughter to that one if he's smart. Still, the fact remains he killed his own dad while trying to avenge his mother, some thirty-seven years later. Crazy stuff, eh?"

Roxy shook her head sadly. "This whole saga is insane. It's horrendous how one drunken night in a foreign land back in 1975 has managed to destroy so many lives."

"And one simple picture was able to bring the truth out."

"Two, actually," said Roxy. "If it wasn't for the restaurant Polaroid showing Sondra and Tony in the background on Father's Day, she may never have cracked."

Gilda nodded. "What do they say about a picture being worth a thousand words?"

"That's it, although I do think the photo at the Survey Congress is the one that really speaks volumes. I looked at it again last night and it gave me a chill. I was so wrong about that one. It wasn't a boring picture at all. If you look closely you can see Berny, staring over towards one side. I thought he was leering at Betty, but he wasn't. He was ogling his idol, Wolfgang, the man who could do no wrong. And there was poor Betty, innocently smiling, Wolfgang wedged right up to her, a little too close to comfort. And in the middle of the photo is the poor hubby Gordon, looking miserable, as if he already knew his life was about to take a terrible turn."

They both sighed and Gilda ordered another round of drinks. As they waited, Roxy had a sudden, bleak thought.

"Do you think Berny mentioned my name as he lay dying to help his daughter out? To make sure she got hold of the deed to the gold mine? Or do you think he said it to show everyone that she had a motive to kill him? To make sure she got caught?"

Gilda's eyes widened. "Oooh, that's creepy! I'd like to think the former, but who knows with families. As Betty's son has just shown, they can be ugly, vindictive beasts."

She paid the barman for the drinks and waited until Roxy had several sips under her belt before she said, "Speaking of which, heard how Max is doing?"

Roxy scowled. "Yeah, he's well. Why wouldn't he be? He's in Berlin, making a small fortune."

"You know this because you've buried the hatchet and are talking or ...?"

Roxy blushed. "Caroline is my informant. She's furious with us both for the way things ended."

"So it *has* ended?" Gilda looked disappointed but not surprised.

Roxy blew a strand of black hair from her face. "I don't know. But he's over there and I'm over here and ..."

"... never the twain shall meet?" Gilda looked at her sideways. "Jesus, woman, there are these new inventions called airplanes. They're amazing. You can catch one and be with him in less than twenty-four hours, you know? Not to mention Skype, e-mail, Facebook ..."

Roxy shrugged. "Yeah, well, maybe one day. We'll see."

Little did Roxy Parker know, she would be heading to Berlin within weeks, and she would be doing it for all the wrong reasons, but that's a story for a future date. For now, Roxy was simply trying to deconstruct another gruesome week in the life of a ghostwriter. So much for her promise to Lorraine and Max.

"Come on," Roxy said, "let's drink up and toast old Berny Tiles. Killed by his own daughter, and on Father's Day. I think *I've* got problems? It doesn't get much sadder than that."

Gilda agreed and raised her glass.

ABOUT THE AUTHOR

C.A. Larmer is a journalist, editor, teacher and author of multiple crime series, stand-alone novels and a non-fiction book about pioneering surveyors in Papua New Guinea. Christina grew up in PNG, was educated in Australia, and spent many years working in Sydney, London, Los Angeles and New York. She now lives with her musician husband, boomerang sons and their very cheeky Bluey on the east coast of Australia.

Sign up for news, views and giveaways:
calarmer.com